Christine Flynn is "...one of the genre's master storytellers."

—*Romantic Times Magazine*

* * * *

"I remember the first time I touched you. Do you remember, Erin?"

Trembling, she gave a little nod, his breath heating her temple when he touched his lips there.

"Do you remember where we were?" His fingers snaked into her hair. "We were right here." He tipped her head back, drawing a line of kisses along the side of her throat. "But we're going to be in that stall behind us in about thirty seconds unless you back away right now."

He was the one with the iron control. He was the one who could hold his passions so ruthlessly in check. She would have reminded him of that. But all she could think about at the moment was that he had been the man who'd awakened her sensuality. And he was the only man who had ever filled her with the raw need consuming her now. What she felt, she felt only with him. Only for him. She didn't know how it had happened, how he'd managed to breach every defense she possessed, but she was falling in love with him all over again....

D0030879

Dear Reader,

Special Edition is pleased to bring you six exciting love stories to help you celebrate spring...and blossoming love.

To start off the month, don't miss *A Father for Her Baby* by Celeste Hamilton—a THAT'S MY BABY! title that features a pregnant amnesiac who is reunited with her long-ago fiancé. Now she must uncover the past in order to have a future with this irresistible hero and her new baby.

April offers Western romances aplenty! In the third installment of her action-packed HEARTS OF WYOMING series, Myrna Temte delivers *Wrangler.* A reticent lady wrangler has a mighty big secret, but sparks fly between her and the sexy lawman she's been trying very hard to avoid; the fourth book in the series will be available in July. Next, Pamela Toth brings us another heartwarming story in her popular BUCKLES & BRONCOS miniseries. In *Buchanan's Pride,* a feisty cowgirl rescues a stranded stranger—only to discover he's the last man on earth she should let into her heart!

There's more love on the range coming your way. *Finally His Bride* by Christine Flynn—part of THE WHITAKER BRIDES series—is an emotional reunion romance between two former sweethearts. Also the MEN OF THE DOUBLE-C RANCH series continues when a brooding Clay brother claims the woman he's never stopped wanting in *A Wedding For Maggie* by Allison Leigh. Finally, debut author Carol Finch shares an engaging story about a fun-loving rodeo cowboy who woos a romance-resistant single mom in *Not Just Another Cowboy.*

I hope you enjoy these stirring tales of passion, and each and every romance to come!

Sincerely,

Karen Taylor Richman
Senior Editor

Please address questions and book requests to:
Silhouette Reader Service
U.S.: 3010 Walden Ave., P.O. Box 1325, Buffalo, NY 14269
Canadian: P.O. Box 609, Fort Erie, Ont. L2A 5X3

CHRISTINE FLYNN

FINALLY HIS BRIDE

Silhouette®

SPECIAL EDITION®

Published by Silhouette Books
America's Publisher of Contemporary Romance

If you purchased this book without a cover you should be aware that this book is stolen property. It was reported as "unsold and destroyed" to the publisher, and neither the author nor the publisher has received any payment for this "stripped book."

 SILHOUETTE BOOKS

ISBN 0-373-24240-9

FINALLY HIS BRIDE

Copyright © 1999 by Christine Flynn

All rights reserved. Except for use in any review, the reproduction or utilization of this work in whole or in part in any form by any electronic, mechanical or other means, now known or hereafter invented, including xerography, photocopying and recording, or in any information storage or retrieval system, is forbidden without the written permission of the editorial office, Silhouette Books, 300 East 42nd Street, New York, NY 10017 U.S.A.

All characters in this book have no existence outside the imagination of the author and have no relation whatsoever to anyone bearing the same name or names. They are not even distantly inspired by any individual known or unknown to the author, and all incidents are pure invention.

This edition published by arrangement with Harlequin Books S.A.

® and TM are trademarks of Harlequin Books S.A., used under license. Trademarks indicated with ® are registered in the United States Patent and Trademark Office, the Canadian Trade Marks Office and in other countries.

Printed in U.S.A.

Books by Christine Flynn

Silhouette Special Edition

Remember the Dreams #254
Silence the Shadows #465
Renegade #566
Walk upon the Wind #612
Out of the Mist #657
The Healing Touch #693
Beyond the Night #747
Luke's Child #788
Lonely Knight #826
Daughter of the Bride #889
When Morning Comes #922
Jake's Mountain #945
A Father's Wish #962
Logan's Bride #995
The Rebel's Bride #1034
The Black Sheep's Bride #1053
Her Child's Father #1151
Hannah and the Hellion #1184
From House Calls to Husband #1203
Finally His Bride #1240

* The Whitaker Brides

Silhouette Desire

When Snow Meets Fire #254
The Myth and the Magic #296
A Place To Belong #352
Meet Me at Midnight #377

Silhouette Romance

Stolen Promise #435
Courtney's Conspiracy #623

Silhouette Intimate Moments

Daughter of the Dawn #537

Silhouette Books

36 Hours

Father and Child Reunion

CHRISTINE FLYNN

admits to being interested in just about everything, which is why she considers herself fortunate to have turned her interest in writing into a career. She feels that a writer gets to explore it all and, to her, exploring relationships—especially the intense, bittersweet or even lighthearted relationships between men and women—is fascinating.

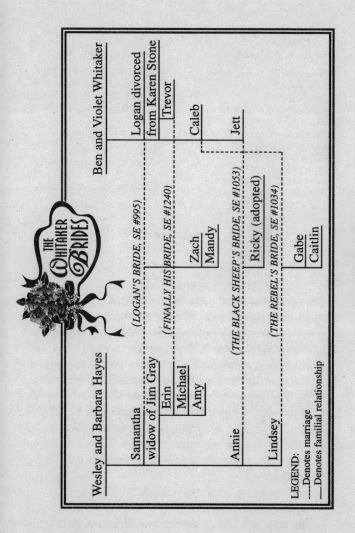

THE WHITAKER BRIDES

Wesley and Barbara Hayes   Ben and Violet Whitaker

(LOGAN'S BRIDE, SE #995)

Samantha — Logan divorced
widow of Jim Gray   from Karen Stone
      | Trevor
Erin
Michael
Amy

(FINALLY HIS BRIDE, SE #1240)
         Caleb
Zach
Mandy

(THE BLACK SHEEP'S BRIDE, SE #1053)
Annie   Jett
      Ricky (adopted)

(THE REBEL'S BRIDE, SE #1034)
Lindsey
      Gabe
      Caitlin

LEGEND:
---- Denotes marriage
—— Denotes familial relationship

Prologue

She wasn't supposed to be with him.

The thought nagged vaguely at the back of Erin Gray's mind as she watched Trev Whitaker shoulder a heavy sack of oats and carry it into the horse stable's storage room. She wasn't supposed to be here, but there wasn't anyplace else she could go that didn't feel like hostile territory, so she dismissed the twinge of guilt tugging at her—along with the thought of how much trouble she'd be in if she got caught—and headed into the storage room herself.

With a surge of corded muscle that belonged more on a man than a boy of not-quite eighteen, Trevor shrugged the sack to the ground and split it open with a quick rip of the sealing string.

"Hand me those buckets, will you?"

"These?"

At his nod, she picked up the half dozen pails stacked by a wall of saddles and straps.

"Just line 'em up right here."

Metal clattering, she did as he asked.

She loved watching him do his chores. She liked helping, too, even though she hadn't a clue what to do until he told her. Twice now, he'd brought her out to his father's ranch after school and they'd talked while he tended the horses and cared for whatever sick or injured animals his dad's wranglers found out on the cattle range.

Trevor talked about the animals, mostly. And she, who knew nothing about anything four-legged, loved to listen. She was drawn by the way his pewter gray eyes became so intent when he spoke about the eagle whose wing he'd set, and about how he was anxious to release it so it could return to the wild. She liked the way a guy as big as he talked so gently to the huge horses. She liked the deep rumble of his voice, his faint drawl and the way he looked at her when she wrinkled her nose or got embarrassed at some of the earthier aspects of ranching life that he simply took for granted.

Mostly, she just liked him. Even though she didn't know that much about him yet. She'd overheard girls at school talking about him, though. Sue Lynn Farley said she'd dump Billy Baxter in a heartbeat if Trevor would pay any attention to her. Donna Gunther and Cindy Weiss practically threw themselves in front of him in the halls to get him to notice them. They both thought he was gorgeous, and Donna had said that his dad owned more land than anyone in West Texas. A major stud, Cindy called him. Not to his face, of course. But even if she had, he would have ignored them all. From what Erin had also overheard, he was very much a loner.

"Just like his father," Cindy had pronounced.

Erin hadn't been able to ask what Cindy had meant by that. She was never included in those sighing, whispered conversations. She was an outsider; the kid from the big city who'd been dumped in their midst less than a month ago and relegated to the land of the untouchables. The girls at Leesburg High had decided her California casual clothes and her lack of a drawl made her a snob, and they'd given her the collective cold shoulder. Not that she cared what a bunch of hicks thought about her, she told herself, wanting badly to ignore the hurt that compounded the ache living in her chest.

In the dying, dried-up town of Leesburg, Texas—the town her mother had been hired to rejuvenate—Trevor was her only friend. And her mom had now informed her that she couldn't see him anymore. Not until she introduced him to her. Erin wasn't about to do that. Since her mother managed to find fault with just about everything she liked, said or did lately, she was bound to find something wrong with him, too.

On top of that, if he knew she needed permission to see him, he'd think she was a child. She was sixteen. At sixteen, her mom had practically been engaged to her dad.

"Did you get a new lock for your locker yet?" Trev asked, glancing up as she leaned a hip against the bare wood wall.

"Not yet." She smiled at the top of his black cowboy hat as he bent to scoop oats into the pails. He'd seen her struggling with the lock a couple of weeks ago and unjammed it for her. That had been the first time they'd spoken. "I just don't push the bar in far enough to lock it."

"Why don't you just get a new one?"

"Honestly?"

His head came up, his sculpted features shadowed by a frown. "Yeah. Honestly."

"I don't want to ask my mom for the money."

"Why not?"

"I don't talk to her any more than I have to." She shrugged, trying to pretend it didn't matter. "You know how moms are."

"No, I don't." The whinny of a horse impatient for its dinner joined the sound of the metal scoop sliding through oats. "I never knew my mother. She walked out when I was around six months old. It's just been Dad and me for as long as I can remember.

"So, why don't you talk to your mom?" he asked, dismissing the matter of his absent parent as easily as he'd brush off a fly.

The ache in her stomach suddenly felt worse. Instead of answering, she crossed her arms and shrugged again. If she pretended hard enough that something didn't matter, maybe, eventually, it wouldn't.

"Oh-kay," he drawled, drawing the word out in a way that made it apparent he knew he'd hit a sore spot. "So why don't you use your own money to buy a lock. They don't cost more than a few bucks."

"I'm saving every cent I can get my hands on so I can get out of here. I want to go back to Los Angeles."

"Didn't you just move here?"

"My mom moved us here. My little brother and sister and I didn't have anything to say about it."

"That sorta sucks."

"Yeah," she agreed, smiling at his conclusion despite the tightening in her chest.

"Where's your dad?"

Her smile faded. Usually the dull ache was simply there, a thing that lay quietly beneath the protective anger she felt toward her mom for uprooting her from everything that had once been familiar. The grieving was so constant, she barely noticed it during the day. It was a little like breathing, she supposed. Something she didn't have to be conscious of to do—unlike at night in her room when the darkness robbed her of ways to avoid acknowledging it. Yet, with Trevor's simple question, that dull ache sharpened to pain, shadowing her face, burning her throat.

"He's dead."

The quiet statement drew Trevor upright, his big, powerful body towering over hers as he tossed the scoop into the sack. In the light from the bare bulb overhead, his expression became as intent as it had been when he'd talked about the eagle.

"What happened?"

She took a breath, blew it out. She'd die if she cried in front of him.

"Daddy was a policeman," she said, her throat tightening, anyway. It had been over a year now, and the department counselor had *promised* that time would make it better. But it wasn't better. Erin couldn't see how it could ever be. She felt as lost without her father at that moment as she had when her dad's partner had shown up at the door and taken her mom to the morgue. Her dad had been her buddy, her friend. They'd laughed at jokes her mom didn't get, and teased her about being overly protective and having no spirit of adventure at all. Her dad was impulsive, a little reckless, and she'd been just like him. He'd said she was like a water sprite, the free spirit he'd always wanted to be—and she missed him horribly.

"He..." She pulled another breath, determined to get the words out without humiliating herself. She didn't talk about her dad. It was just too hard. "He was shot by a gang."

She was staring at Trevor's battered boots, but scarred brown leather suddenly blurred with golden straw. Before she could stop them, the tears that had gathered in the corners of her eyes streaked down her cheeks.

She swallowed. It didn't do any good at all.

"God, Erin," he murmured, sounding as if he were actually praying for help. "I don't know what to—"

Trevor cut himself off when she looked up at him. She barely met his eyes before tightening her hold on herself and glancing back down. She looked embarrassed. But mostly she looked small and fragile and as lost as the frightened, injured fawn he'd once found in a thicket.

Like that fawn, he found himself reaching for her. He'd never seen a girl cry before. Not in person. And he didn't know why it was that the tears she tried to hold back suddenly began to fall in earnest when he pulled her against his chest. He just recognized pain when he saw it. So he held her, awkwardly lifting his hand to stroke her long, sun-kissed hair and marveling at how she hadn't hesitated to come to him, and how delicate she felt in his arms.

"I don't want...to cry." Her words were muffled, the sobs shuddering through her body making the words hard to understand. "I don't want...any of this."

"I'm sure you don't," he agreed, not knowing what else to say.

"I want my dad...back."

"Hush," he whispered, holding her tighter.

"Can't."

"Okay. Then go ahead and cry."

Her slender shoulders rose with another shudder, then fell with a muffled, "'Kay."

"What else do you want?" he asked, when he couldn't bear to hear the sobs that had her barely able to breathe.

"The...old...house."

"The one you lived in?"

He felt her nod, or maybe she just rubbed her nose.

"What else?"

Her fingers bunched his shirt, her tears soaking the fabric. "My...friends."

The ones she'd left behind, he thought. The ones she couldn't seem to make here. The girls all seemed jealous of her. And she rarely made eye contact with any of the boys. He knew. Like every other red-blooded male in school, he'd been watching her. He just hadn't thought about approaching her until it had been obvious that no one else was around to help her with her lock.

He'd be her friend. He didn't mention that, though. It was hard for her to talk, so he finally just let her weep while he held her and tried to ignore the way his body responded to her slender curves. There wasn't much to her, really. He doubted she weighed a hundred pounds, not even as much as the sack of grain he'd just carried. But she smelled like some impossible combination of sweetness and seduction that tightened the muscles in his stomach every time he breathed. And soft. He'd never felt anything as soft as the silk of her hair, or her skin when he skimmed her cheek and pressed her head to his chest.

The only woman he'd ever held was ten years older than he was; a waitress who worked at a roadside café outside of town. Lily was divorced and a little jaded, but she was fun. She'd made it clear the first time he'd stopped for supper on his way back from delivering a horse that she had a weakness for men with broad shoulders—and that she'd be more than willing to give a young cowboy a ride. He'd stopped there a few times since, and after her shift was over, he'd spent the evening in her bed.

He'd learned a lot from Lily.

But this...

Holding Erin was like nothing he'd ever experienced before. She seemed to need the comfort of his arms, and he couldn't believe how much like a man that made him feel.

Her sobs eventually eased. By then, he'd sat down with her on a bale of hay, cradling her closer, and it no longer felt awkward at all to smooth the hair back from her face. Careful not to abrade her translucent skin, he slipped his work-roughened hand along her cheek and tipped her chin up. As he did, he ducked his head to see her face.

"How you doing?"

"I'm sorry," she whispered, still gripping his shirt.

"Don't be," he whispered back and touched his lips to the corner of her eye to catch the tears on her lashes. "I'm not."

Another tear slipped down her wet cheek. "Okay." She laid her head back on his shoulder. "Then I'm not, either."

With his head still bent, he caught another tear, and nudged her face up to catch one trailing to her jaw. Her breath felt warm on his neck. Her skin felt like slick satin. And kissing her seemed like the most natural thing in the world.

With the salt of her tears on his tongue, he curved his hand at the side of her face and settled his mouth over hers. He felt her stiffen for an instant, then she made a little sound. It wasn't protest. It was more like the tiny mewl of a kitten as her entire body relaxed against him. Her lips stayed closed, though, soft but unmoving beneath his.

His heart was already beating like a trip-hammer. But when she pressed closer, he thought it might come right through his chest. It wasn't that she didn't want him to kiss her any deeper, he realized, feeling her breathing quicken. She just didn't know how.

With the tug of his thumb below her bottom lip, he coaxed her lips apart. Erin felt his tongue stroke hers, the light touch gentle and utterly devastating. But even as a strange, intriguing heat joined the first real security she'd felt in over a year, Trevor lifted his head and pressed hers back to his shoulder.

She asked him a week later why he'd done that—what she'd done wrong. He told her she'd done nothing wrong. He just hadn't wanted to take advantage of her when she was upset.

That had been the day he'd shown her what a real kiss was.

He taught her a lot of things over the next few weeks. And she'd wound up nearly grounded for life the day her mom came to the huge RW ranch and found her there with him. Her mom had been so upset she'd actually been arguing with his father before she and Trev had shown up. She never had known why her mom had been so irritated with Logan Whitaker. But in the months before her mom married Trevor's dad, Trevor had become far more than a friend.

That was why it was so hard when he stopped speaking to her.

Chapter One

Nine years later

"I've been back three days, Erin. How much longer did you plan to avoid me?"

Trevor's deep voice skimmed along Erin's nerves, the rich, husky sound slamming defenses into place on the way. From where she knelt in the stable beside a restive bay gelding, she glanced over her shoulder, caution stealing around her like a cloak.

She'd known she would have to see him sooner or later. But she'd never expected him to seek her out. He stood at the end of the wide breezeway, six feet two inches of solid muscle and tension in blue chambray and worn denim. The afternoon sunlight streamed in behind him, hay dust shimmering in the sultry June air. She couldn't see his face, shadowed by the wide, low brim of his hat. But she didn't need to see his expression to know how he felt about having returned home to find her at the ranch. The edge of resentment in his tone said it all.

"I haven't been avoiding you." Resigned to getting this particular encounter out of the way, she didn't bother pointing out that for nearly nine years, he had been the one who'd avoided her. "I've just been busy. Welcome back," she said, and turned to smear ointment over a lemon-size sore on the horse's foreleg.

She refused to be rattled. She refused to let him know he rattled her, anyway. She'd promised herself only two things when she'd left Los Angeles six weeks ago. Three, actually, if she counted her intention to have a job by the time Trevor returned, but she'd already blown that. She'd promised herself that she would stay at the ranch absolutely no longer than she had to, and that she'd do nothing to disturb her family's peace. Since Trevor was family, sort of, and he actually seemed to be making an effort at peace, the least she could do was meet him halfway.

He didn't appear to trust her unexpectedly cordial greeting, however. Either that, or the way he hesitated meant he was trying to decide if he really wanted to pursue the question he'd asked. But even as she rose, she saw him step from the blazing sunlight.

His boots thudded on the cement floor as he moved down the rows of empty stalls, his stride measured as he glanced around him. The cutting horses were on the range or in the pasture this time of day, and the colts and yearlings were out in the corrals where the breeze offered respite from the heat. The ceiling fans rotating slowly overhead provided little relief from the humid warmth, but the determined squeak of one at the far end of the long building could be heard when Trevor stopped a foot from where she stood.

Ignoring her, he reached up to stroke the horse's sleek neck.

"Easy," he soothed, catching the leather sidestrap of the horse's hackamore when the big animal snuffled and tried to dance away. "What did you do to yourself, fella?"

Beneath the brim of his hat, his dark sable hair was neatly trimmed. A tiny nick on the underside of his angular jaw told of a recent encounter with a razor. He was close enough that she could see where tanned skin met paler at his temple. Close enough that the breath she drew brought the unnerving combination of crisp citrus and warm male. But she didn't move away. Not like she once would have. He was crowding her on purpose.

"He did battle with a cactus. One of the hands said a rattler spooked him and he tore through a patch of cholla."

"When?"

"Yesterday."

She watched him run a practiced hand down to the raw, swollen spot she'd just medicated, tipping his hat back slightly to get a better look. His hands were broad, blunt-fingered, strong. A couple of silvered scars marked his knuckles from pulling cattle out of briars when he was younger, and there were fresh knicks from doing heaven-only-knew-what around the ranch the past couple of days. He'd rolled the sleeves of his shirt to his elbows, exposing the corded muscles of his forearms. That blue chambray pulled across his shoulders, defining their breadth. Worn denim delineated his powerful thighs and narrow hips.

He'd been impressively built when he was eighteen. At twenty-seven, he possessed a hard, honed masculinity none of the gym-jocks she'd seen in L.A. could hope to match.

She wished he'd been built like a donut.

"You should bandage this."

Eyeing the crown of his coal gray Stetson, she held out a roll of gauze. "I'd planned on it."

"What ointment did you use?"

She held that out, too.

"Good," he murmured, glancing at the tube of antibiotic before checking the scratches she'd already treated on the horse's black-stockinged fetlock. "So, what have you been busy with?"

"What?"

"You said you'd been busy," he reminded her, pulling his hat back down as he rose like a pillar of granite in front of her. "Doing what?"

Looking straight ahead, all she could see were the buttons on his shirt. She couldn't remember the last time they'd been this close. She didn't remember his chest being quite so broad, either. But he'd always been tall. She'd once had to stand on tiptoe to get her arms around his neck. Even then, he'd had to bend to kiss her. He would catch her by the waist, his big hands closing possessively around her, and he'd draw her up until their lips met. Once they'd nearly even made love.

She blinked, swallowed. The memories had come out of nowhere, catching her completely off guard. So did the odd bump of her heart when her glance slid over his blatantly sensual mouth and she found his hooded gray eyes locked on hers.

Time had honed him, sharpened the hard angles and planes of his compelling features. There was no denying that he was a remarkably attractive man. But it was his air of quiet control that made him truly formidable. There was an inbred confidence about him that she couldn't help but envy. Unlike her, he'd always known who he was and where he was going. He'd known where he belonged and what was expected of him. More than that, he'd always known his own mind.

Nothing stood in his way when he had a goal. And from the rigid set of his jaw, Erin had the uneasy feeling that Trevor had something quite definite on his mind now.

Beneath the dark slashes of his eyebrows, his narrowed glance moved to her mouth, lingering long enough to make her wonder if he had a few memories of his own, before his eyes shifted to the tree on the Save the Rain Forests T-shirt she'd tucked into her jeans. She had no idea what made the muscle in his jaw tighten before his eyes met hers once more. As far as she was concerned, it didn't matter what he thought. Or what he wanted. All she needed to remember was that she'd once thought herself in love with him, and that when she'd told him how she felt, he'd frozen up like a creek in the dead of winter.

She'd been only seventeen when she'd made that particular mistake, and he'd gone out of his way ever since to let her know he wanted nothing to do with her. Well, she'd gotten over it. Over him. And, in her usual, inimitable style, promptly gone on to make an even bigger mess of her life.

At least with her latest judgment error she understood what had gone wrong.

A muscle in his jaw jumped, his voice sounding oddly tight in the strained silence. "I asked what else you've been doing," he quietly reminded her.

Movement always helped her dispel anxiety. But pacing wouldn't present the calm, controlled front she was striving for, so she turned to the horse, rubbing her hand over its deep cinnamon withers. "I've been going on job interviews."

"What kind of work would you do in Leesburg?" he demanded before she could say anything else.

"I'm not looking for work in Leesburg. I'm looking in San Antonio and Austin." She eyed him dully. "Small towns aren't exactly overrun with public relations firms."

"Your car hasn't moved for two days."

"I also work around here to earn my room and board," she informed him, openly frowning at his implication that she wasn't looking very hard. "And I help Aunt Lindsey," she told him, referring to the sewing all the women in the family got roped into on occasion for her aunt's boutique in town. "Not all of us have jobs to come back to like you do."

He'd returned finally to take his rightful place on the ranch. She was simply stuck there until she found a job. She couldn't afford to go anywhere else.

"By the way," she added, determined to be adult, "congratulations on joining Doc Henderson's veterinary practice. I was a little surprised you did that, though. I thought you'd want to open your own."

"I only want to work part-time so I can help Dad here."

That made sense. He'd loved this land.

"So, what is it you do around here?" he prompted, refusing to be sidetracked.

"I help Dusty take care of the stables," she replied, referring to one of his father's many employees, "and I've been helping Hank break cutting horses."

"You're helping break horses?"

She couldn't tell if his scowl was of displeasure or disbelief. Either way, her back stiffened. "I'm sure your dad told you that."

"Dad hasn't told me anything about you," Trev muttered. "Except that you'd come back."

What his dad had actually said to him was "If you want to know what Erin is doing here, ask her." He'd also made it abundantly clear in their little discussion in the barn this morning that Trevor was to "work it out and get along with her."

His father hadn't been upset with him over much of anything since Trev was thirteen years old. He wasn't exactly upset with him now. But he disapproved of his attitude. Having his dad feel that way about him on account of her didn't predispose Trevor to liking her any better, either.

"I'm sure you're not all that interested in my activities, Trevor. What is it you really want?"

"What makes you think I want something?"

She met his frown with admirable aplomb. "You and I haven't had a single conversation in over eight years that's gone beyond 'please pass the salt.' We've even managed to avoid any conversation at all the past three years simply by not being home at the same time. And you were the one who started avoiding me," she reminded him, wanting to keep that straight. "So when you suddenly show an interest in what I'm doing, I guess I get a little suspicious.

"You want something," she concluded flatly. "I'm sure of it."

He skimmed a glance from her delicate features to the tendrils of wheat-colored hair framing her face. Her hair was caught high and loose in a clip rather than hanging down her back in the thick braid he remembered. But it was still shot with streaks of silver that reminded him of sunlight bouncing off polished gold.

There wasn't much else about her that he found familiar at the moment. He'd always thought of Erin as fragile, mercurial, needy. And while she still looked as innocent and lovely as an angel, he found no trace of the troubled young girl he'd once known. There was confidence in her melodic voice, challenge in her lovely hazel eyes. But it was her demeanor that was truly unfamiliar.

The top of her head didn't even reach his shoulder, and there still wasn't enough meat on her coltish frame to keep a good breeze from blowing her over, but she no longer deferred to him the way she once had. She hadn't backed away from him as he'd thought she would when he'd stepped into her space. Nor had she hesitated to meet his eyes. She'd simply tipped her chin, answered his questions and forced his hand.

The muscle in his jaw jerked, much the way his father's had done when they'd talked a while ago. "What I want is a truce."

The delicate wing of her eyebrow arched. "A truce?"

"Is that so impossible?"

"You tell me. You're the one who just made the word sound as if it were spelled with four letters."

"Look, Erin. Coming out here wasn't my idea. Dad wants us to get along, so that's what I'm trying to do. Are you going to cooperate or not?"

She hesitated, her soft voice becoming even quieter. "This was Logan's idea?"

"He was talking about how it took him years to get his brothers back together, and how he's not going to have any other members of his family avoid each other. This is important to him. Now that I'm home, we're going to have to…"

"Be civil?" she suggested when he couldn't seem to come up with any ideas on his own.

"Yeah."

For a moment, she said nothing. She just stared at the strong column of his throat, wondering how he'd avoided choking on the request. She didn't understand Trevor's attitude toward her, but she understood completely where his dad was coming from. Family was important to Logan, and the last thing in the world she wanted was to cause a problem between him and his son. Or worse, be a problem for her mom and Logan because of the strain between her and the man defensively watching her now. She'd caused her family enough grief over the years as it was, and she'd be more than happy to be rid of this particular feud. But the realization that Trevor had been coerced into seeking her out was too humiliating.

Defenses she didn't even know she possessed kicked into place as she reached for the horse's lead. She'd actually forgotten how adept Trevor was at pushing her away.

"I'll make an effort to get along if you will," she told him, thinking she'd do anything for her stepfather as she unclipped the long leather lead from the wall. "I don't want to cause trouble for anyone while I'm here."

She shot him a glance, letting it graze off his jaw rather than meeting the cool gray of his eyes. "I don't imagine you do, either." Looping the free end of the lead in her hand, she walked back to the horse. "So, maybe the best way for us to avoid problems is to stick to the weather when we find ourselves in situations where we have to talk, and otherwise stay out of each other's way.

"Since the stables are temporarily my space, that includes the horses I'm working with," she informed him, desperately needing to feel she could do at least one thing right. "If I need a vet, I'll call one."

Her back was as stiff as bailing wire as she turned the animal around and led it down the wide breezeway separating the stalls. Over the syncopated beat of hooves on concrete, Trevor heard the whinny of a horse from one of the corrals outside and the sharp bark of a dog. The sounds scarcely registered. She hadn't even given him a chance to ask why she'd come back from California, or how much longer she planned to stay.

Dragging in a breath of the stifling air, wishing the breeze would kick up and cool things down, he jerked the brim of his hat lower and headed into the sunshine. Lips pursed, he gave a short whistle for the dog waiting patiently in the stable's shadow. Within seconds, forty pounds of exuberant yellow Lab was dancing around his legs, tail wagging and bright, onyx eyes watching his master's every move.

"Come on, Max," Trev muttered, motioning his little buddy into step beside him. "Let's find some lunch."

He didn't really want food. What he wanted was Erin gone. Now. Through college, veterinary school and the two years he'd spent researching cattle breeding in Argentina and Australia, he'd dreaded coming back to the ranch he loved, his home, because she'd been there; the ex-girlfriend who'd become his stepsister. Once she'd headed off for college herself and gone to work on the west coast, he'd thought the awkward situation had resolved itself. And it had, he told himself, giving the brim of his hat another yank, until she'd suddenly quit her job and moved back.

He headed through the sprawling compound, past the enormous white breeding-barn and maintenance buildings, and followed the rise of the dry gravel road toward the main house. It sat nestled in an oasis of green grass and majestic live oaks, sprawling, gleaming white, and solid as the red brick planters hugging its angles.

Within seconds, his steps slowed, the crunch of pea gravel dying beneath his dusty boots. He'd yet to become accustomed to seeing the house as it was now. Heaven knew, it had never looked so good when he'd lived in it himself. Back then, the paint had been gray, the finish chosen to protect the wood from the elements rather than for eye appeal. Neither he nor his dad had given any thought to such a thing. Now, the once barren planters overflowed with pink periwinkles and red geraniums. Lace curtains hung in the sparkling windows. Children's toys were scattered in the shaded yard.

He didn't belong up there. Not anymore. When he'd lived in that house, he hadn't been afraid to walk in with dirt on his boots. It had just been him and his dad—and the crew of wranglers and ranch hands who lived in the camps on the range and in the bunkhouse beyond the barn. That was how it had been until he'd gone off to college and his dad had married Samantha, Erin's mom. Now, the house was overrun with a new family of stepsiblings and half siblings he didn't really know at all.

Then there was Samantha herself.

He never had felt comfortable around her. The first time he'd met her, the day she'd come out looking for her daughter, the look she'd given him would have frosted a hot branding iron. She'd thawed a little after she and his dad got together, and she'd tried to make him feel welcome, but the temperature had dropped again when he'd started avoiding Erin. Since Erin had once told him that her mom didn't like the idea of them being serious anyway, he'd have thought Sam would be pleased he wasn't hanging around.

He'd never understood anything about the female mind. To be honest, he admitted, turning back toward the stables, he'd never tried. But whether he understood women or not, he would do what he had to do to get along with Erin. After all, she wouldn't be there forever.

The thought would have buoyed his spirits considerably had his steps not just stalled again.

There were changes in this direction, too. A new, twenty-stall stable had been built on the other side of the corrals from the weathered old building he'd just left. But the addition of the new structure wasn't what gave him pause. It was the thought that he'd always planned to live in the apartment above the old stables when he finally came home—at least until he could build himself a house of his own somewhere on the ranch. On a rise above the river, perhaps. Or beyond the meadows surrounding the old homestead that his uncle Jett had refurbished. But with Erin living in the apartment, however temporarily, even that small bit of familiarity had been denied him.

Telling himself he was far too old to be feeling like an outcast stepchild, irritated for even having the thought, he cut a path to his Bronco and signaled Max into the front seat. He wasn't due to meet with Doc Henderson for another hour, but there wasn't much to eat in the trailer he was staying in. He'd have gone down to the cookhouse, but Leon, the cook for the men in the main compound, was with one of the chuckwagons feeding the crew moving herds and he would only have prepared enough lunch for the mouths he'd planned to feed. That left the refrigerator up at the house. Since he definitely didn't feel comfortable raiding that, he'd grab a hamburger in town. He'd been raised to fend for himself, anyway.

"Stop teasing your sister, Zach, and finish your homework. And Mandy?" Erin's mom raised her voice over the chatter of cartoon characters drifting from the family room as she shoved a foil-covered casserole into the oven. "I want you to turn the television off and tell Amy to come set the table. Dad and Mike will be home soon."

"It sounds just like it always did around here," Erin observed, picking up a spool of thread from the sewing box she was riffling. Frowning at the color, she dropped it back in to continue digging. "Only the names have changed. Now it's Zach teasing Mandy instead of Michael teasing Amy.''

"Michael still teases Amy," Samantha Whitaker replied, speaking of her oldest son and middle daughter. Zach and Mandy were her children by Logan. "Only now instead of chasing her with bugs, he bugs her about boys."

She swiped her feathery blond bangs back with her forearm, strands of silver glinting in the overhead light. At forty-three, she was beginning to gray, but she made even that look good. "Thank heavens, she isn't showing any real interest in them yet." Setting the oven timer with one hand, she motioned with the other toward the oak cabinets above the long, white counter. "Hand me the green bowl, will you? There's plenty if you want to stay for supper."

Abandoning the sewing basket, Erin grabbed the big ceramic mixing bowl that, over the years, had held countless salads and batches of cookies. "Thanks, but I'm only here to borrow some thread. I'm working on a batch of shirts for Aunt Lindsey and I ran out of pink."

"Didn't you just do a dozen?"

"She's back ordered. Aunt Annie and I both took another batch." The lace appliquéd T-shirts her mom's sister designed had been enormously popular for years. Erin had always enjoyed working on them, mostly because she liked seeing what patterns she could come up with for the ribbons and lace. "I want to have these done by Friday so I can drop them off on my way to Austin. I have an interview with a PR firm at one o'clock."

"Anything promising?"

"An account assistant position. It just opened. With any luck I can be out of your hair in a week."

"You're not in my hair. You've kept so busy, I hardly know you're around." Perpetually busy herself, her mom toed open a bottom drawer to get a fresh dishtowel, then turned with a frown of concentration to the open window over the sink. Along with the breeze fluttering the buttercup yellow curtains came the distant hum of an engine.

"That sounds like Trevor's Bronco."

Erin didn't question the conclusion. Her mom could identify a ranch vehicle by its sound as easily as she could a human voice. It was a knack Erin herself had developed. The pitch of the approaching vehicle was too low to belong to Logan's or his brothers' trucks, and it was too even to be the battered old Jeep Hank, the ranch foreman, always drove.

"Yeah, it does," she agreed, spotting a spool of carnation pink. Picking it up, she glanced toward the window, a strange little knot forming under her breastbone. "Well," she murmured, having found what she'd come to borrow, "I guess I'd better get going. I'll see you tomorrow. Okay?"

"You don't have to leave, Erin. He hasn't been coming to the house."

It seemed to Erin that her mom's tone held as much assurance as it did exasperation. Everyone in the family knew that she and Trevor had once been involved. Just how involved was something she and her mom had never discussed. When they'd broken up, though, she knew her mom had felt nothing but relief. Trevor was only two years older than she was, but her mom had regarded him as a man even back then, and light-years more mature than her little girl had been at the time. She'd just never understood why something that had been so brief and so long ago hadn't been resolved by now.

Erin had never understood it, either.

"He probably hasn't been coming to the house because he's afraid he'll run into me."

"I don't think he's comfortable with any of us," Samantha allowed, determined as always to downplay the tension that had existed for so long between her daughter and her stepson. If there was nothing she could do to fix a situation, she simply gave it no import. It was a trait Erin had adopted herself. "He's only come up here once without his dad, and that was to get Max. Zach and Mandy adore that dog. They were trying to introduce him to Spot.

"Anyway," she continued, stepping over the spoiled, spotted mongrel asleep in front of the sink, "he hasn't come to dinner once since he's been back. We've asked him up here three nights in a row and every time he's had other plans."

"Did you know Logan had him talk to me?"

Her mom glanced up, something suspicious sweeping through her eyes. "I knew he was going to. I didn't know that he had."

"You knew?"

"I don't want tension in the house," she quietly defended, chopping radishes with fervor. "Once it became apparent that you'd still be here when he got back, I asked Logan to talk to him. He said he'd planned on it, anyway, if the matter didn't resolve itself…though his reasons for wanting things straightened out are different from mine."

"You didn't get into an argument, did you?"

The quick disquiet in Erin's voice had her mother turning from her cutting board. Defensiveness eased. "No, honey, we didn't argue. We just had a difference of opinion about when something should be said. He wanted to wait and see what Trevor did and I wanted something done before things started getting uncomfortable again. It's perfectly natural that I would side with you and he would side with his son," she explained, well versed in the art of blending his, hers and theirs. "At least you weren't in the habit of leaving the room every time Trevor walked in."

She returned to her task, but Erin didn't move. Logan and her mom might not have argued this time, but she had the awful feeling that this was not the first time the difference of opinion her mom referred to had reared its ugly head.

Only that morning, she'd told herself that the last thing she wanted was to cause a problem between her mom and stepdad. But the problem obviously existed anyway. According to her mother, they'd even taken sides, a phrase that made it sound as if the guys had lined up on one end of the room and the women on the other. Backs to the wall. Ready to charge. Had her aunts and his uncles taken sides, too? With Logan's brothers married to her mom's sisters—a phenomenon that probably still had the town talking—she could only imagine the impact on family get-togethers.

Clutching the thread, she crossed her arms. The ripple effect of a stone dropped in a pool flashed in her mind. ''I think I know Logan's reasons for wanting this resolved. Trevor mentioned the problems he'd had with his brothers.'' She hesitated. ''But what's your reason?''

Radishes landed in the bowl. ''This is your home, too, Erin. I don't want you feeling you have to leave before you find a job because he's here.''

She looked just the way she sounded. Protective. Determined. ''But in all fairness, you need to get along with him, too. Mike and Amy are at ages where they couldn't care less what's going on with adults, but Zach and Mandy pick up everything. They need good examples from their oldest siblings.

''If you run into him, and if he seems receptive,'' she continued, having delivered her warnings and her concerns, ''tell him we're having chicken and rice and he's welcome to join us.'' Enormously adept at leaping from one fire to another, she reached for a bunch of scallions on the counter, noting the drawing paper and crayons scattered over the old, antique pine kitchen table. "Mandy? I asked you to get Amy. Where is she?"

A tow-headed little girl with a headful of springy curls and eyes as blue as her father's appeared around the corner. Mandy was only four years old, but she was already tired of being the baby in the family.

"She's upstairs in her room," came her faintly exasperated reply. "She's on the phone again."

"Go tell her to cut it short and come down here. Then come clear your project off the table."

"But you said not to interrupt on the phone. Not unless we're bleeding."

Erin watched her mom open her mouth as if to explain the difference between waiting until a parent was on the phone to ask questions and interrupting a teenage sibling who'd hogged the instrument for an hour. But her mom apparently decided it wasn't worth the effort at the moment. Having dealt with her oldest children, she took her youngest offspring by the shoulders and nudged her toward the table. A moment later, she called for Amy from the foot of the stairs, then reminded Zach, who'd burst into the room complaining that he was hungry, not to run in the house. The freckle-faced six-year-old, all elbows and appetite, slid to a stop by the refrigerator.

To the casual observer, things might appear a tad chaotic, but Erin knew her mom had everything under control. As she helped her little half sister gather papers into a pile, then quietly called out that she was leaving, she couldn't help wonder if she'd ever be that together herself. Her mother had a husband, four children living at home, and she was the director of Leesburg's chamber of commerce.

All Erin was responsible for was her own life—and she wasn't doing such a hot job of managing even that.

They needed a good example from their oldest siblings. The admonishment made her feel like a child herself.

Hating the feeling, wondering if Trevor even suspected he was supposed to be a role model, she stepped outside, closing the screen behind her with a muffled thud.

The hum of the heavy-duty engine had grown to a deep-throated purr. In the gathering twilight, she could see a cloud of dust moving along the mile-long road that led to the ranch from the highway. By the time it reached the curve that led down toward the compound, she could see Trevor behind the wheel.

Since he could also see her and she was obviously on her way to the compound herself, there was no way she could gracefully avoid him. Wondering when she'd become a masochist, she tipped her chin up and reminded herself she wasn't even going to try.

Chapter Two

The mottled shade of the yard gave way to heat rising from the road as Erin left the main house and headed for the apartment above the stable. In the distance she could hear the muffled buzz of a saw from the workshop and the pitiful bawling of calves recently separated from their mothers. Her route would take her directly past the long, open garage Trevor had just turned into, but she didn't allow her steps to slow. Her mentor at the huge public relations firm she'd resigned from last month, a forty-something dynamo who'd clawed her way to the top by possessing the persistence of a gnat and the face of a twenty year old, had firmly believed that appearance was everything. It didn't matter what you were inside, it was how you were perceived.

If you can't dazzle them with brilliance, baffle them with bull. The phrase her mentor liked to quote had actually been a bit more descriptive than that, but it was the philosophy that was important. Erin had always had trouble with the clawing part and she'd never been able to accept that looks and connections were more important than integrity. But if she had learned anything in the wilds of the Los Angeles public relations market—beyond the fact that she didn't belong in it—it was the value of never letting the opposition know where you were most vulnerable.

The opposition had just killed his engine.

Erin heard the Bronco's door slam shut. The sharp report carried like a gunshot in the sultry evening air and drew her glance to where Max spun in a circle by his master's long legs. There was still enough pup in the dog that his tail wagged constantly. Even when Trevor motioned him to sit and the dog immediately obeyed, that tail simply couldn't stay still.

It was no wonder Zach and Mandy adored him, she thought. Spot, the aging family pet, still had a few bursts of energy left in him, but like an old man who preferred a nap to horseplay, his tolerance for exuberant children was limited. Max was a kid himself.

She was twenty feet away when that bundle of canine enthusiasm caught sight of her. Tail whipping like a wiper blade, he bounded over for a pat, then wheeled to search out his water dish.

Ten more feet and Trevor saw her, and promptly went still as stone.

He'd stopped by his back fender to frown at the layer of dust that had settled over the black paint. This time of year, with no rain and the temperature gaining another degree every day, there wasn't much of anything that wasn't covered with a layer of the pale tan stuff. Erin's little red Mustang, parked three spaces down, definitely needed a bath.

She thought he was frowning at the dust, anyway. Considering that the quality of his scowl didn't change when he turned to fully face her, she had the distinct feeling he'd actually been thinking about her.

"Mom said to tell you they're having chicken and rice for dinner up at the house, and that you're welcome to join them. You don't have to worry," she added, her tone deliberately light. "I won't be there."

Having delivered the invitation, she offered a small smile and turned on her heel. Getting along was going to be a piece of cake.

"Why did you come back?"

The blunt question froze her in her tracks.

"There was a time when all you talked about was moving back to L.A., Erin. L.A. had been your home. It was where your friends were. You were completely obsessed with going back to live in the city."

Trevor watched her slowly turn to face him. He hadn't intended to challenge her so bluntly. But habits where Erin was concerned were hard to break. Since his tone had been less than civil, he braced himself for more of the defensiveness she'd treated him to that morning. Yet all he saw in the delicate lines of her face was a strange sort of withdrawal he didn't recognize at all. Or maybe, he thought, it looked more like defeat. He dismissed the disquieting conclusion even as it occurred.

"I wanted a job closer to home," she said simply.

Skepticism slashed his brow. The agreement he'd made with his father managed to keep most of that doubt from his tone. "That's it?"

"Pretty much."

The skepticism deepened, anyway. "What happened to that promotion you were up for? Didn't you get it?"

She matched his frown. "How did you know about that? The promotion, I mean."

"Dad mentioned it. Is that why you came back?" he asked, refusing to be diverted. "Because your job wasn't working?"

"I got the promotion, Trevor. I was given an office with a window, which happens to be a big thing in a city, and a secretary and my own accounts. I just didn't want it. Any of it. What I wanted was a job in a smaller city and as I said, one closer to home."

Despite the ease of her remarkably patient responses, Trevor could practically see her pulling into herself. That withdrawal was in the way she couldn't quite hold his glance, the restraint in her tone and the protective way she'd crossed her arms. That wasn't like Erin at all. The girl he remembered had worn every emotion on her sleeve, and there hadn't been a thought she'd kept from him. Granted, it had been years since they'd had that ease. But he would bet every one of the ten thousand acres of the ranch he'd inherited at eighteen that there was more going on than she was admitting to him. More, perhaps, than she'd admitted to anyone else.

"I don't get it." He liked things straightforward, reasonable. "You earn a degree. You land the sort of job you always talked about having. In the city you always talked about living in," he emphasized, "and you give it all up to come back to a place you once claimed to hate? You even ran away," he reminded her, sweeping his arm in the direction of the town she'd run from. "I gave you a ride to Austin so you could catch a bus. Remember?"

His attitude goaded her, but she wasn't about to let him know it. In the barn that morning, she'd let herself be hurt by the knowledge that he'd had to be pushed to make peace with her. And being hurt made her defensive. It was patterned behavior where he was concerned. The same sort of action-reaction response a horse had to someone who'd mistreated it. The animal shied or lashed out. She'd simply pushed him away like he'd pushed her.

"Of course I remember," she replied, quite aware that he was still pushing. "I wound up taking a plane instead of the bus." That was after her mom and his dad found them, which was totally beside the point. She didn't want to think about that awful time in her life. She'd felt so confused, so frightened. So alone. "But I was sixteen at the time. It took a while to…"

Her words trailed off with the slow shake of her head. It had taken her a while to accept that nothing could ever be as it was—that Leesburg and eventually the ranch would be the closest thing she'd ever again have to home. But at first, she'd fought everything about the laid-back little town. The move to it. The people in it.

Her only friend had been Trevor. He'd helped her through the pain of losing her father, her anger with her mother for tearing up what roots they had left and moving them from the only home she'd ever known. He'd been solid and strong and far more sensitive than anyone she'd ever known.

"And I missed my family," she admitted, wondering at the distance he'd put between them since then. "And the horses," she added with a little laugh that said she'd been as surprised as anyone by how much a city girl had come to adore something so innately wild. "I had a client outside L.A. who raised quarter horses. After we became friends, I'd spend weekends exercising them for her, just to be around them again."

She was searching for common ground, hoping to find something that could get them past their differences. She didn't believe for a moment that they could ever be friends, but she couldn't deal with the agitation she felt around him, either. She'd come home to start over, not to dredge up old animosities. And since she'd never known anyone who possessed the affinity he did for animals, she felt certain he would know what she meant about missing them herself.

The connection she sought simply wasn't there. The steadiness of his steel gray gaze as he considered her made it clear that he either didn't like what he was hearing. Or, that he didn't believe her.

Irritation vied with defeat when she realized that. She was being as cooperative with him as she knew how to be. And every word she'd uttered was the absolute truth. It was the parts she'd omitted, however, that kept her from indulging annoyance and forced her glance from his. He would be the last person to sympathize with how difficult it had been to come back after the fuss she'd put up about moving to California to begin with. And her experience with the man she'd come disastrously close to marrying— a humiliating little affair that had proved what happened when a woman like her tried to swim with sharks—wasn't something she cared to share with someone who'd done a number on her himself.

"None of that should be hard for you to understand, Trevor. I'm sure there were things you missed while you were gone, too. As for family," she defended, preferring to focus on his shortcomings rather than her own, "you won't be able to duck the dinner invitations from Mom and your dad forever."

"Who said I was ducking them?"

She slanted him a droll look.

Unbelievably the tips of his ears colored.

"I've been busy since I got back."

The excuse was every bit as lame as it sounded, but she

had the negligible satisfaction of seeing his glance falter before she tightened her arms around herself and took a step back. Something else she'd forgotten about Trevor was how much of a loner he'd been. Still was, for all she knew. He'd always preferred the company of his horses and the stock to any of the kids at school. The only friends he'd claimed had been among his dad's ranch hands. Men who were content by themselves. The way his dad had once been. When she'd first met him, she'd been the first female on two legs that had set foot on the ranch in years. Logan had told her so himself.

She edged back, wondering as she did if that had been part of the reason Trevor hadn't wanted her. Maybe he was a man who simply preferred to go it alone.

"You should try giving the family a chance." She couldn't let it matter why he'd pushed her away. And it didn't, she assured herself. All she cared about was that, while she was here, everyone got along. "You might find you actually enjoy being part of it."

It seemed to Trevor that there was a lot of strain in the smile she offered before she turned away, but it was the advice she offered that gave him pause. There was a ring of helpfulness to it that he never would have expected. Not from her.

He wasn't an unreasonable man. Nor was he an ungrateful one. He was just a man trying to find where he fit in a place that wasn't what it had once been. Erin had been right when she'd said he didn't want trouble. All he wanted was to get on with his life. And his life was not the one up at the main house. Despite the offer she had just passed on, he doubted that Sam wanted him up there. She was just being polite. And since he didn't want to be there, either, the only thing for him to do that made any sense

at all was to mind his own business and stay out of everyone's way.

Minding his own business was exactly what Trevor was
doing when he strode through the compound at ten o'clock
the next morning. He'd been up at five, downed breakfast
and a pot of coffee strong enough to wrestle a steer and
headed out to cut potential breeders from a lot of heifers.
As soon as he showered and changed he'd be on his way
out to the Eiger place to see what had put their daughter's
champion barrel-racing horse off its feed. He would check
with Verna, Doc Henderson's office assistant, after he finished to see if there were any other calls in that direction
before looking in on a foundering mare out by Dry Creek
and inoculating a couple of calves the Withers boy was
raising for a 4H project. Unless an emergency arose, he
could be back by six to help feed the five hundred cow-
calf pairs that were being shipped out in a couple of days.

Those plans were always subject to change. On a ranch,
what a man had planned for the day wasn't necessarily
what he accomplished. A rancher woke each morning
knowing what he planned to do, and usually got about half
of it done before something else demanded his attention.
There was always a fence to repair, a water supply to
check, animals to sort, move, inoculate, deworm, dehorn,
breed, wean.

And that was if the weather held.

That he wanted to do all that and work as a vet, too,
would have daunted most men. It was the only life Trevor
had ever contemplated.

He passed the protective fencing leading to the bull pens
and the nose-ringed masses of muscle and testosterone
snorting inside, purpose in his step and Max at his heels.
The summer sun beat down on his shoulders, dampening

the collar of his shirt and trickling perspiration down the small of his back. Whipping his hat off, he wiped the sweat from his forehead with his forearm and jammed his hat back on.

When he glanced back up, a mischievous little dust devil was whirling its way across the road, picking up bits of leaf and twig and bending the dry grass along the fence. Absently following its path toward the stables, he noticed Erin in the training corral.

The purpose leaked from his stride. Even at a distance, he could see that she had her slender back to the sleek chestnut pacing nervously behind her.

The thought that she shouldn't have her back to an agitated animal lodged on top of the thought that she had no business being alone in that ring at all. Leg muscles tensed to sprint, he saw Hank, the grizzled foreman of the RW, hanging on the fence watching in absolute silence. The fact that Hank wasn't shouting at her to keep her eye on the thousand pounds of power and muscle behind her made no sense to him at all.

It didn't occur to him to question that he was on his way to haul her out of the ring. He didn't even bother to remind himself that it was none of his business if she broke her graceful little neck. He was too busy trying to imagine what had possessed his dad and Hank to let her handle the horses in the first place. An inexperienced trainer could ruin a good horse.

He was within a hundred feet of the corral when he noticed one of the wranglers sitting on the railing near the gate. Dusty had a wad of chew ballooning one cheek, a circular can of the stuff visible in the pocket of his checkered shirt and a lasso draped over his chaps.

The realization that the wrangler was prepared to rope the horse if it posed a threat registered a scant second before Hank turned toward him. Holding up his gloved hand, the older man silenced the warnings and questions so obviously etched in Trev's scowl.

Erin still had her back to them, and to the horse. Only now, the horse had lowered his head and was moving toward her. Its movements were tentative, and the little whinny it gave sounded nervous, impatient or maybe a little of both.

Trevor's glance shifted to Erin. She was wearing a white T-shirt with the face of a gray wolf silkscreened above the words Wolf Preservation Society tucked into jeans that made her legs look a mile long. A single, wheat-colored braid hung a few inches down her back. He remembered when that braid had been long enough to hang between her narrow shoulder blades, but the sunlight still caught shades of silver and honey in the intricate weave. Those glints of light shifted as she turned, her motions deliberate and slow.

The horse whinnied again. Definitely nervous, Trevor thought.

Erin took a single step forward, ducking her head slightly to catch the horse's eye. As she raised her head, the horse raised his.

Trevor instantly knew what she was doing. The fact that *she* knew what she was doing stopped him cold.

"I've only known two other people who can gentle a horse that way. You and your dad," Hank admitted, nudging back the brim of his battered brown hat. A wealth of wrinkles creased skin tanned the color of saddle leather. "Who'd have thought a city girl would have the touch." He shook his head, the gray bristles of his thick mustache moving like a wave as he switched his perpetually unlit cigar from one corner of his mouth to the other. "Amazin', isn't it?"

Hank's question was more statement than query. He wasn't looking to Trev for an answer, anyway. He wasn't looking at Trevor at all. His rheumy blue eyes were trained on the young woman now slowly moving toward the horse, trailing a sash line behind her. When she was two feet from the chestnut's head, she held out her hand and waited for the animal to step forward. The coppery tips of the horse's ears cocked toward her, his big nostrils twitching.

Trev kept his voice deliberately low. It wouldn't take much to spook the horse, not as skittish as it was. "How'd she pick that up in a month?"

"In a month?" Hank's voice was a low rasp, a little like gravel rolling around the bottom of a barrel. "What are you talking about?"

"She's only been here about that long, hasn't she?"

"I suppose so. Give or take." He watched Erin ease herself along the horse's flank. The horse sidestepped and she waited a moment before moving forward and touching him again. This time the horse stayed still, clearly waiting to see what she would do next. "But she's got a dang sight more than a month's experience doing this. When she was living here before, she spent near every weekend and all summer working out here with the yearlings. All the summers she was in college, too." He hooked a boot on the low rung, his focus on the slow dance of budding trust taking place in the corral. "When she came back this time, I don't think she even had herself unpacked before she was out here checking on her favorites. Twilight here's one of Firelight's throws."

Firelight was the horse she'd learned to ride on. The only reason Trev remembered that was because he'd picked the horse for her himself. He'd wanted something gentle, something that wouldn't frighten her. Erin had been skittish as a filly herself when she'd first encountered the massive animals, and totally reliant on his experience to keep her safe.

He felt the muscles in his jaw tighten as he breathed in the familiar perfume of warm earth and animals. There was no reason the memory should have been so clear. No reason he should have been so disconcerted by it. He shook it off, reminding himself that the girl he'd known would never have possessed the patience, the confidence, or the interest to work the magic he witnessed now. She seemed to communicate with the beautiful young mare in a way he'd seen few others master; her touch, her voice and her movements conveyed meaning far better than any trainer with a whip or spurs. Her empathy and expertise were that of someone who'd been born in a saddle. Yet, he knew she'd never touched horseflesh until he'd held her hand and guided it to Firelight himself.

He was about to tell himself that she'd never shown any interest in horses beyond wanting to learn to ride when he felt his conscience kick hard. He had no idea what her interests had been after he'd started backing away from her. Or maybe he had known, but it just hadn't mattered. Once he'd left for college, he'd blocked her out the same way he had most everything else concerning his new "family."

"Well, I ain't got time to stand here watching this," Hank muttered, cranking his head toward the sun to check the time rather than looking at his watch. "Did you need me for something?"

"No. No," Trevor repeated, ignoring the fact that he'd been on his way to snatch her out of the ring. "I was on my way to get cleaned up and just came over to see what was going on. I've got a couple calls to make."

A grin split the old man's weathered face. "Doc Whitaker," he drawled, doing another shift with his cigar.

"Still can't get used to people calling here asking for you by that name. That's all you talked about from the time you were nine years old. Being a vet, I mean. Kinda hard to believe it finally happened."

For the grizzled old cowhand, the blunt observation was downright sentimental. Embarrassed to have shown a soft spot, he mumbled something about how the day wasn't getting any younger and sauntered off, his shoulders rolling with his bow-legged gate. The man could go from companionable to cantankerous in the blink of an eye, and sixty-some years of sitting a saddle had definitely left their mark.

The groan of a metal gate joined the beat of hooves on hard-packed ground. His attention nudged by the sounds, Trev saw Erin turn the chestnut into a connected corral. He had no idea how long she'd worked the horse before he'd noticed her, but she was giving it a break now. Or maybe, he thought, watching her wave to the wrangler as he headed off to the horse pasture, she had other things she needed to do.

He should let her go.

He should go.

"Got a minute?" he called.

She was pulling off her gloves when her head came up. Fisting the chamois-colored leather in one hand, she hugged her arms beneath her breasts, obliterating the words below the wolf's face, and started toward him. If her body language was any indication, she felt more unease with him than she did a half ton of green-broke and potentially dangerous equine. She'd been open to the horse, vulnerable in a way that said "I'll trust you if you'll trust me." With him, it was as clear as the caution shadowing the delicate lines of her face that she didn't trust him at all.

There had been a time when he wouldn't have cared. He told himself he didn't care now.

"How long did that take?"

She stopped a foot from the railing. In the morning light, her skin looked smooth as cream, its perfection marred only by the faint shadows beneath her eyes. She looked tired, he thought, as if sleep hadn't come easily to her last night.

"To let me touch him, you mean?"

"Yeah," he murmured, wanting to blame the heat, but knowing it was thoughts of her that had been responsible for his own little battle with the sheets.

"About an hour. I was getting ready to let him go and try later when he finally dropped his head." Her own head tipped to one side. "Why?"

"Just curious. I didn't know Dad had taught you how to do that."

Puzzlement swept her features, her brow lowering in incomprehension. "Your dad helped me a lot," she admitted. "But I learned that from you."

"I didn't teach you that. The only thing I taught you was how to ride."

"No, Trevor. You were the one—" As if suddenly deciding the reminder wasn't worth the effort, she cut herself off. Skimming a glance over his face, she slowly shook her head and turned away with a quiet "Never mind."

In one breath Trevor damned the rail that kept him from reaching out to stop her. In the next he was thankful the barrier was there. Considering that he'd spent half the night wondering if her skin felt as soft as it looked, touching her didn't seem like such a hot idea. Even if it was just to keep her from leaving. "Why do you have to do that?"

She glanced back over her shoulder, snagging back the

strand of hair that blew across her face as she did. "Do what?"

"That," he emphasized. "You get upset or something doesn't go your way and you walk off."

"No, I don't."

"Yes, you do. You just did it. You did it yesterday morning in the stable. You used to do it all the time." His dark eyebrows knitted tighter. "It irritated the hell out of me."

She wasn't upset. She couldn't see where she wasn't getting her way, either. If she walked off, it was strictly a defense mechanism.

Not caring to share that with him, she said nothing—which put the ball back in his court.

For a moment, he didn't seem to know what to do with it. Then, surprisingly, he murmured, "I'm sorry. I just don't remember working with you and the horses."

The last thing she ever expected to hear from Trev Whitaker was an apology. Not to her. And not for anything.

"You'd bring me out here after school," she reminded him, cautiously eyeing the man cautiously eyeing her. "I used to watch you. With the horses," she explained, thinking it apparent that she'd cherished more about the time they'd spent together than he did. "You seemed to have a ritual every time you entered the corral with a green horse. You would say the same things. Do the same things. You said you and the horse were just learning to talk to each other."

It had been years, but she could clearly remember him telling her how hard it must be for a horse to know what a human wanted it to do. The huge animal was torn from his herd, taken from everything familiar, and the only way to calm it was to let it know you meant it no harm. Beating a horse into submission as some trainers did didn't break the horse. All it did was break its spirit.

That was rather how she had felt herself, she thought. She'd been torn from the life she'd known when her father had died and it seemed as if the Fates had tried to beat her into submission by piling one change on top of another. She'd kept bucking those changes and getting nowhere. That had to be why she'd been so drawn to Trevor at the time. It took incredible compassion and patience to work with something so frightened. And she'd been scared to death by the changes taking place in her life at that time.

In some ways, she felt just like that now.

Reminding herself she'd be fine once she was away from the ranch and back in the routine of projects, meetings and deadlines, she glanced from the V of sweat darkening his denim shirt to where his left hand idly stroked Max's head. He scarcely seemed aware of the gentle motions that were second nature to him.

"After you left, I started coming down to the stables," she continued, wondering what had caused him to lose that gentleness with her. "Your dad found me down here once, and when he asked what I was doing, I told him I wanted to learn how to talk to the horses the way you did."

Surprisingly, Logan hadn't balked at all. He'd told her that anyone who'd learned to ride as quickly as she had, must have an affinity for the animals. She'd liked that, the idea that she had an affinity for something. Heaven knew, she'd needed something to feel good about.

A faint smile touched her mouth. It had been during those unexpectedly companionable times that Logan's wariness of the teenager he'd inherited when he'd married the woman he loved finally began to ease, and Erin's respect and affection for the big, intimidating rancher had begun to grow.

"It was a long time before he let me work without him," she confided, aware that Trev's glance had shifted to the curve of her lips. "Even then, he had Hank watch me like a hawk."

Trev didn't doubt that for an instant. Hank would have been there to make sure she stayed out of trouble. But he would have been there, too, to keep his eye on any of the men around her. No one was more particular than Logan Whitaker about who he hired, but there wasn't a monk in the lot. And Erin, with her shy eyes, peach-soft mouth and those incredible legs, had looked like pure temptation even then.

Temptation, he thought, rolling the word over in his mind. That was exactly what she was, though the shyness was long gone. Yet, what struck him over the physical appeal he'd have to be dead to deny, was that something that mattered so much to him had made such an impression on her.

"I can't believe you remember what I did in the ring."

"I think I remember everything you ever told me about horses," she quietly admitted. "Actually, I remember a lot of things you taught me." A self-deprecating smile lit her eyes, turning them more gold than green. "Like never to stand under a tree in a thunderstorm. And never to leave the stall gates open when you're preparing feed."

His dark eyebrow arched. "Or when a mare is in heat?"

"Especially that," she agreed, clearly remembering the day the stallion Trevor had ridden had cornered a little mare she'd gone into the stable to see.

Her smile faltered. His glance held hers, his gray eyes darkening as that memory triggered another.

That was also the day he had taught her how to kiss.

To this day she didn't know how she'd made it out of that stall so fast, or how Trevor had managed to muscle

the stallion away from the pretty little bay. She had only
the impression of Trevor moving like lightning to get the
big roan back before he hurt the mare or himself in the
confined quarters.

Horses needed room to mate, and there was no room for
the stallion to mount. That didn't mean he wouldn't batter
down a wall trying, though. Nature could be pretty demanding. But they hadn't wanted that mare mated, anyway. It was her first season and they liked to wait until
their mares were more mature before producing a foal. Or
so he explained after the stallion had been corralled.

He'd talked of mating as easily as most people discussed
the weather, but she was sure she'd been blushing furi-
ously. She'd told him she was sorry, that she hadn't meant
to cause a problem. He'd simply looked at her, told her
no harm had been done and pushed the hair back from her
face. The next thing she knew he'd lowered his head.

Kiss me back, Erin, he'd coaxed, framing her face with
his big hands. *That's it, honey. Open your mouth. Breathe
into me.*

He'd coaxed her to relax, gentling her with his hands,
his voice. She'd been a little nervous and enormously curious to know what a real kiss felt like. She'd been dying
to know since the week before, when he'd held her while
she cried. Her experience until then had been non-existent.
But Trevor taught her how to kiss him back, how a woman
responds to a man. How to want so badly she ached.

The memory shouldn't be so clear. So compelling. But
as Trevor's glance lingered on her mouth, his own looking
too hard to feel as soft as she remembered, she felt certain
it was only the memory that gathered the heat low in her
stomach.

Or so she tried to convince herself just before she saw
him raise his hand toward her. It hovered by her head for

a frantic heartbeat before she felt his fingers brush the hair above her ear. The touch was featherlight and seemed to disappear for an instant before she felt him smooth back the loosened strands.

His eyes were steady on hers when his hand fell away.

"Straw," he said, holding out a two-inch piece that had lodged in her hair.

He could have dropped it. Let it float to the ground where it would disappear among the maze of other stalks that had been trampled into the dirt. But he just held it there, waiting for her to take it.

Erin had no idea why she did. His gesture seemed to be part curiosity, part challenge and, had she been thinking, she might have simply taken the straw and tossed it away. But her fingers brushed his, the contact jolting heat up her arm, and she closed the broken stem in her palm.

Trevor was already pulling back when the muffled drone of men's voices drifted toward them. He had no business touching her. And that was all removing the straw had been. Nothing but an excuse to feel the texture of her skin and to see if her hair was as silky as he recalled. There were some memories of her that hadn't been buried as deeply as he'd thought. If the awareness she'd tried to hide in her eyes was any indication, she had a few memories of her own.

"Hey, Trev. I thought you were heading out."

Max was first to respond to Logan Whitaker. Wheeling with a sharp bark of recognition, the dog darted toward Trevor's dad. Tall, broad-shouldered and powerfully built, the oldest of the Whitaker men strode toward them, calling out to the hand unloading hay from a flatbed to take two bales over to the bull pens, then stopped to give Max a pet when the animal plopped himself at his feet.

Even with his dad's eyes shadowed by the brim of his

tan Stetson, Trev was aware of his shrewd glance shifting from him to the woman in the ring.

"Mornin', Erin."

"Good morning," she greeted, strain shadowing her smile as she backed up a step. Looking oddly self-conscious, she motioned behind her, explaining that she had tack to polish. A moment later, she was headed across the corral.

Trevor watched the curve of her backside as she slipped between the horizontal rungs and disappeared into the stable.

Logan watched his son.

"Everything okay?"

The two men were nearly identical in size and physique, and while Logan's features had forty-six years of wear and tear reflected in them, the physical resemblance between them was strong. Trev had his mother's eyes, though. Unlike the intense blue the Whitaker brothers shared, his were the cool, clear gray of his mother's, the only reminder he possessed of a woman he'd never known.

"I don't know if I'd go that far."

"At least you're talking."

"I suppose."

"Look. I know she's a woman," Logan said, sounding as if that somehow put a man at an automatic disadvantage. "But she's also family."

Logan Whitaker could say more with less words than anyone Trev knew. And what Trevor got from his dad just then was that he realized their circumstances weren't exactly normal. Usually, when a relationship ended, the parties simply went their separate ways. He and Erin had never had that luxury. Yet, while he appreciated that his father understood that, Trevor didn't understand the emphasis his dad put on family. As far as Trev was concerned, family was his dad and whatever animal he happened to have living with him at the time. To his dad—and to Erin, too, it seemed—the concept obviously meant something totally beyond him.

"I told you I'd get along with her."

Logan's mouth pressed in a hard line as he clapped his son on the shoulder.

"Appreciate the effort," was all he said before he dug his heavy key ring from the pocket of his jeans and headed for one of the battered white ranch Jeeps parked by the tractor shed.

Trevor had work to do, too.

With the flick of his fingers, he signaled Max to his side and made for the single-wide trailer next to Hank's, down by the pecan orchard. His father had never interfered in his life. He'd raised him by example, and all he'd ever asked of Trevor was that he be honest, fair and keep his sights on his goals. He'd had to drop out of vet school himself to take over the ranch when his own father died. And since his wife had wanted no part of ranching life, or motherhood, he'd also been left to raise his son alone. That he didn't want Trevor repeating his mistakes was understandable. And he'd always regarded marrying young and never having the opportunity to travel as the two biggest mistakes he'd ever made.

The only thought Trevor had ever given marriage was to avoid it. As for travel, his dad's feelings over the years about missed opportunities had undoubtedly influenced his decision to take on the research projects he had after he'd completed his training. He'd spent two years trekking between Argentina and Australia getting any wanderlust he possessed out of his system and waiting for the day his contract was up so he could come home.

In a way he supposed he'd done what he had for his father's sake as much as his own. And for his father's sake he was doing what he'd asked where Erin was concerned.

What he really needed to do, however, was keep his hands to himself.

"Next time, bite me or something," he muttered to the dog trotting alongside him. "Okay, Max?"

The dog barked in response, his tail going a mile a minute.

A tug of amusement made Trevor smile, but the expression was fleeting. There wasn't going to be a next time. But even if there had been, Max wasn't going to be around to help.

It was too bad he had to give him up, he thought, knowing he was really going to miss that sweet little canine face. Without Max to pitch balls to in the evenings, he'd have to resort to pacing.

And Trevor knew there would be a lot of that in the days ahead.

Four hours wasted, Erin thought, her high heels tapping on the wooden steps that led to the stable apartment. Four hours that she could have spent working with Twilight, or appliquéing shirts, or looking for some other job. It wasn't that the interview with the public relations firm of Putney & Robinson hadn't gone well. They'd seemed impressed enough with her credentials, but she'd been halfway through a tour of their beautiful, spacious offices when she'd known the job wasn't for her. Beneath the creative energy she'd thrived on at Lowell and Associates was the almost tangible stress of competition. Competition for another company's clients. Competition among the account execs to create the best campaign, to put out the biggest media fire, or to start one. Competition to stay competitive.

She wasn't sure why she'd felt it so keenly. But it hadn't been a pleasant feeling at all. Certainly not one she wanted to confront every day. She felt certain it was just that particular agency, but she'd wondered all the way back to the ranch if maybe she shouldn't be looking for a job in a smaller company, not just for one in a smaller town.

On top of that, she reminded herself, the salary they'd mentioned had been ridiculous. She was already prepared to earn less than she had in L.A. But just because the cost of living wasn't as high in Austin didn't mean she could live on half of what she had been earning.

Peanuts, she thought, reaching for the door. They'd offered peanuts for a job they should have offered double, for anyone to take. Antacids alone would cost a fortune.

The temptation to stew vanished with the rush of blessedly cool air when she stepped inside the functional little space of her apartment. She couldn't wait to strip off the suit and panty hose it was entirely too hot to wear. But she'd no sooner crossed the threshold than she felt a vague sense of disquiet.

Something wasn't right.

Leaving the door open, she took a single step inside. The beige blinds were slanted against the heat of the sun, slashing stripes of light on the cool white walls. A basket filled with lace medallions, ribbons and pearls obscured the magazines on the little coffee table, and the shirts she'd finished last night still lay folded over the arm of the old brown Naugahyde sofa. The place had always been used by men, and even though the spare quarters were only temporary for her, she kept a vase of whatever she could find blooming in the garden on the green Formica table.

Skimming a glance past the fist-size yellow sunflowers she'd picked yesterday, she dropped her purse on the counter by the two-burner stove.

Everything looked as neat as it had when she'd left that morning. But the commotion coming from her bedroom definitely captured her attention. Specifically, the whimper of a dog and the muffled sound of children's voices.

The bedroom closet was behind two mirrored sliding doors on the right wall of the narrow little room. Over the blue swirls of the bedspread, she could see Zach kneeling on the floor inside the closet and the back of Mandy's pink denim shorts as the little girl peered at whatever he was doing.

"Don't cover him up," she heard Mandy whisper loudly. "He'll smothercate."

"We need a water dish."

"I'll get one. And some food."

Erin planted her hands on the hips of her tailored, chocolate brown suit. "What have you got in there?"

At the curious demand, Mandy swung around, blond curls bobbing, and stifled her gasp of guilt with her hand. Blue eyes fixed on her oldest stepsister, she blinked back the suspicious brightness in her eyes while her brother backed his denim-covered backside out of the closet.

Looking just as guilty as his little sister when he straightened, Zach quickly shut the door and blocked it protectively with all three feet of his bony little frame.

Zach had a tendency to grin like an imp when caught red-handed. He'd been caught, all right, but at the moment, he, too, looked ready to cry.

Concern joined curiosity. "What's going on?" A thump from inside the closet was followed by a decidedly insistent bark. "Zach? Mandy? Do you have one of the dogs in there?" Erin asked, crossing the room.

"It's Max," Zach admitted.

"Don't let him out," Mandy begged, grabbing Erin's arm. "We have to hide him."

"Hide him? Whatever for?"

Wanting to be heard first, Zach pushed Mandy aside. "'Cause Trevor's going to give him away."

"An' we won't ever get to see him again." Undaunted by her bigger brother, Mandy pushed right back. "Can we hide him here? Please, Erin. Please?"

"I'll feed him and take him out after it gets dark and everything," Zach promised, swiping a hand over his buzz-cut, desperation shining in his innocent blue eyes. "Just don't tell Trevor where he is. Please?"

"Wait a minute. Both of you."

The last thump inside the closet had been accompanied by a whine. The one she heard now was joined by what sounded like her suitcases hitting the wall. Setting Zach aside, she slid the door back to see Max trample over the only other pair of heels she hadn't put in storage and emerge with a brightly colored afghan draped over his back.

Figuring the dog had survived the worst of his little ordeal, she left him to fend for himself and sat down on the end of her bed with an arm around each child. "Let's just calm down for a minute, okay? I'm sure you must have misunderstood something here. What makes you think Trevor is going to give Max away?"

"We heard him tell Daddy this morning." Mandy sniffed, rubbing her nose with the back of her hand. "Daddy said he's going to miss him, too."

"Well, I can't imagine Trevor would do that." What

they'd heard made no sense. Trevor doted on that dog. "Do you know where he is now?"

"I'm right here."

Erin's head snapped up. From where she sat with the kids, she could see that the outer door still hung open. Trevor stood at the threshold, his shoulders filling the doorway. Even though he blocked much of the midday light, it was easy enough to see that he didn't look pleased.

Chapter Three

Trevor didn't wait for the invitation Erin wouldn't have offered, anyway. Ducking as he removed his hat, he stepped inside. As he did, Max wandered over to greet his master, trailing the afghan like a royal robe.

"Hey, fella," Trev said quietly, hunching down to toss the afghan aside. He scratched behind the dog's ears, soothing him as if to make up for the indignity. "I've been looking all over for you."

Zach and Mandy both turned pleading eyes to the woman who was more like an aunt to them than a stepsister. Do something, those silent pleas seemed to say.

The pure affection Erin heard in Trevor's murmurings to Max had her more convinced than ever that the kids had somehow misunderstood. Wanting to be sure, she extricated herself and rose from the bed. Trevor straightened, too, his glance moving from her legs and the slim skirt brushing her knees to the chunky gold necklace at the jewel neckline of her jacket.

She had no idea what crossed his mind as his glance moved openly to the sophisticated sweep of hair coiled at the base of her neck. She wasn't concerned with his impression of her at the moment. Her only concern was the two children who expected her help.

"Zach and Mandy are under the impression you're giving Max away."

"I am."

"You are?"

"No," Mandy cried, running past Erin to throw her arms around the dog's neck. "You can't. Don't let him, Erin."

"Mandy. Zach," she said, not at all sure why Trevor suddenly looked so confused. "Take Max outside to play. I want to talk to Trevor."

"I want to stay here."

"Me, too," Zach echoed.

"Then take him in the bedroom," she conceded, peeling the little girl from the dog so she could grasp his collar and turn him in the right direction.

Turning back to the man watching the trio reluctantly depart, she planted her hands on her hips. "Do you have a minute?"

"Why do I have the feeling you won't take no for an answer."

"Maybe it's because you're very perceptive."

"What's going on with them?"

"That's what I'd like to know," she said, as soon as the children closed the bedroom door. "Why are you giving Max away?"

"Because it's time. Max is a companion dog. Or he will be," he amended, shifting his frown between her and the door the kids had cracked back open. "I've socialized him, now I have to turn him in to the center for training. When he's ready, he'll be matched with a handicapped person." Watching the mother-hen look slip from her face, he mirrored her stance. "What's the big deal?"

Erin glanced behind her. Seeing the door partially open, she checked the edge as if to make sure she wouldn't catch any fingers and pulled it shut. A moment later, she'd moved past him, tightening his gut with the light scent of spring she wore and the subtle shift of her hips beneath crisp linen. There was nothing particularly provocative about the way she was dressed. The color and cut of her suit were all business. Her jewelry simple. Her hair restrained. Her legs...unbelievable. The overall effect was sophisticated. Understated. And as different from the cotton shirts and denim she normally wore as night was from day.

Even as the thought occurred, he was forced to amend it. He'd seen her in cotton and denim because that was what a practical person wore working around stables. For the past several years, she undoubtedly looked much the way she did now. Competent. Capable. Classy.

She'd stopped by the sink in the corner kitchenette. "The 'big deal,'" she explained, her soft voice deliberately low as he approached, "is that the kids don't want him to go. They were trying to hide him so you couldn't take him."

"You're kidding."

The look she gave him was as tolerant as her silence.

"I have to take him," he defended, still at a loss. "When you get one of these dogs, it's with the understanding that you'll give it back. It's not like he's really mine."

"Did you mention this to them before?"

He barely talked to the kids at all. Rarely saw them, for that matter. "Why would I?"

In disbelief, she lowered her voice to nearly a whisper. "You would mention it because it would be easier on them," she explained, looking as if she couldn't believe he didn't know that. "If you'd warned them from the beginning that Max wouldn't be around long, they wouldn't be so disappointed that he has to go. At the very least, they'd have been better prepared for this."

"He's only been around for a week. How attached can they be?"

A moment ago, he thought she'd seemed confused. Now, the mother-hen look was back.

"They're children, Trevor. They don't measure their feelings or protect their emotions. It's not a skill they've acquired yet. If they care about something, that's all that matters. They care about Max and they're upset because they won't see him again."

"Then explain the situation to them," he told her, exasperated. Casting an uneasy glance toward the door, he noticed that it was open again. His deep voice dropped like a rock in a well. "It's not like I'm trying to upset them on purpose. Just talk to them and tell them to hand over the dog."

Erin couldn't believe how insensitive he was being. Or, incredibly, how generous. The incongruity of his actions would have confused her completely had she thought about it. As it was, all she considered was the wary way he'd looked back toward the kids, who were now watching him just as uneasily from around the corner.

Seeing the three of them eye each other, the basic problem with the predicament was suddenly too glaring to miss.

"You explain it to them," she countered, thinking it

interesting that a man she'd known to wrestle breeder bulls and soothe newborn calves would actually be intimidated by small children. "They're your siblings, too."

"But you could—"

He broke off suddenly, a muscle in his jaw bunching as he considered her. He had the look of a man who would rather be anywhere than where he'd just found himself. And, though the temptation was strong, she couldn't stand there and let him flounder on his own.

"If you don't know how to talk to them," she began, telling herself she was only thinking of the children, "you might start by getting down to their level." She looked from the hat dent in his dark hair to the tips of his scarred boots. Six foot two had to be awfully intimidating to someone in the three-foot range. "You look like a mountain to them."

He looked like a mountain to her, too, but it wasn't intimidation she felt at the moment. It was surprise. And an odd sort of sympathy. He hadn't bothered to deny how uneasy the children made him. He'd simply looked to her for help.

"Then what?" he asked.

Trevor would be the first to admit he knew squat about kids—of the human variety, anyway. Goats, he could deal with. Sheep. Dogs. Cats. Cattle. Horses. Put four feet on a mammal and he was home free. With children, especially female children, he'd discovered, he felt like the proverbial bull in a china shop.

Mandy, with her cornsilk curls and impossibly innocent eyes, had her arms around Max's neck. Max, tongue lolling and tail working in a slow wave against the floor, sat happily panting up at him.

He felt Erin move beside him, her voice quiet near his

ear. "You could start by telling them you really don't want to let him go yourself."

It was pretty clear to him that the children huddled with the dog expected one of them to explain what was going on. Dead certain he'd get nothing from Erin but advice, he decided he might as well take it.

Hunkering down by the stove, he avoided the two sets of unhappy blue eyes and held his hand out to Max, who promptly leaned his big head forward and licked his knuckles.

"I like Max, too," he said, sounding as uncomfortable as he looked. "He's my buddy. But I made an agreement with the people I got him from that I'd give him back when he was a year old." His brow furrowed when he glanced at the woman quietly watching him. "Do they know what an agreement is?"

She raised one shoulder in a rather elegant shrug. She was only going to help him so far.

He looked back to the kids.

Mandy's pink little mouth twisted in concentration, an expression he found oddly sweet.

Zach nodded vigorously. "It's like a promise."

"Yeah. Like a promise," Trev echoed, focusing on the little boy since he, at least, grasped the concept. "Anyway, I promised I'd give him back, and that's what I have to do. I've had to do it before."

"You gave Max back before?" Mandy asked, clearly confused.

"Not Max. I raised two other dogs just like him. They're both helping blind people right now."

"But Max can help us right here," Mandy insisted. Her bottom lip quivered. "He can be a herd dog for Daddy."

The kid was crying. Big, fat tears gathered in her eyes and rolled down her cheeks. Trev looked from her to Zach, who was trying hard to be braver than his little sister, and felt a knot of helplessness twist in his gut.

"I'm afraid that's not possible," he began, only to see the child's face twist with a sob as she darted for Erin.

Feeling like the town bully, he rose and stepped away. Erin was right there, crouched down by the trio, one arm around the little girl and her free hand rubbing Zach's back. Her skirt rode up her thigh and one heel slipped from the back of her pump, but she seemed oblivious to everything except the need to tend the tears.

"Hey," she coaxed, "it's not like Max is going to doggie heaven," she explained, her voice as gentle as spring rain. "He's going to go help people. Don't you know how special that is?"

Trevor wasn't sure what else she said. Or what the kids said in response. He wasn't really listening. He was aware more of the calming effect of her voice, and how natural she looked soothing two kids while a blissfully panting dog nosed her arm so he could get a pet, too.

Something tugged in his chest, something totally unfamiliar and more than a little disturbing. He'd witnessed countless animal births, assisted in dozens more, and he knew the importance of maternal bonding. He'd just never considered that the same bonding process would also take place between a woman and her child when she gave birth—until he saw Mandy lay her head on Erin's shoulder and Erin pressed a kiss to her forehead.

Trev took a step back and jammed his hands in his pockets. Why he should have thought of such a thing just then made no sense to him at all. Yet, as he watched her, listening to her explaining how helpful Max would be, he couldn't help but think that she'd make a wonderful mother herself.

"He isn't taking him away to be mean," she assured

Zach, who'd just mumbled the accusation. "What he's doing is really an unselfish thing. Isn't that right, Trevor?"

She was trying to draw him into the conversation, to have him help her make the children understand his intentions. He didn't know if he was being unselfish or not. He hadn't thought about it. Raising the pups was just something he did because the need was there and he could fill it. He wasn't sure, either, what it was he felt as he stood there with her hazel eyes locked on his. He knew only that picturing her pregnant was not a good idea.

Focusing only on his discomfort at having made the kids cry, he held up his hands and shook his head. "I'm sorry, guys," he muttered, feeling more like a heel by the second. "But there's nothing I can do to change this. You have to say goodbye to him. We're supposed to be in Austin right now."

There really wasn't anything he could do but take the dog and go. To his amazement, Erin seemed to understand that. At least, she didn't argue with him about it or ask for more time for the kids to say their goodbyes. She just told Zach and Mandy to give Max a hug, which they did. Twice each. Then, she remained kneeling beside them on the floor when he walked to the door with the dog, three pairs of eyes staring at his back.

He didn't believe for a moment that she was thinking of him when she spoke in his defense. She was only trying to make things easier for the little ones, but he could still hear her explaining that Max would get lots of love and attention, when he closed the screen door behind him.

"I still think he's mean," Zach muttered, preferring anger to the tears he probably thought he was too big to shed. Six was getting up there, after all.

Erin gave her head a firm shake. "He'd be mean if he was hurting Max, but he would never do that. He loves animals. And a person has to care a great deal about people to do what your brother is doing.'' Or not care at all, a little voice warned in the back of her mind.

A few minutes more of talking and soothing and the kids had calmed enough for her to leave them with the last of her Oreo stash while she changed clothes. But all the while she was trading her suit and panty hose for jeans and a T-shirt she wondered if Trevor realized how much he'd just revealed of himself.

She couldn't help but admire him for wanting to help someone less fortunate. But he raised dogs from puppies, bonded with them, cared for them, then simply…let them go. Either he could turn his emotions off and on like a faucet, or he simply didn't invest them to begin with. Either way, it explained more about him than she'd ever known before.

Unwinding the coil at the back of her head, she reached for a scrunchee from the basket in her tiny bathroom and whipped her hair into a ponytail. As she did, her glance caught on the little piece of straw she'd taped to the mirror above the sink. It was the straw Trevor had pulled from her hair the day she'd remembered how he'd taught her to kiss.

She'd taped it there as a reminder of something else he'd taught her. That she had never mattered to him at all.

Knowing what she did about him, she'd have to be out of her mind to get involved with him again.

The slice of orange sun low on the horizon cast everything in a peach-tinted glow as Erin left the main house that evening. She'd never thought about how restful this time of day could be, but there was something calming about the quiet transition into night. Animals began to bed down. Birds went silent in the trees. It wouldn't be long before, come sunset, the shrubs would be alive with the steady hum of cicadas and the heat of the day would linger long into the night. That was when the summer thunderstorms would start; the "monsoons" that sent humidity skyrocketing and taunted man and animal with torrents of rain. But for now, the warm air was quiet, comfortable and breathlessly still.

She should have felt the peacefulness, she told herself. She should have appreciated the calm that settled over the land she had, however reluctantly, come to miss. She felt incredibly lucky to have a mom who hadn't said "I told you so" when things hadn't worked out in California and a stepdad who'd made it clear she was always welcome at home. Considering the grief she'd given them when she was younger, her mom especially, they could have easily balked at her request to return—or questioned her explanation for why she'd wanted to do it. But neither had questioned her reasons. The explanation she'd given was the same she'd given Trevor. It was the truth, after all. As far as it went.

She tried to shake off the thought, to find the quiet. Yet all she felt as she skirted the drying grass by the split-rail fence was the same empty sensation that had accompanied her all the way from Los Angeles. The fact that the feeling was worse since Trevor had returned was a phenomenon she didn't care to explore.

With a disgusted sigh, she glanced back toward the house. She didn't want to think about Trevor at all. What she wanted to do was find something to do that would occupy her mind—which was why she'd gone up to the house in the first place. Her mom was up to her pearl studs in preparations for the town's upcoming Fourth of July celebration, and Erin knew she could use help. If not with the celebration itself, then for the plans she was making for a family gathering the day after. But her mom was in town at a meeting. Or so she'd been told by Amy, who'd peeled the phone from her ear long enough to suffer the interruption.

Instead of spending the evening being useful, Erin had scanned the want ads from Logan's Austin and San Antonio papers—finding absolutely nothing new—while Mandy told her about Trevor's visit to the house to show them his new puppy. Mandy really hadn't said much other than that he had a new one, and that she and Zach didn't want to play with it. But her little sister's comments were enough to make it apparent that Trev had immediately replaced Max—and to make Erin wonder if he replaced people in his life as easily as he did his animals.

Was that what he'd done when he'd dumped her? she wondered, rubbing at the tension at the back of her head. Had he promptly replaced her with someone else? Or had there been someone else already?

It doesn't matter, she hastily admonished herself. What had happened between her and Trevor was ancient history. Right up there with the Dead Sea scrolls and the fall of the Roman Empire. It was just that she'd seen a side of him that she'd never suspected and, whether she wanted to think about him or not, she couldn't avoid it.

She couldn't avoid giving him the credit he deserved, either. After the little scene he'd prompted that afternoon, he was obviously going to let the kids know up-front what the deal was with the replacement pooch. As she turned to lean against the fence, wanting to avoid the confines of the apartment for as long as possible, she couldn't help thinking it was too bad he couldn't be as up-front with the dog itself. Poor Max wouldn't understand why his beloved master had turned his back on him any more than she'd understood why, years ago, Trevor had started treating her like a leper.

With a disgusted sigh, she toed away a rock encroaching on the efforts of a bluebonnet trying to grow by a post. It was truly pathetic that she could identify so strongly with a Labrador retriever.

From a patch of low scrub grass below the road, Trevor hunched by the puppy squatting a few feet away and watched Erin stop by the split-rail fence. With her back to the sprawling limbs of the live oaks shadowing the rolling pasture, she leaned against the rail and pulled off the band holding her hair at her nape.

It must have felt good to get rid of the binding. Pushing her fingers through the hair at the back of her head, she closed her eyes and tipped her head back, ruffling her hair as she did. Had there not been so much weariness in her movements, what she was doing would have been rather provocative—all that thick, sun-shot hair cascading over her shoulders. As it was, she just looked tired. Or, maybe, he thought, seeing the slump of her slender shoulders, how she looked was…lost.

The thought settled uneasily on him as he watched her drop her hand and open her eyes. That was when she noticed she wasn't alone.

He hadn't intended to talk to her tonight. What he'd planned to do was hit her up for help first thing in the morning—when he'd be too rushed for her to refuse to help him out. Not that he thought she would refuse. She might regard him as one step behind the Neanderthal in emotional development, but the woman was a soft touch where children and animals were concerned. She'd proved that in spades when she'd bailed him out with the kids.

The tiny yellow Lab, a pretty little gal that was all snug-

gle and paws, had done her duty and wandered back over
to curl up beside his boot. Scooping her up with one hand,
Trev decided he might as well approach Erin now and get
it over with. He couldn't just walk off without seeming
rude, anyway.

Cradling his peace offering in the crook of his arm, he
rose and started toward her. As he did, she straightened
herself, her glance moving from him to the pup whose eyes
had closed within seconds of getting comfortable. It was
a sure bet that Erin didn't share the animal's ease. The
smile that formed at the sight of the pup died before she
met his eyes.

Her reaction to him wasn't much different from Zach's
a couple of hours ago. She was just too poised to turn
around and run.

"I heard you'd brought back another one."

"I imagine you did." He picked up a hint of accusation
in her observation. Needing her help, he ignored it. "I took
it up to the house a while ago, but the kids didn't want
anything to do with it."

They hadn't wanted anything to do with him, either. She
undoubtedly already knew that, too.

"They just need some time." She watched the puppy's
black button of a nose twitch as it slept. It looked so comfortable tucked against Trev's solid chest, so blissfully secure in his muscular arms. "I understand what you were
trying to do," she admitted, unwillingly drawn by the
powerful combination of his strength and gentleness. "But
it's a little soon to introduce them to another of your dogs.
Especially a puppy."

Kids were suckers for puppies. Unable to keep herself
from touching the furry little head, she had to admit, she
was, too. "I can't imagine how you keep yourself from
getting attached to something so sweet."

She hadn't intended to voice the thought. But as she pulled her hand away, conscious of Trev following her every move, she found herself torn between wishing he'd explain and wondering if he even could.

He didn't seem to think her observation even mattered.

"This isn't my dog, Erin."

"I know. He—"

"She."

"She," Erin corrected, "belongs to the program. Look, Trevor, it's great that you want to let the kids know that up-front this time. And that's exactly what you need to do. But you would have had a better response if you'd given them a while before you sprung this on them."

"This isn't a companion dog. I brought her for them." He glanced from the quick confusion in her eyes, feeling awkward and hating it. Those feelings were exactly why he avoided the people in the house. He felt that way every time he set foot in it. "I tried to give it to the kids, but they wouldn't stick around long enough to let me explain that it's theirs."

He never walked into the house the way he had when it had been his home. Not unless he knew his dad was right inside. So he'd knocked on the open screen door, halfway hoping Samantha would answer so he could just give the dog to her and leave. A moment later he'd heard Amy yell for someone to get the door, and Zach had come flying into the mud room like a rookie stealing third. Mandy had raced to a halt behind him, hollering that she wanted to be the one to answer the door. Then they'd both looked up to see him standing on the other side of the screen holding the puppy, and neither had said another word. At least, they hadn't until he'd said he wanted to introduce them to their new friend.

"You'll just take it away," Zach had accused and stomped off with his little sister trailing right behind.

A muscle in his jaw jerked. They hadn't even given him a chance to hunch down to their level.

"I don't think they trust me."

"I don't imagine they do. It's hard to trust someone once they've hurt you."

The feathery crescents of her lashes drifted down, swiftly hiding her eyes. As if fighting a sudden chill, she crossed her arms over the tree on the green Save the Rain Forests T-shirt she seemed particularly fond of wearing and nodded toward his little companion.

"I don't suppose you asked Mom about giving them a pet."

"Give me a little credit, will you?"

"Is that a yes or a no?"

"Yes," he said, thinking she looked awfully self-conscious all of a sudden. "I called your mom from Austin. The last thing I wanted to do was bring them a puppy, then have someone else tell them they couldn't keep it. I'm not as insensitive as you seem to think."

Her only response was to shoot him a glance that said that particular point was debatable. But it was the way she tightened her hold on herself that gave him pause. No way was she cold. The sun had set, deepening shadows, graying the twilight, but the temperature still hovered in the eighties. Her stance was purely protective.

Culpability kicked hard at his conscience. Mandy and Zach weren't the only ones who didn't trust him. Erin didn't, either.

The thought was hard to acknowledge, even though he knew he couldn't blame her. Not after the way he'd treated her. But it wasn't as if he'd scarred her somehow.

Or had he?

The unwanted question taunted, humbling him, demanding he acknowledge the possibility. He'd always been able to justify what he'd done, but he'd always known at some level that he'd hurt her. His discomfort over that was one of the reasons he'd starting avoiding her in the first place. Yet, uncomfortable as those thoughts were, he considered something that disturbed him far more than he was prepared to admit: every time he was with her, he sensed an indefinable sort of withdrawal, as if something inside her was tender and in need of protection. Injured animals often retreated to their den, or someplace they perceived as safe, to lick their wounds and heal. Had someone else hurt her? Was that why she'd come home?

"So what do you plan to do with her now?" she asked, running a finger over the puppy's head again.

"I'd thought you could give her to the kids. I was going to ask you in the morning." With her focus on the dog, he studied her more closely. This afternoon she'd looked polished, unflappable. Now, with her hair hanging loose, her lipstick worn away, she seemed as vulnerable as the little animal he held. The weariness he'd sensed when he'd watched her leave the house was visible in the faint shadows beneath her eyes. And the wistful smile curving her very inviting mouth when the pup licked her fingers seemed almost…dispirited.

He didn't trust the vague sense of protectiveness he felt at that moment. Nor did he care for the guilt that came with it. "If you wouldn't mind, maybe you could do it now."

"The morning would be better," she replied, careful to avoid brushing his arm as she continued stroking the silky fur. "It's almost their bedtime and they'll never get to sleep if they get hold of her tonight." She glanced up to find him studying her. Suddenly aware of how close she'd moved to him, she reluctantly withdrew her hand and stepped back. "You should be the one to give her to them, anyway."

"I doubt they'll accept her from me. As far as they're concerned, I might as well have shot the Easter Bunny."

"True," she agreed, finding it easier to focus on the pup than on him. "But they'll accept her if you start by telling them she's theirs."

He didn't plan to tell them anything at all. "I need to leave here by six-thirty. That's too early to show up at the house."

One eyebrow arched in tolerant disbelief. "You *need* to leave that early?"

"It's not an excuse," he muttered, knowing she thought it was. The fact that he would have invented an excuse to avoid the kids and the house was beside the point. "I have an appointment with a bull over in Dry Creek at seven."

"So you planned to just show up with her at my door at the crack of dawn?"

"Six-thirty is hardly the crack of dawn. You're in the stables by then."

"You're evading."

She was right. "Look, Erin, I can't take her with me. And I can't leave her alone. I'm doing the only thing I know to do to make amends with the kids. Help me out here, will you?"

He hated to ask. She was as sure of that as she was the fact that he would have put off asking for as long as he could, had she not seen him minutes ago. Had he appeared the least bit impatient, the perverse streak he tended to bring out in her would have surfaced and made her tell him she'd have to think about it. But all she could see in the masculine angles of his face was the same guardedness she felt.

"If you give her to me now, you won't have to worry about it in the morning."

He didn't bother to hide his relief. "Great," he murmured, slipping his free hand under the pup's belly to hand her over. "Her food is back at the trailer. I'll bring it up."

He wasn't going to give her time to rethink the offer. He stepped toward her, still cradling the sleepy little dog. Erin automatically reached to accept it, their arms brushing as her hands slipped beneath his.

"Got her?"

Erin nodded, her voice evaporating as the heat of his palms seared the backs of her hands. She could feel calluses at the base of his fingers. Their roughness contrasted starkly with the gentleness in his touch when he reached out to push her hair from her shoulder so it wouldn't be trapped by the warm little body snuggling over the curve of her breast.

His motions were instinctive, nothing more than a simple reaction to something that needed to be done. His long fingers skimmed the bare skin of her collarbone before sliding over to tug her hair free with a nudge from the back of his hand. But the instant he realized what he was doing, his glance collided with hers and he went as still as the evening air.

She thought he'd pull back. She knew she should. But he didn't move and she couldn't seem to make her legs work. He held her there with nothing more than his touch, her hair draped over the back of his hand and her pulse scrambling beneath his fingers.

The puppy squirmed against the erratic beat of her heart. She scarcely noticed. Trevor loomed over her, his big, solid body blocking her, overwhelming her. Only she didn't feel overwhelmed. What she felt was confusion, longing and a vague sense of panic.

Her breath shuddered in, drawing Trevor's glance to her mouth. Her lips remained slightly parted, full and inviting. Her hair felt like strands of silk in his hand. And her skin felt like warm satin when he slipped his fingers behind her neck. He tipped his head, heat jolting his gut when he breathed in the scent of spring clinging to her skin.

He scarcely knew her anymore. Didn't understand much of anything about her. What he did understand was that he wanted to know how she would feel against him, how she would respond. He couldn't remember. And the fact that he'd been trying to recall the intimacies they'd shared only made the hunger that much sharper. He wanted to know her taste. How she would move. He wanted his hands tangled in her hair and those incredible legs locked around his. And if he had the brains God gave a gelding, he'd let go of her before he did something incredibly stupid.

"I'd better get her food."

Erin nodded. At least she thought she did before he brushed his thumb to the corner of her mouth.

"I'll just leave it by your door."

He dropped his hand, deliberately stepping back.

Erin hesitated. "She's already been fed tonight?"

"About an hour ago. She shouldn't need anything but water before morning." He ran a glance from where she hugged the seven pounds of peace offering she was to baby-sit, to the wariness in her eyes. Moments ago, he'd seen awareness in the amber-flecked depths, heard it in the hitch of her breath. He'd seen a truckload of caution, too. He felt both himself. In spades. "Thanks for helping with the kids."

Her only response was another quiet nod. She clearly didn't know what to think of what he'd done. As he turned away, he had to admit he wasn't too sure what to make of it himself.

His dad had asked him not to avoid her. But avoiding her was probably the only way he was going to keep his sanity. The last thing he needed was to complicate the way he felt about her. The only problem with that thought was that he wasn't at all sure how he did feel about her anymore.

Chapter Four

"Is that Trevor out there with Logan and Jett?" Annie Hayes Kendall Whitaker wiped her hands on a towel as she peered out the window over Samantha's kitchen sink. Over the row of peach pies cooling on the windowsill and the heads of five children and a puppy playing in the yard, she could see three brawny men hoist sacks of charcoal and mesquite branches from the back of a pickup truck.

"It has to be," she decided, tossing the towel aside to lean her petite frame against the sink to get a better look. The feathery cap of her light brown hair gleamed in the sunlight. "He's the spitting image of his dad and his uncles."

Lindsey Hayes Whitaker, Annie and Samantha's statuesque, and very blond youngest sister, moved closer. "How can you tell? All you can see from here is a cute butt and great shoulders." Her eyes narrowed, concealing the artful touch of bronze eyeshadow that perfectly matched the top and shorts outfit Erin recognized from her boutique. "Come to think of it, there is a definite resemblance. They do have great genes," she concluded, turning her smile to two of the children outside playing with their cousins. Lindsey had married Cal Whitaker, the middle Whitaker brother, not long after Erin's mom had married Logan. Annie had married the youngest brother, Jett, the following year.

People in Leesburg still talked about the fact that three sisters from the city had actually caught and tamed the three elusive loners. Since rumors flew fast and furious in a town as small as Leesburg, Erin had overheard the comments and speculation herself. Only she knew, from what she'd witnessed of her aunts' tumultuous courtships, that you didn't tame a Whitaker. They settled down when they were ready, and not an instant before. Except for Logan's brief marriage at twenty, the brothers had been well into their thirties when that had happened.

Erin pulled her attention from her aunts, skimming a glance past her mom. They were finishing preparations for tonight's Fifth of July barbecue. Since her mom was always too involved with the town's festivities on the official day to have a true family celebration, the odd date had become a tradition for the Whitakers. All morning long, the kitchen had been filled with wonderful aromas and animated conversation. This was one conversation, however, Erin didn't care to join.

Thinking about Trevor in any context unsettled her in ways she didn't care to explore. But thinking about his "great genes" felt downright dangerous. He had caused heat to flow through her with nothing more than the touch of his hand. And the way his eyes had darkened when he'd brushed his thumb over her mouth had nearly stopped her heart. Heaven only knew what would have happened if he'd kissed her.

She grabbed another potato, sectioned it, cubed it and scooped it into the big green bowl. She had absolutely no business letting her mind wander into that particular minefield. The man had burned her before, and she wasn't about to stick her hand back in that fire again. If she felt attracted to him, it was only because he'd charmed her with the puppy.

Feeling she could live with that bit of rationalization, she reached for another spud—and found a hand waving in front of her face.

"Erin?"

Her head snapped up. "I'm sorry. Were you talking to me?"

She hadn't even noticed when Annie had come up beside her. Lindsey was back at the stove, reading aloud the ingredients for the last batch of baked beans to make sure she hadn't forgotten anything. Her mom was in the walk-in pantry, muttering something about brown sugar.

It was apparent that she'd missed something.

It was also apparent from the way Annie glanced toward the pantry that she'd been waiting for Erin's mother to leave. "I asked if Trevor is still walking around with a chip on his shoulder."

"It's more like a block of ice," Lindsey interjected, barely missing a beat before her voice dropped to continue reading from her list. Smacking her head, she muttered, "Dry mustard," and headed for the spice rack.

"She's right." Annie's agreement was for her sister. Her concern was for her niece. "I never could understand the reason for the big chill, either. How long has it been, anyway?"

"That depends on what you're talking about," Erin quietly replied. "We met nine years ago. He started backing off a few months after that, around the time Mom and Logan married. And he stopped speaking to me the following Thanksgiving."

By then, she'd been a senior in high school.

He'd been a sophomore in college and home for the break.

"I wish you weren't so far away," she'd told him the night he'd come home. "I really miss you."

She hadn't seen him since summer, but even then he'd spent most of his time out on the range. That was why it had meant so much when he'd told her he'd missed her, too. He'd kissed her then, something he hadn't done in a long time. But before she could get her arms around his neck, he'd pulled away.

"What's wrong?" she'd asked.

"Nothing's wrong. I just don't want to start something we can't finish."

"We wouldn't have to stop," she'd told him. "I love you, Trevor. Don't you know that?"

For a moment, he'd said nothing. He'd just stood holding her wrists and looking at her in a way she didn't understand at all. He'd seemed taut as a wire, but all he'd said was that he had to go help with chores.

She'd offered herself to him, told him she loved him. His response from then on had been to avoid her.

She drew a painful little breath, the sharp scents of vinegar and spice jolting her back to the kitchen. Rubbing her nose with the back of her wrist, she noticed that both of her aunts had stopped what they were doing.

Identical expressions of concern were mirrored in their eyes.

"What?" she asked.

"For something that happened so long ago," Annie observed, "you're awfully specific with your timetable."

Erin glanced from the quiet, soft-spoken woman to the mountain of potatoes she was turning into salad. She'd lived with Annie for a while when she'd run off at sixteen, so her aunt knew how much Trevor had once meant to her. And Lindsey had certainly witnessed enough during family get-togethers over the years to understand how far Trevor had carried his rejection. For the most part, everyone overlooked the occasional tension—rather like some families ignored a great-uncle who snored through holiday meals by talking around him.

"It's natural that I'd think of it since we're both here," Erin defended. Getting dumped had been hard enough. Having her entire family witness the aftermath for the next several years had moved the experience to a new level of humiliation. "It doesn't mean a thing."

Lindsey looked dubious. "I know we're talking ancient history here, but how involved were you two, anyway?"

"For Pete's sake, Lindsey," Annie muttered. "There are some things we really don't need to know."

"It's not like she's a teenager, Annie. She's a twenty-five-year-old woman. By that age, everyone has a past."

"I didn't."

"Which explains a lot. Anyway," she continued, undaunted by the droll glance her sister shot her, "it seems to me that there had to be something pretty intense going on for him to have acted like such a jerk for so long."

"It wasn't that intense." Not on his part, Erin mentally muttered. "We never slept together, if that's what you're getting at."

"Well, there goes that theory," Lindsey mused.

"Now *that* I wish I had known." Annie actually looked relieved. "Your Mom was worried to death about you. So was I. You were head over heels about that kid and we were so afraid you'd wind up pregnant.''

''You don't know how comforting it is to know the entire family was discussing my nonexistent sex life.''

''We were concerned, Erin.'' It wasn't admonishment in Annie's voice. It was simply explanation. ''Those were a rough couple of years for you. As inexperienced as you were and as experienced as he probably was, he could easily have taken advantage of you.''

Erin could have let it go. She probably should have, because she really wanted to change the subject. But in this instance, Trevor had been misjudged by her mom and aunts and her basic sense of fairness couldn't let it pass. ''Trevor wasn't like that. He never tried to take advantage of me,'' she quietly admitted. ''Ever.''

Her defense of him was obviously unexpected. But whatever Annie had been about to say was cut off when Samantha bustled back into the brightly lit room and handed her a box of brown sugar.

''It was buried behind the cereal boxes,'' she said, explaining why it had taken her so long to find it. ''Now, where were we?''

Annie hesitated. ''I asked Erin how Trevor is behaving since he got home,'' she finally said, mercifully letting the rest of the conversation go.

''Oh, he's better than he was,'' Samantha replied, her head bent as she searched a drawer for a clean measuring spoon. ''We don't see much of him up here at the house. But he did bring the puppy for the children. Actually,'' she amended, smiling when she found what she was looking for, ''he gave it to Erin to give to them. I thought that was nice, don't you?''

Annie's puzzled glance slid to her niece. ''Trevor gave the puppy to you?''

Not totally sure what her expression betrayed, Erin turned to the fridge for the mayonnaise. Her mom wanted everything to be settled. Annie clearly suspected it wasn't. "It was late when he got back with her," she said, scanning the rack on the refrigerator door. "And he had to leave early the next morning. There wasn't much else he could do."

"Weren't you surprised he came to you instead of asking his dad to take care of it?"

"A little."

"It certainly surprised me," Samantha expanded, handing Erin what she was looking for. "But then, I hadn't expected him to call me at the office to ask if I minded him giving Zach and Mandy a dog, either. Since they seemed to like Max so much, he thought they might like having one of the same breed themselves." She shook her head, her expression equal parts amazement and skepticism as she turned back to the batch of barbecue sauce she was concocting on the stove. "I didn't think he'd even noticed his brother and sister, much less given them any thought."

"I find that hard to believe myself," Annie admitted. "I was always under the impression that he avoided the kids as much as he avoided Erin."

With her tasting spoon poised at her mouth, Lindsey immediately agreed. "Me, too. I never actually saw him break out in hives, but I figured he was just one of those men who are allergic to small children."

"Well, Zach and Mandy aren't just children. They're his siblings." The back screen door groaned open as Samantha tapped the metal measuring spoon against the side of the big pot. The scent of cloves joined the sweet and savory scents filling the air.

"But to be fair," she continued, clearly torn where her

stepson was concerned, "he'd never been exposed to children before I came along. At least he seems to be trying to do what his dad asked. Logan told him he wanted his family to get along, and it seems he's taken the request to heart."

"So it's his dad who's responsible for the change," Annie concluded, sounding as if that explained everything. "What did he say to him?"

"Actually, he talked to him about Erin—"

Lindsey's elbow hit Samantha in the ribs, cutting her off as the screen door slammed shut. An instant later, her tone bright, she looked past them all and smiled. "Hi, Trev."

All three women glanced up from their respective bowls and pots, their expressions taking on various shades of guilt when they saw Trevor in the mudroom. A dark V of perspiration stained the front of his work shirt, and he'd rolled its sleeves to his elbows, exposing an angry red scratch on his tanned forearm. Loaded down with a large box of corn, freshly picked from the looks of the tassels hanging over the sides, he couldn't take his hat off as the men tended to do when they entered a home. With the additional height, he completely filled the doorway.

He looked about as comfortable as a freshly branded calf with the four females openly staring at him. The muscle in his jaw bunching, his glance landed briefly on Erin before shifting to her mom. Even if he hadn't heard the conversation, the silence ricocheting through the room made it painfully apparent he was being discussed.

"Where do you want this?"

Nudged into action by the question, Sam handed Lindsey her spoon and headed across the kitchen. "Just leave it on the dryer."

Slipping past him to clear the top of the appliance, her

eyes narrowed on the angry, red abrasion running the length of his forearm. Concern as real as she would feel for any other member of her family washed over her face. "What did you do to yourself?"

"Oh, that's nothing," he muttered, seeing where she was scowling. "Just a scratch from a branch."

"Hang on and I'll get some peroxide and ointment."

"No need. Really." He held up his hand, clearly anxious to be gone. "I'll take care of it later. I need to get back and finish the fire pit. Dad wants to know where you want the tables."

"Mommy?"

There were three women in the room who answered to that name. And all three automatically turned toward the little voice coming from behind Trevor. An instant later Caitlin, Lindsey's precocious five-year-old, squeezed past the big man blocking the doorway and in a flash of neon pink headed straight for the refrigerator. Right behind her came Mandy, wearing the same style of romper in electric blue and toting the squirming puppy.

"We're hot," the cousins announced in unison.

"Yeah, Mommy. I'm hot, too." Three-year-old Ricky, Jett and Annie's adopted son, came barreling in as fast as his sturdy little legs would carry him. Erin caught him before he could collide with a counter stool, but he immediately squirmed from her grip. His cousins were at the refrigerator, and he wasn't about to miss out on whatever they were getting.

"Have your brother turn on the sprinklers," Lindsey replied to her daughter, catching the pitcher of lemonade before her busy little girl could hoist it off the shelf herself.

"He's helping Uncle Logan."

"Would you mind turning it on, Trev?" Samantha asked, picking through the corn.

Busy eyeing the whirlwind in screaming pink, he hadn't kept up with the conversation. Confusion slashed his brow. "Pardon?"

"The sprinkler," Samantha repeated. "Would you turn it on for the kids? It's the spigot outside the back door."

It seemed to Erin that Trevor didn't actually have a chance to respond. While her mom was talking, Mandy had come back to him and was holding up her puppy. Clearly dubious, he looked down at her peering up at him. Her blue eyes were as bright as the smile on her sweaty little face.

"Guess what we named her?" she coaxed, grinning. "We named her Jasmine and she sleeps with me. 'Cept when Zach comes in and sneaks her out of my bed." Clearly displeased with her brother's behavior, her little face crumpled. "But you know what?" she asked, suddenly brightening again. "Spot sleeps with Amy and he growls when Zach tries to take him, so Spot can teach Jasmine how to growl, too."

Apparently, responses were not necessarily required in conversations with small children. The conclusion occurred vaguely to Trevor as he watched the little girl trot back across the room to see what was happening at the fridge. He knew Spot was the dog that had come with Sam and the kids when they'd moved into the house. What threw him completely was that *this* particular child was the same one who, three days ago, had nearly burst into tears at the sight of him. Now she was acting as if she'd never had a problem with him at all.

"Will you lift me up, please?" The whirlwind was back, the one in glowing pink who belonged to Cal and Lindsey. He thought she was theirs, anyway. They all looked sort of alike to him. "I'm suppose to get glasses to take outside for you and Uncle Logan and I can't reach."

"I've got it," Sam assured him, slipping past to open the cupboard above the little girl. "If you'll just get the sprinkler..."

Erin could have sworn she saw a muscle in Trevor's eye twitch. To the best of her knowledge, this was the first time he'd ever been surrounded by all the Whitaker preschoolers. They were clearly more comfortable with him than he was with them. To the children, he was a relative. A relative who looked very much like their respective fathers. There was no hesitation on their part, no wariness. Nothing but the uncomplicated, completely innocent trust a child has in someone they believe will help and protect them simply because that was what family did.

She didn't know if that easy acceptance registered with Trevor. Or, if it did, she wondered if he realized what a gift it was. He just stood back from the blur of color and controlled chaos, two-hundred pounds of male muscle in denim and a cowboy hat, looking totally out of his element.

Her protective instincts had slammed into place the moment she saw him. Feeling them falter, she ruthlessly quashed the twinge of sympathy yanking at her heart.

"Definitely allergic," she whispered to Annie, her comment inaudible to anyone else over the commotion of small voices demanding attention. "But I think he's also completely overwhelmed. Call me cranky, but it does my heart good to know there's something he can't handle.

"I'll get it, Mom," she called, moving to the sink to wash her hands. "The kids need to be stripped down, anyway."

"I can turn on the water," Trevor muttered, shooting a glance over all the little heads to where Erin ignored him at the sink. "I just need to know where you want us to put the tables."

''Oh, Trevor, I'm sorry,'' Sam replied, clearly having forgotten he'd asked. ''Just set them away from the trees. It'll be dark by the time we eat and I don't want bugs dropping onto the plates.''

''Bugs on the plates?'' Caitlin screeched. ''Oh, yuck!''

Mandy echoed the sentiment, making a face to match her cousin's that seemed to encourage Caitlin to make a gagging noise. That particular sound effect earned an admonishment from her mother and had Trevor backing toward the door. He'd never thought of himself as claustrophobic, but he found himself dragging in a long, deep breath the instant he stepped outside. The incredible smells inside the house had reminded him that it had been hours since he'd wolfed down breakfast, but tantalizing as the scents had been, there was no substitute for the pure, fresh air of wide-open space.

Maybe he did have a thing about confinement, he told himself, as he turned on the faucet by the back door. Maybe that was why he'd always preferred working outdoors to working inside. A room with a window to one without. He certainly liked that explanation better than thinking he felt so edgy because he couldn't handle being in a room with four women and a swarm of children. Yet, he'd rather think that than admit his edginess was due to the jolt he'd felt when he'd seen Erin standing at the counter.

He hadn't realized she was there.

''Thank you.''

He glanced around to see her standing in the doorway. She held the screen open with her hip. In one hand was a pitcher of lemonade. In the other, she held a stack of plastic tumblers. Something like amusement danced in her eyes, but he couldn't tell if it was because of the kids marching past her like little soldiers, or because of him.

Suspecting the latter, he muttered, "For what?"

"For turning on the water," she replied, making it sound as if she'd thought him too rattled to handle the minor request. "By the way, they love the dog."

The sun touched her hair, lighting it. Her skin glowed, teasing him with its softness. "Glad to hear it."

"I'm sure they'd be happy to show you the trick they taught her."

The pup under discussion had commandeered a sock and was presently shaking the life out of it. "Some other time," he murmured, and started to turn away.

"This is for you and the guys." She hoisted the pitcher when he glanced back. "Would you take it with you? Or," she added as if she suddenly couldn't resist, "do you want to take care of the kids while I do?"

His instinct was to reach for the pitcher. Another instinct, this one prompted by the glint in her eyes, stopped him. At the barbecue pit some thirty yards away, he could see Zach and Gabe, Cal and Lindsey's seven-year-old. They were still watching his dad and Jett unload the tables that had been stored in the barn. The men hadn't taken the day off. There were no days off on a ranch. The chores for the evening's festivities had just been added to the list.

He should be down there helping. Yet what he should do and what he would do bore no resemblance to each other. From the light in Erin's eyes, he knew she expected him to bolt from anything that had to do with the kids. But his desire to keep his contact with her and the rest of the family at a manageable minimum was outweighed by the challenge suddenly shimmering in the air.

As challenges went, this wasn't even a contest. She should have him with the boys a while ago. The way Zach had been tagging after him, asking the same sort of questions he'd asked at that age—why, the two of them were practically buddies.

But then, he reminded himself, Zach was a guy.

''Tell them where your mom wants the tables,'' he said mildly, not totally sure why it felt so necessary to prove her wrong. ''I can handle this.'' Enormously satisfied to see her amusement falter, he planted his hands on his hips. ''You said something inside about stripping them,'' he reminded her. ''How far down do I take them?''

She thought he was bluffing. He was sure of it.

''To their underwear.''

He didn't so much as blink. He merely held her glance long enough to let her know he'd learned a thing or two about kids lately and that he wasn't going to be cowed by a bunch of munchkins. Now that they were outside, he could see that there were only three of them, anyway. They'd just created such a clamor inside that it had seemed as if there were more. At the very least, he now knew they wouldn't run from him screaming.

Letting the door close behind her, Erin watched him give the brim of his hat a tug, the motion reminding her of a bronc rider getting himself set to enter the ring. His long-legged stride carried him to where the three children sat on the grass pulling off their shoes. There was no way he could feel as confident as he looked, not as uneasy as she knew he was around the children. But he seemed to hesitate only a moment before he gave the knees of his jeans a yank and hunkered down in front of them. A moment later, little Ricky scrambled to his feet and held up his arms.

Glancing over at Caitlin wriggling out of her rompers, Trevor tugged the little boy's striped shirt over his head, exposing a skinny little belly. Beside him, Mandy shim-

mied out of her romper and T-shirt and dropped it on top
of Caitlin's.

Obviously figuring the kids knew what they were doing
even if he didn't, he dropped Ricky's shirt on the pile of
clothing, too, then reached over and caught the little boy
before he could dart into the sprinkler in his shorts. By the
time he'd added the shorts to the pile, the kids were running off to dash through the slowly oscillating spray wearing underwear in cartoon prints she doubted he knew underwear even came in.

She was standing right where he'd left her when he rose,
tall and solid as an oak, and turned around. As if he knew
exactly where he'd find her, his glance locked on hers. He
didn't look cocky. He didn't look smug. He didn't even
look relieved to have survived his little bout of stubbornness, though that was actually how she'd thought he'd feel.
Not that she felt sure of anything at the moment. Two
minutes ago, she'd have bet her next interview that he'd
opt for a walk over hot coals before doing what he'd just
done.

The children's giggles and screeches as cool water hit
their warm little bodies were accompanied by the yip of
the puppy bounding after them. But Erin's attention was
on the big man silently watching her. His expression was
carefully blank when he walked back over, not stopping
until he was so close she had to tip her head back to see
his face.

His smoky gray glance brushed her lips as softly as a
caress, then settled, dark and unreadable, on her eyes. "I
might as well take that with me," he said, relieving her of
the pitcher and tumblers she was to have delivered. "Save
you the trip."

She didn't want him to be thoughtful. She didn't want
him to surprise her. And she definitely didn't want him

jerking around with her heart rate the way he did when he looked at her that way. But what she wanted didn't seem to matter at the moment. He was doing as he pleased, and it seemed to please him that she couldn't think of a thing to say before he left her staring after him.

She'd felt safer when he treated her like a pariah.

The thought of just how very dangerous he could be had her disappearing into the house before he could turn and find her still watching him. For over a week she'd tried to convince herself that his presence didn't bother her, and for over a week she'd been lying through her teeth. He did bother her. In more ways than it was wise to consider. But she'd never been a very wise person. There were times when she hadn't even qualified as being reasonably bright.

Intent on preventing the development of another one of those instances, she decided on her way past the kitchen table that she was not going to the barbecue tonight. It wasn't as if she were needed for anything once the preparations were finished. No one would even miss her. Yet, necessary as the decision felt, it was axed within seconds.

It was apparent that no one had seen what Trevor had done. Lindsey wasn't even in the room, and since Annie and her mom had known Erin was outside with the children, there had been no need for them to check out the window themselves. But even without witnessing Trevor's slightly startling behavior, her mom was going on about how much he had matured the past few years, how much like his father he was and how nice it was going to be to have everyone together without someone being at odds. Tonight would be the first time that had *ever* happened, and she badly wanted that for her husband.

After hearing that, Erin figured there was no way she

could avoid going. But she couldn't think of any reason she couldn't slip out after putting in a brief appearance. After all, with family and all the friends her mom had invited, who'd even notice she was missing?

Chapter Five

"Hey there, Trevor. Heard you were back." Ty Murdock, Jr. slapped Trev's shoulder, then pumped his hand good-ol'-boy style. "Good to be home, I'll bet. My dad was just telling yours that he's going to ship me off to school so he can have a vet in the family, too. Thanks a lot, buddy."

The teasing was good-natured. So was Trevor's smile when he returned the bear-trap handshake and lifted his beer toward the man he hadn't seen since he'd last been home. Except for Doc Henderson and a couple of ranchers whose stock he'd tended lately, it had been ages since he'd seen many of the people at the party. Ty was a few years older than Trev and they were acquaintances more than friends, but, like him, Murdock was the third generation on family land. "How're you doing, Ty?"

"I'd be a sight better if beef prices would go back up, but the Rocking R is holding its own."

"Glad to hear that."

"Sure would like some rain, though. I've had to double the irrigation on our alfalfa."

Understanding the man's concerns perfectly, Trevor told him the heat had increased water needs on their feed crops, too. Weather, specifically the lack of rain, had been the main topic of conversation that evening, but after three hours of socializing, Trevor had parked himself against the back fence. It was quieter on this end of the enormous yard. At least, it had been. He didn't mind Ty, though.

Or so he thought.

Purpose clear in his raw-boned features, the tall, rangy rancher turned to face the crowd. "You wouldn't happen to know where that oldest stepsister of yours is, would you?"

Stepsister? he thought. "You mean Erin?"

"Yeah. Pretty thing, isn't she?"

The observation rankled, though he didn't know why it should. It was accurate enough. "I suppose."

"She involved with anybody?"

That one gave him pause, too. "Not that I know of."

That seemed to please Murdock. Lipping a cigarette from his pack, he lit up and shoved the pack back into the pocket of his Western-cut shirt. Squinting through smoke as he exhaled, he scanned the crowd gathered along the lawn leading down to the river. The smell of tobacco tangled with the scents of blooming sage and spicy barbecue.

"I saw her down there dancing with Hank a bit ago," Ty said, seemingly oblivious to the silence coming from his left, "but by the time I got over there to ask her to dance myself, she'd disappeared. Thought maybe I could see her from here."

"I thought you were married."

"Divorced. Vicki split a couple of years ago."

Trevor didn't know if he was supposed to offer condolences or congratulations. Getting no clue from the man next to him, he said nothing. Ty was a decent guy, as far as he knew. Hardworking. Honest. He supposed he didn't have any trouble attracting women, either. They seemed to go for guys with wide shoulders and dimples.

"She calm down any?"

"Who?"

"Erin."

Trevor felt an odd sort of tension creep up his back. "I'm not sure I know what you mean," he said carefully.

"Maybe you were gone by then." Still scanning, Ty missed the measured way Trev watched him. "Didn't she give y'all a rough time there for a while? Seems I heard the folks talking about her skipping school and running away and such years ago."

Erin had definitely had her moments. And Trev, like it or not, was feeling a little defensive for her sake. "Like you said. It was years ago."

"Hey, I'm not being critical," Ty conceded with an easy smile. "A little trouble once in a while isn't necessarily a bad thing. A man doesn't want a filly with no spirit now, does he? Tell you what." He pointed across the crowd, oblivious to the sharp glance Trevor sent him. "I'm over there with the folks. When you see her, maybe you could bring her by."

"If she's agreeable," Trevor replied, having no intention of taking her anywhere. "I'll do that."

Trevor swore the rancher swaggered as he headed over to where Cal's wife was serving peach pie. Lifting his long-neck Lone Star, he jerked his glance from the man's back to the lights glowing from the house and took a pull on the beer. The last he'd seen of Erin, she'd been with her other aunt and little Ricky. She was probably inside putting him in bed. Maybe she'd stay there, he thought, and frowned back at Ty.

He hadn't liked the guy's eyes, he decided, watching his uncle Cal slip his arm around his wife's shoulder while they talked with Ty themselves. Or maybe it was his aftershave.

"Who put the vinegar in your beer?"

Suddenly conscious of his scowl, he glanced toward his dad as the big man strolled to a stop beside him. Ignoring the question, he looked back toward the crowd. "What kind of guy is Murdock?"

Logan raised his own beer, along with his eyebrow at the odd tightness in his son's tone. "Okay, I suppose. Never had reason to think otherwise." The eyebrow kicked higher. "Why?"

"Just curious." Trev shrugged, the motion too tense to be dismissing. "What's up?"

"Just taking a breather."

Like father, like son. Except his father wasn't anywhere near as solitary as he'd once been, Trev thought, shaking off his odd reaction as he watched Ty walk off with a slice of pie. "I'm kind of surprised you'd even do something like this," he said, referring to the party his dad was escaping.

A rueful smile deepened the vertical lines carved in Logan's cheeks. "There was a time I wouldn't have even considered it." He made the admission easily, his glance drawn to the beautiful, flower-bordered house, then to the pretty blond woman motioning to him from near the dance floor. "But then, I wouldn't have considered a lot that I was missing."

"You do all this for her?" Trevor asked, following the path of his father's glance.

"*For* her?" his dad repeated, considering his son. His

expression lost its edge. So did his voice. "I'd say it's more *because* of her.

"Looks like she needs something," he said, speaking of the woman who'd mellowed him like a bottle of vintage wine. "Get yourself some dessert, Trev. One of these women see you over here without a plate, they'll take it as a personal offense."

From where he remained leaning against the fence, Trev watched his dad move off though the crowd. The Fifth of July party wasn't a big gathering by Texas standards. Downright intimate, some might say. But the hundred or so friends, relatives and ranch hands seated under the lights strung between the utility poles and those dancing to the two fiddlers trying to outplay each other from their hay-bale stage, were having a great time.

Feeling edgy, not sure why, his glance skimmed over the crowd. Amy sat at a table twenty feet away, hiding her braces with her hand as she smiled. Her pale blond hair was caught up in a high ponytail that was duplicated by all four of the teenage girls giggling with her over Michael and his friends. The boys were hanging out down by the keg, so he doubted they even noticed the girls' bids to get their attention. They were more interested in sneaking a beer.

He tipped his bottle, his glance straying toward the house before he could tell himself it wasn't Erin he was looking for. He hadn't spoken to her all evening, but he'd seen her looking like a breath of spring in a yellow sundress that bared her shoulders, hugged her tiny waist and had every young buck in attendance drooling after her like hounds in heat.

Steadfastly refusing to identify the sensation tightening his gut, he looked to the heads bobbing to the beat of the Texas two-step. Over the course of the evening he'd seen her turn down offers to dance from everyone except his dad, his uncles and old Hank. She'd smiled, laughed, her eyes bright as she'd turned and twirled. He'd watched her skirt flip to expose a flash of slender thigh and her graceful arms curve to catch the hand and shoulder of her partner. Then she'd seen him watching, and the light in her expression had faded like the last rays of the sun.

Their eyes had locked, held, and he'd felt electricity jolt him to the tips of his hand-tooled dress boots. That wasn't a sensation he was accustomed to feeling, either. Not in a crowd. But it was the moments when she thought no one was watching at all that bothered him the most. It was then that he'd caught glimpses of the fragile young girl she'd once been, and a dispiritedness he never would have suspected had he not seen it in her only days ago.

A flash of yellow caught his eye. He hadn't been conscious of looking back toward the house, but he could see her slipping along the shrubs beneath the dining room window. Like a wraith wrapped in soft lemon, she disappeared from the pool of light beyond the gables and eaves and melted into the shadows of the road that led to the work compound.

He didn't consider what he was doing. Pushing himself upright, he left his bottle by an empty plate and moved past the people knotted around the pie table. There was something about Erin that just didn't fit. Something that had nagged him since the day she'd stood in the stables and glibly told him she'd come back because she missed her family. Since then, he'd begun to suspect that she'd been hurt somehow. By whom he hadn't a clue. But as he threaded his way through the tables, stopping to get Mandy a glass of punch because she thrust her cup at him and asked him to please fill it for her, he was more convinced than ever that she'd come home for reasons that had little to do with wanting a job closer to home.

Why he found it so necessary to know what that something was, was something he didn't take time to consider.

He found her in the newly constructed stable. Through the open grillwork atop the stall walls, he could see her settling a piebald mare.

"Why didn't you ask Dusty or Pete to bring the horses in?"

Erin looked up, her heart sinking when she saw Trevor lean against the doorpost. It hadn't been five minutes since she'd breathed a sigh of relief for getting through the evening without incident.

Obviously she'd gotten ahead of herself. "They were having a good time. I didn't want to interrupt them."

Trev tipped his head in the direction of the corral. His expression was unreadable, his tone quiet. "How many more horses are out there?"

"Four. We left the older ones out because it was so hot earlier. All I need to do is bring them in and put in fresh feed."

"You bring them in. I'll fill the feed buckets."

"That's not necessary."

"Yeah, it is." His glance skimmed her bare shoulders and the expanse of skin above the curved neckline of her dress. Two straps, thin as ribbons, held up the snug bodice. If she was wearing a bra, there was no evidence he could see. "You'll ruin your dress."

Pulling out one side of her skirt, she shrugged, then let the fabric fall softly back around her knees. The white shoes she'd worn earlier had been traded for a pair of rubber boots.

He couldn't imagine any other woman looking as comfortable in the incongruous outfit as she did.

"I thought I'd give the horses a treat," she said over the snuffle of the animal behind her. Most of her clothes were in storage, so she'd had to borrow what she wore from Lindsey. "It's not often that I dress up for them. Is there something you wanted?"

"Yeah. There is," he admitted bluntly. "But we'll finish the chores first."

We? "Thanks, but I can do this myself."

He gave her a look she couldn't read at all. "Do they all get the same thing?"

"I said I'd do it."

"No special diets?"

"You aren't listening."

"What about supplements?"

"Trevor."

"You know, Erin," he muttered, his shoulders looking a mile wide when he planted his hands on his hips, "I don't recall you being this stubborn about accepting a little help. Now, I'm going to put feed in these buckets. Do they get the same thing or not?"

"I'm stubborn? You're the one—"

"I'm the one trying to get along. You're the one who's not cooperating."

He had the same look in his eyes that he'd had when he'd walked away from her after calling her bluff with the kids that morning.

The look in hers made it as clear as the crystals winking from her ears that she didn't think he was playing fair at all.

"Ginger here gets a cup of vegetable oil in her oats," she told him, refusing to be the first to break their truce,

such as it was. "Slugger and Charlie worked hard today
so they could use some molasses."

"Which stalls are you putting 'em in?"

She told him, then watched him open the swing-outs on
the end stalls to remove the feed buckets and disappear
into the supply room. She couldn't tell if he was irritated
or just determined, but she could hear every jab of the
grain scoop into the big feed bin while she unclipped the
mare's lead and swung the stall gate closed. She didn't
bother trying to figure it out, either. When Trevor wanted
something, nothing stopping him. The fact that he wanted
something now, however, made the trait a little difficult to
admire.

It took him half the time it would have taken her to hay,
grain and water the horses, simply because he could carry
more weight than she could. Leading in another mare, she
watched him move between the stalls, his corded muscles
bunching and shifting beneath crisp white cotton and snug
denim as he lifted heavy buckets into place. He sweet-
talked the horses the same way he had when she'd helped
him with these same chores years ago. And like years ago,
she couldn't help being drawn by the contrast of those
deep, gentle sounds and his sheer physical strength.

He didn't say a word to her, though. And she said nothing to him. They went about their tasks, moving past and
around each other as if they performed this particular
dance every day, yet there was no mistaking the fine tension filling their silence. The only sounds were of their
movements, the bump of horseflesh against a stall wall, a
nicker, a whinny.

It was over the rush of water in the storage room sink
that the silence was finally broken.

"I need the soap when you're through," he said, coming
up beside her to stick his hands under the flow.

There wasn't much room at the gunmetal gray utility tub. His arm brushed hers, his big body crowding her, though she didn't think he was doing it on purpose. Not this time. A quick glance at his profile when she handed him the bar revealed nothing but preoccupation.

"Were you planning to go back to the party?" he asked, lathering up.

Since she'd already traded boots for shoes, the question seemed logical.

"No," she murmured, edging back.

"I didn't think so."

"Why not?"

"You didn't want to be there to begin with."

His tone was unremarkable, the observation spoken with an easy assurance that had her staring at his profile while he finished up and tore several sheets of paper towels from the holder on the wall.

He held out half.

"You have no way of knowing that."

"Do you deny it?"

She'd forgotten how easily he'd once been able to read her. Totally disconcerted to know he still possessed the ability, she ignored the question completely. "You said you wanted something," she reminded him, taking what he offered. "What is it?"

"I want to know why you came back. The real reason," he quietly insisted. Doing a three-pointer with his wadded up towel, he leaned against the tub. "Not the story you gave me about wanting a job in a smaller city and missing your family."

It was only because she'd turned to dispose of her own towel that he didn't see the hesitation wash over her. "It wasn't a story," she replied, forcing calm over the quick surge of anxiety. "It was the truth."

"Then I want the rest of 'the truth.' There's more to it than what you've said."

"How could you possibly know that?"

"Because I know you. At least, there was a time that I did." The admission took the force from his voice, softening its demand. "When something's bothering you, you can't hide it. Maybe you can from everyone else," he conceded, his eyes steady on hers. "But not from me."

He'd proven that only moments ago. Yet, he didn't bother pointing out the obvious. He knew she understood the connection they'd had. He was simply waiting for her to acknowledge it.

The fact that he acknowledged it himself would have amazed her had his questions not been so disturbing.

No one else had questioned the reasons she'd given for her return. And the fact that Trevor questioned them now felt as threatening as it did inevitable. He was right. No one else had ever known her quite as well as he once had. There had been a time when he'd been so attuned to her moods, her thoughts. He'd been her friend when she'd thought she had none; her mentor when she'd badly needed one.

Without thinking, he reached over and smoothed back the hair veiling her cheek. "What hurt you, Erin? Or," he amended quietly, "should I say, 'who?'"

The question jarred her, even as his touch so unexpectedly soothed. The combination was startling in its familiarity. So many times before, when she'd been upset or troubled by the changes taking place in her world, Trevor had found the spot that hurt the most and drawn her out. Invariably he'd absorbed the sting of his probing with his touch, the contact letting her know that she wasn't alone in her struggle. But she didn't believe for a moment that he cared the way he once had. Not, she reminded herself, that he'd cared that much even then.

She was struggling now. And she hated for him to know that.

"It was a 'who,' and it was nothing but a relationship that didn't work. Okay?"

"Why didn't it?"

"It doesn't matter."

"Did he break up with you?"

The question jabbed at her pride. "No, Trevor. I broke it off."

"Why?"

"It doesn't matter," she repeated, feeling too susceptible, too much in need of the friend he'd once been. "You wanted to know all the reasons why I came back and I told you." She'd had to be burned twice to get the message, but she knew now that it was a mistake to confide that much in a person, to trust that much. "What more do you want?"

What he wanted was to know why the light in her eyes died when she thought no one was watching. He wanted to know why, even when she was trying to be defiant, she reminded him of a hurdle-shy yearling, a young horse who'd been hurt or intimidated leaping an obstacle and now feared every approach. It was almost as if the confidence had been beaten out of her.

The thought caught him up short, the possibility that she'd been mistreated knotting something ugly in his gut.

Hating the mental images forming in his mind, he brushed past her bristling. All her defensiveness had done, anyway, was tell him he was getting close to his mark.

"There's more to this." His dark expression matched his tone. "Did you come here so he can't find you?"

All Erin saw was disapproval. "I came back because I

want a job closer to my family. Why can't you believe that?''

"Because you spent too many years wanting to be away from here. And you didn't answer my question."

"Is that what's wrong?" she returned, more concerned with Trevor's narrow-mindedness than his off-the-wall query. "You can't accept what I'm saying because in your mind no one is allowed to grow or change? Because my reasoning doesn't fit what you remember?"

"What's wrong," he countered, mentally ducking the dart of truth she'd so skilfully aimed, "is that you're hiding something. Or from something." *Or someone*, he would have said had she given him the chance.

"I'm not hiding from anything," she snapped, struck by the audacity of the accusation. "I know exactly what got me right where I am. And I'm who I am and where I am because I've been blessed with a combination of lousy judgment and a weakness for men who don't give a damn about me. Not that there've been that many," she expanded, too agitated by his dogged persistence to care that Trevor actually flinched. "I made up in quality what I lacked in quantity. Scott just happened to be a first-class con artist. He said all the things I wanted to hear, *needed* to hear," she emphasized, splaying her hand over her chest. "But I was nothing to him but a means to an end. That's why I broke up with him." She let her hand fall, fisting it to keep him from seeing it tremble. "Are you satisfied now?"

If he found any satisfaction in her humiliation, she couldn't see it in Trevor's shadowed expression. She hadn't only shown her weaknesses to the opposition, she'd just exposed her underbelly. But all he did was look at her as if he didn't know what to say. As verbal as he'd been moments ago, it was the silence she simply couldn't handle.

She made it to the wide doorway at the end of the stable before she heard him call her name. But not until the night had surrounded her did it register that he was behind her. As she moved through the pale glow of the security lights she heard his heavy footfall, the rustle of his clothes, the snap of a twig on the hard ground. A heartbeat later, she felt his hand slip around her upper arm. His grip was gentle, insistent, and burned all the way to her heart.

"Erin."

"Let me go."

"No."

He stepped in front of her, his hand still circling her bare arm. "When I asked if you were hiding, I meant from him." His glance flicked over her face, his eyes searching hers. He looked as unsettled as she felt. "I thought he might have been abusive or something…and that you didn't want anyone to know."

She hadn't expected concern. But that was what she heard in the honeyed tones of his deep voice. She hadn't expected protectiveness. She had the feeling he hadn't, either. Yet, that was there, too. But it was the possessiveness glittering in his eyes when he tipped up her chin that made her throat feel tight. She doubted he realized it, but at that moment he actually looked as if he'd be willing to slay dragons for her.

"It was nothing like that," she repeated, assuring herself it was only the principle he was prepared to defend. She couldn't let herself believe that he'd have come to her rescue. The thought was too seductive, too certain to sabotage her defenses. And she needed those defenses with him. They were becoming more necessary by the second. "What he did was bad enough. But it wasn't…that."

A muscle in his jaw jerked as he lowered his hand. For a moment he said nothing. He just stood there looking very big and very solid, taunting her with the thought of how it would feel to be wrapped in his arms. She'd always felt so safe there. So protected.

"Do you want to tell me what you meant about him being a con artist?"

He was no longer demanding. He was inviting. The difference was so subtle anyone else might not have noticed it. Yet, it was definitely there. In his phrasing, if not in his tone. And something about it seemed to put a rather large crack in their barriers.

"He was after your dad's money."

Incomprehension shifted over his face as he tipped his head. "I don't get it. You don't have access to anything." His eyebrows merged in question. "Do you?"

She told him she didn't. But that didn't seem to relieve the deep scowl that settled over the hard angles of his face. "It wasn't direct access he was after," she explained, turning her back on the comfort that wasn't being offered anyway. "He had his own methods of getting his hands on what he wanted."

She moved toward the shadows, seeking some place where she'd feel less exposed while she dispassionately related what it had taken her all of two minutes to figure out after she'd overheard her snake of an ex-fiancé talking to one of his buddies.

Moonlight glowed around them, turning trees and fence posts into stark silhouettes. She stopped at the pasture gate, listening to the burble of the creek that ran through it. Fireflies bounced over its surface. In the distance, low on the inky black horizon, she could see heat lightning illuminate clouds that still refused to give up their rain.

"Scott was an accountant at the PR firm where I

worked," she said, aware of Trevor beside her. "I'm still not sure how he found out that my stepfather owned the largest cattle ranch in West Texas. I assume that with access to everyone's personnel files he checked out everybody. Anyway," she continued, "he found out how much Logan was worth, and went to work on me."

Scott had pushed all the right buttons, too. He'd romanced her with notes, flowers and evenings in charming little restaurants. He'd been the perfect suitor, the *Cosmo* dream date, which had later made her suspect that he'd probably bought the magazine so he'd know just which buttons to push to begin with. He'd even stopped calling for a while, just to keep her on her toes.

"He would get me talking about my family," she recalled, remembering one particularly useful ploy he'd used, "and I'd tell him about everyone here and about how I wished I were closer so I could be part of them again." Every time she'd talked to her mom, she'd hear about Michael's soccer games and Amy's makeup experiments and what was going on with her aunts, and she'd feel less connected instead of more. She'd gone away searching for home, but it had been home that she'd actually left. "I might as well have handed him a script. He knew exactly what to say to get me to fall in love with him.

"Only now," she confessed, pulling her glance from the rigid line of Trevor's jaw, "I know I wasn't in love with him. I was in love with the idea of the life he said we'd have when we moved here to be closer to my family.

"He had it all worked out," she continued, shaking her head at how hopelessly, impossibly gullible she'd been. "He said we could live in Austin and he'd open an accounting firm. Since he was a CPA, he'd specialize in farm and ranch operations and he could help Logan by handling the RW's accounts for him. He said he could save him a bundle in accountant's fees." Her voice fell. "But saving Logan money hadn't been his plan at all."

She turned away, crossing her arms over the knot in her stomach. She could still remember the abject disbelief she'd felt when she'd discovered just exactly what Scott's plan had been. Her family had known she'd been dating someone for the past year, but she'd never indicated she was serious about him. She hadn't been. Not until last May. That was when they'd planned a trip to the ranch to announce their engagement. But three days before they were to leave, during a dinner party at his condo, she'd overheard him tell one of his buddies that he was going out to Texas "to survey the goldmine."

He'd made the RW sound like the spread in old "Dallas" reruns. The RW was big, but it was far from ostentatious. The "gold" was in the cattle, the land and hard work.

"I heard him tell a friend he figured it would take him a couple of years after we were married to win Logan's confidence enough to let him work with his money, and another one or two of squeaky-clean performance on the accounts before he could start skimming off them. But he'd assured his buddy he was a patient man," she said, her tone utterly flat. "He said he'd even stay faithful to his wife, until he no longer needed her. In case anyone got suspicious later on, it wouldn't hurt to have her solidly in his corner."

The faint strains of music could be heard in the distance, the joyful sound caught on the ebb and flow of the shifting breeze. That faint movement of warm air fluttered her skirt around her legs and teased strands of hair around her face.

She was aware of little beyond the knot in her stomach and the man standing still as stone beside her.

"What did you do?"

She lifted her shoulder in a shrug. "I opened the door to his study," she said, not knowing what else she could have done. The sense of betrayal, the hurt, the anger—all that had come later. When she'd opened that door, she'd felt so numb it was all she could do to breathe. "I've thought of a hundred scathingly brilliant things I could have said since then. But all I did was stand there telling myself to breathe. I don't think I even appreciated how white Scott went when he saw me and realized he'd just kissed his little nest egg goodbye. I just picked up my purse without saying a word to anyone and left."

She drew a breath and slowly blew it out. Trevor watched her slender shoulders rise and fall with the movement, her skin glowing like alabaster in the pale blue moonlight. He wasn't sure what he felt at that moment. Anger was high on the list, though. And an inherent need to protect his own, though he wanted to believe that feeling had more to do with his father and the land than with the lovely young woman whose trust had been so badly abused.

"Please, don't tell anyone what I just told you," she begged, suddenly turning to face him. "Please, Trevor. Especially your dad. He's been so good to me, and I couldn't bear him knowing what I almost did to him. When I think of what could have happened because of my lousy judgment, the damage I could have done bringing someone like that—"

Her voice caught, but Trevor clearly heard the litany of self-recrimination battling inside her. The realization that the man had used her had merely shored up her defenses. But the thought that she'd almost brought someone like that into the lives of the people she cared about still left her horrified.

"I won't say anything," he assured, struck by the fact

those defenses were woefully lacking at the moment. "No harm was done, anyway."

Not to anyone but her, he thought, engaged in a little battle of his own. Not trusting the need he felt to reach for her, he pushed his hands into his pockets. "His own arrogance tripped him up."

"But what if it hadn't?"

"Come on, Erin," he murmured. He had his answers. He just hadn't bargained on the little achy spot they'd put in his chest. "You're being too hard on yourself. You were being manipulated by a pro."

"I don't know why that doesn't make me feel better."

"Because the wounds are still fresh. And he hurt what can take a long time to heal."

My heart? she thought.

"Your pride," he said. "He beat up your self-respect."

For a moment she said nothing. She just stood marveling at his certainty—and wishing he would hold her. It wasn't a wise wish. It was just a feeling that rose from deep inside, an ache that had been there longer than she cared to consider.

"You always could get right to the heart of a problem."

"Not always."

"Sure you could." When he wanted to, he could cut through the fog of emotional confusion and nail its source with the accuracy of a laser. He'd once tried to tell her that it wasn't her mother she was angry with; it was the circumstances. He'd tried to tell her, too, that fighting the changes in her life wouldn't make them go away—and that running back to California wouldn't give her back her home. He'd been right on all counts, though it had taken her years to appreciate his insight. "Maybe it's because you were always so sensible. So…practical."

It was his turn to hesitate. "One of us had to be."

He was referring to her tendency to let her emotions get in the way of her logic. She was sure of it. And it was only because she was feeling a little raw inside that the reminder of his rejection got the better of her now. Her glance shied from his, but not before she could shield the hurt that flashed through her. That pain was totally different from anything else she'd felt, and the fact that she felt it now told her she was definitely in trouble where this man was concerned.

She missed the ease she'd once felt with him. And she thought it totally unfair of him to tease her with it when there wasn't another soul on earth that she'd ever felt as comfortable with as she'd once felt with him.

"Would you answer a question for me?" she asked.

"Considering the answers I badgered out of you, that seems fair."

She glanced back up. "Did you have to stop talking to me?"

Chapter Six

The music had stopped. The only sounds Trevor could hear as Erin's question echoed in the still night air were the drone of cicadas and the murmurings of his conscience. She looked as fragile as glass in the moonlight. Yet, unbelievably brave. He knew she tried to be tough, but there was no way she could ever be. Under the facade of survival skills she'd developed beat the soft heart of a woman who cared deeply about what mattered to her—and who hadn't deserved the lousy hands she'd been dealt. Especially by him.

Lowering his head, his hand gripped the back of his neck, his mind searching for the insight she'd assured him he possessed. When he'd come after her, he'd known only that he wanted answers. Maybe he'd thought that once he had them he could stop thinking about her. Maybe he'd wanted to prove she wasn't what she seemed. Either way, he hadn't counted on having to answer a question he'd never considered.

He didn't know why the memory was suddenly so clear, but he could picture Erin alone in the hall at the high school, totally frustrated with the lock on her locker. He even remembered how her hair had hung down her back like a curtain of cornsilk, and that she'd worn snug jeans and a little pink shirt that had made him hard just looking at her. But it had been her eyes that had kept him from walking away after he'd unjammed the lock and handed it to her. Even though she'd smiled, he'd never seen such sadness.

She'd been sixteen at the time, confused and angry over the unfortunate death of her father, and he'd been drawn to her much as he was drawn to any wounded creature. But as he'd befriended her, she'd become his friend, too, and he'd shared his dreams with her, his plans. And he'd wanted her to the point of pain.

He'd thought about sleeping with her almost constantly. He'd kissed her. Caressed her. Held her while she'd cried, torturing himself with the feel of her until he ached. He even remembered the first time he'd unbuttoned her shirt, and the way she'd buried her head against his shoulder because she was so shy. She'd trusted him and she'd allowed his touch, allowed him to explore her, to taste her. Yet the one time she'd made it clear she wouldn't stop him from going further, he'd stopped himself before anything started. He'd had no protection for them to use, and the last thing he'd wanted to do was compromise the plans he'd made for himself by getting her pregnant.

He might not have considered the question she'd asked, but in the weeks he'd been home, he'd considered nearly everything else about their relationship.

"No," he finally conceded, his body taut as a trip-wire.

"I didn't have to just stop talking to you." Something that felt like apology edged into his voice as he raised his head and made himself meet her eyes. "My only excuse is in-experience. I didn't know how to break up with you, so I figured I'd just avoid you." Finesse hadn't been high on his list of accomplishments at that point. Having pretty much skirted any situation calling for it in the meantime, he wasn't sure he'd acquired much since, either. "I was at school most of the time, anyway, so it wasn't that hard to do."

"But why avoid me for so long?" She lifted her hands at her sides, the supplicating motion drawing his glance to the silky fabric flowing over her slender hips and up to the soft swells of her breasts. "I know what scared you off. I'd fallen in love with you. But I got over it," she told him, ignoring the little voice whispering "liar" in the back of her head. "What I don't understand is why you hated me all these years."

Trevor felt a muscle in his jaw jerk. He was as lousy at this sort of thing now as he'd been years ago.

"I never hated you, Erin. But I knew you felt something I didn't. I didn't even know what love was. I still don't," he admitted, deciding the only way to handle the situation was to be as honest with her as she'd been with him. "All I knew was that I had to cool the relationship before I got in over my head."

He'd backed off a little more each time he'd seen her, but he'd missed her too much to completely let go—until he'd realized there was no other way. "You were a threat to my future." There was no kind way to explain how he'd felt. No gentle words to soften what he'd done. "And a man either runs from a threat, or he fights it. With you," he concluded quietly, "I guess I did both."

For a moment Erin said nothing. She just wrapped her

arms over the hollow ache in her stomach and watched him plant his hands on his hips. She had to admit that he'd caught her off guard when he said he didn't know what love was. Knowing him as she did now, she supposed that didn't surprise her as much as it saddened her. For his sake. She had, however, already known that his feelings had been far different from her own. She just hadn't bargained on having him spell it out so clearly.

Salvaging what she could of her badly trampled pride, she offered a rueful smile.

"That wasn't so hard, was it?" She didn't know what it said about her that of the only two serious relationships she'd ever had, it hurt more to have been in the way than it did to have been used. She'd always known of Trevor's dreams. They had been part of what she'd loved about him—what she'd admired. She hadn't wanted to stand in the way of them. She'd wanted to share. "We could have saved ourselves years of hard feelings if you'd told me that before."

His glance was as droll as his tone. "I don't think it would have been that simple."

Probably not, she conceded to herself. "Sure it would," she insisted. "All you would have had to do was tell me I was an obstacle. It would have been easier than avoiding me."

Her reassuring smile didn't fool him in the least. Or maybe it was the way her glance barely met his before she looked away that made her armor so transparent. Something about her expression, the vulnerability in it, reminded him of the way she'd looked the day he'd found the dog in her apartment—the day he'd realized he'd scarred her sense of trust.

He hadn't wanted to believe that what he'd done had made that much difference to her. But the attempt proved as futile now as it had then. The jerk who'd nearly manipulated her into marrying him clearly hadn't been the only one who'd battered her self-confidence.

"I don't think you quite get the picture here."

"I'm sure I do," she assured him, turning away.

He turned her right back, his hand a band of heat circling her arm.

"You were more than an obstacle, Erin. You were a temptation. I could fight you. And I could fight myself. But I couldn't fight us together. I had to be where I couldn't touch you. I didn't *trust* myself around you."

The moonlight carved his features in shades of gray granite. His eyes glittered hard on her face. "You have no idea how badly I wanted you." His voice was a rough rasp, dark as the heavens, heated as the evening air. "All you'd have to do was walk into the room and all I could think about was how your body felt against me, the little sounds you made when I touched you. I damned myself a thousand times for not making love to you that night, just so I could stop thinking about what it would have been like."

Erin swallowed, her throat suddenly as dry as the dust beneath her feet. "It probably wouldn't have helped if you'd told me that."

"No." He dropped his tone to match hers and eased his grip as much as he could without letting her go. "It probably wouldn't have."

"Well, I'm not a threat anymore. Whatever plans you have—"

"Don't underestimate yourself."

His glance lingered on her mouth as he issued the blunt command, then slipped to the bare skin above her bodice. She looked cool as marble. Night shadows defined the del-

icate hollow of her throat, her collarbone, the enticing
swells of her breasts.

Unwilling to resist, he lifted his free hand and touched
the tiny strap curving over one shoulder. "I still don't trust
myself around you. I keep telling myself I don't want you
here. But I still want you." With the tip of his finger, he
traced the ribbon of fabric over the edge of her collarbone.
The thought that only those two tiny scraps held up the
top had taunted him all evening. "I don't know how much
longer I can keep my hands off you."

He could stop himself if he wanted to. Trevor's command over himself was even more formidable than Erin
had realized. He'd wanted her before, yet he'd ruthlessly
denied himself what she would have freely given.

She glanced down, thinking to remind him that his
hands were already on her, but that bit of bravado lodged
in her throat. His touch stalled where strap met bodice, and
the fingers circling her arm flexed against her skin.

"Actually," he whispered, his head inching lower as he
tilted her face to his. "I don't think I want to."

She should have moved. She should have stepped back
and let him know that he wasn't the only one who found
their situation a struggle. Then his breath brushed her
cheek, his mouth settled over hers and the thought disappeared like dust in a dry wind.

A mouth as hard as his shouldn't feel like velvet. Callused hands shouldn't feel so gentle. She knew she reached
for his shoulders because the bones in her legs seemed to
melt and she needed something solid to hang on to. He
was all there was, and he was definitely solid. Rock had
more give than the muscles of his biceps. Steel would have
felt softer than the wall of his broad chest. Sensations
swirled through her. Heat where his hand pressed low on
her back drawing her against his hard body. Tightness in

her stomach where he moved against her. And a delicious, dangerous softening deeper inside.

She felt herself straining toward him, her body seeking the contact as if it instinctively remembered what she had forgotten. She had no memory of this. She had no memory of feeling hunger in him, of him wanting her the way he'd claimed. But when he angled her head to deepen the kiss and his tongue slipped over hers, it was hunger she felt.

Need caught like wildfire. Like a spark set to dry tinder, it swept through him, raw and urgent, heating his blood, taunting his body. He felt her sag toward him, and he groaned at the feel of her slender body melting against his. She was so small, so soft. Yet he could feel the strength in her supple muscles as he bent lower and lifted her arms around his neck. Skimming his hands down her sides, he pulled her closer, tighter, shaping her feminine curves while he shifted to align them more intimately. His tongue mated with hers, her taste filling him as he brushed his palm over the tantalizing curve of her breast.

A moan caught in her throat. Or maybe the sound had been torn from him when her breathing altered and he felt her move to accommodate his touch.

He could sense that she was nowhere near as immune to him as she wanted to be. He would have found the thought infinitely more satisfying had she not stiffened a few moments later and drawn his hand away.

"No," she whispered, her breath warm and ragged against his mouth. "Please, Trevor." She turned her head, her temple brushing his chin as her arms slipped from his shoulders. "I can't do this again."

Completely unsettled by the urgency of her response, she curled her hands into fists between them. Her heart was hammering, her breathing shallow when he cupped his hand at the back of her neck and pressed her forehead to his chest.

She didn't know if he was accepting her claim, or if he was calming himself down. She knew only that she could feel his heart beating as erratically as her own.

"Trev? You down here?"

Michael's voice rang out from somewhere beyond the buildings behind them. He wouldn't have been able to see them, protected as they were by shadows. But she was already pulling away.

"Trevor?"

"Over here," he called over her head, his hands sliding to her shoulders. "I'll be with you in a second."

His glance fell to the top of her head. "That wasn't supposed to happen."

"No. No," Erin repeated, though she wasn't sure if he was referring to the interruption, the impact or the fact that he'd kissed her in the first place. "It wasn't."

"Erin—"

"Trevor," Michael called out. "Bill Farley wants to talk to you. Says his horse has HPY or YP or something like that."

HYPP. Hyperkalemic periodic paralysis. "Great," he muttered. Bill had a buffed-up horse that couldn't properly metabolize potassium. Uncomfortably aware of a few metabolic problems of his own, he watched Erin move from his touch.

"You'd better go." She took another step back, her glance skimming his chin. "Good night," she murmured, and turned away.

Before he could decide whether or not he should stop her, she was moving through the shadows, her skirt swaying around her long legs, and heading for the stairs leading to her apartment. She wasn't running, but he couldn't help thinking she might as well have been when, moments later, he left the shadows himself.

"Why isn't he cooling down?"

"It's this blasted heat and humidity."

Erin heard Hank swear under his breath as he ran his hand over the sweat-soaked gelding. One of the hands had ridden him in ten minutes ago. Now the beautiful cinnamon bay with its black tail and mane just stood in the breezeway of the dim old stable, eyes glazed, his breathing rapid.

"It's bad enough that it's over a hundred out there, but these clouds roll in every afternoon and hang there just long enough to clam everything up. Tease like a dang female."

His rheumy eyes darted to her. A film of sweat stained the band of his hat, and perspiration gathered in the creases of his weathered skin. It was a testament to the heat that he wasn't chewing on a cigar. The taste of tobacco, he'd said, just made him more thirsty.

"Sorry," he muttered, looking none too pleased to have to offer the apology. "I keep forgetting you're female yourself."

Most women would have been completely offended by the grizzled old cowhand's remark. Coming from Hank, Erin regarded his comment as the highest form of flattery.

Not that he was in a flattering frame of mind, she thought. He could be cranky on his best days. But the heat had tempers as brittle as dry grass and the discomfort of breathing air that felt like fire from a furnace hadn't improved his disposition a whit.

In the week since the party, the temperature had soared, taking its toll on man and animal alike. The cowhand who'd come in on the badly dehydrated bay, a ten-year veteran of the ranch she knew only as Carter, had been suffering the effects of the heat himself. His leathery face had been the color of an habañero pepper, and he'd headed for the bunkhouse with a pounding headache.

Before he'd gone, he'd told Hank that a couple head of cattle had wandered into a ravine where the water supply had dried up and that he and Tom, one of the other hands, had gone down to roust them out. They hadn't counted on having to run the steers out one by one. But for some reason, the normal herd-and-stampede mentality had failed, which meant the horses had worked three times harder driving them out one at a time.

The weather was even making the cattle cantankerous.

Hank checked the horse's glazed-looking eyes and muttered another oath. "We're going to lose this one if we don't get some water into him."

"He won't touch it." Uncomfortable herself, she tried to disregard the moisture trickling between her shoulder blades. Her gray Save the Whales tank top felt as damp as the waistband of her jeans. "I put a bucket right under his nose and he just turns away."

"Is Trevor back yet?"

Cupping her hands, she scooped water and held the offering under the horse's muzzle. She wished she could have told Hank she didn't know if he was or not, because that would mean she hadn't been listening for Trevor's vehicle. His Bronco had been gone since sunup and she hadn't heard anything with a motor come or go since Logan and Jett had taken off in the helicopter two hours ago to make sure no one else was in trouble. "I don't think so."

"That boy hasn't been around all week," Hank muttered, swearing at the weather again. "Everybody's having heat problems with their animals. But we need him here."

He scratched his unshaven jaw, his brow furrowing as he considered all that had to be done and just who was going to do it.

"You're going to have to track him down," he concluded. "But first, cool this horse as best you can. Keep sponging him off. His head, neck and underbelly," he instructed, tossing a sponge into the bucket the animal wouldn't drink from. "But stay away from his back and rump so he doesn't cramp. I'm taking the trailer out to pick up Tom and his mount. Carter said he left them two miles out from the East camp."

Erin cast a worried glance back to the horse. The big animal really didn't look good at all. He just stood there, panting like a steam engine and looking as if it took all his energy just to breathe.

Not having a clue what she'd do if the horse got worse, she hurriedly sponged down the places Hank had mentioned, then left the horse in cross ties in the breezeway to head for a phone. The closest one was inside the door of the breeding barn across the compound. She headed there at a dead run.

The interior of the breeding barn, with its long, presently empty pens and glass-walled lab was no cooler than anywhere else. The only rooms that weren't the temperature of fondue were the office and the laboratory that formed the heart of the ranch's insemination program. Tempting as it was to use the office phone just to feel the air-conditioning, the one inside the barn's side door was closer.

Trevor wasn't the first person Erin tried to reach. Wiping sweat from her forehead, she snagged the receiver and called Annie. Since Hank tended to worry more about creatures on four legs than two, someone needed to check on Carter to make sure he wasn't suffering sunstroke or something. Her mom would still be in town, and Annie was only five minutes away. She would know what to do if the man needed help. After all, she'd taken care of Jett when he'd shown up out of nowhere, broken, battered and sick as a dog. If she could nurse him, she could nurse anyone.

"I'll wake Ricky from his nap and be right there," Annie said, and hung up before Erin could even say thanks.

Her next call was to Verna at Doc Henderson's office, who told her that Trevor was at the Circle J. The Circle J was Bill Farley's place. So Erin called there, and Mrs. Farley had her hold the line while she ran down to their barn where Trevor was forcing fluid into one of their calves. Trevor was on the phone himself two minutes later.

She recalled once telling him, rather sarcastically, that if she needed a vet, she'd call one. She desperately needed one now. Trying to keep the panic from her voice, she quickly described the horse's condition.

"He needs water and electrolytes," he said before she'd even finished.

"Do we have any here?" she asked, thinking of the assortment of medications and remedies that were kept in both stables' storage rooms.

"Probably not the kind he needs. I think all Dad keeps on hand is the kind to treat scours. If he won't drink, you can't get them into him, anyway. You'll just have to keep sponging him down until I get there." His tone was all business, reassuringly matter-of-fact. "Make sure you stay away from his back and big muscles," he warned, repeating what Hank had already told her. "And check his heart and respiratory rate every five minutes. Write them down so we can see if he's getting better or worse. I'm just finishing here. It'll take me half an hour to get there."

FREE Books! FREE Gift!

PLAY THE

LUCKY 7

SLOT MACHINE GAME!

$$$

Extra Bonus

..AND YOU CAN GET **FREE Books!**
PLUS A **FREE Gift!** →

PLAY "LUCKY 7" AND GET
THREE FREE GIFTS!

HOW TO PLAY:

1. With a coin, carefully scratch off the silver box at the right. Then check the claim chart
see what we have for you — **FREE BOOKS** and a gift — **ALL YOURS! ALL FREE!**

2. Send back this card and you'll receive brand-new Silhouette Special Edition® nove
These books have a cover price of $4.25 each in the U.S. and $4.75 each in Canada, b
they are yours to keep absolutely free.

3. There's no catch. You're und
no obligation to buy anything. W
charge nothing — ZERO —
your first shipment. And you do
have to make any minimum numb
of purchases — not even one!

4. The fact is thousands of readers enjoy receiving books by mail from the Silhoue
Reader Service™ months before they're available in stores. They like the convenience
home delivery and they love our discount prices!

5. We hope that after receiving your free books you'll want to remain a subscriber. B
the choice is yours — to continue or cancel, any time at all! So why not take us up on o
invitation, with no risk of any kind. You'll be glad you did!

YOURS FREE!

PLAY LUCKY 7 FOR THIS EXCITING FREE GIFT!

*THIS SURPRISE
MYSTERY GIFT
COULD BE
YOURS FREE WHEN
YOU PLAY*

LUCKY 7!

©1998 HARLEQUIN ENTERPRISES LIMITED.
® and TM are trademarks owned by Harlequin Books S.A. used under license.

NO COST! NO OBLIGATION TO BUY!
NO PURCHASE NECESSARY!

DETACH AND MAIL CARD TODAY!

PLAY THE

LUCKY 7

SLOT MACHINE GAME!

Just scratch off the silver box with a coin. Then check below to see the gifts you get!

YES!

I have scratched off the silver box. Please send me all the gifts for which I qualify. I understand I am under no obligation to purchase any books, as explained on the back and on the opposite page.

335 SDL CPRP

235 SDL CPRH
(S-SE-04/99)

Name: _____
PLEASE PRINT CLEARLY

Address: _____ Apt.#: _____

City: _____ State/Prov.: _____ Postal Zip/Code: _____

WORTH TWO FREE BOOKS PLUS A BONUS MYSTERY GIFT!

WORTH TWO FREE BOOKS!

WORTH ONE FREE BOOK!

TRY AGAIN!

Offer limited to one per household and not valid to current Silhouette Special Edition® subscribers. All orders subject to approval.

PRINTED IN U.S.A.

The Silhouette Reader Service™ — Here's how it works:

Accepting your 2 free books and mystery gift places you under no obligation to buy anything. You may keep the books and gift and return the shipping statement marked "cancel." If you do not cancel, about a month later we'll send you 6 additional novels and bill you just $3.57 each in the U.S., or $3.96 each in Canada, plus 25¢ delivery per book and applicable taxes if any.* That's the complete price and — compared to the cover price of $4.25 in the U.S. and $4.75 in Canada — it's quite a bargain! You may cancel at any time, but if you choose to continue, every month we'll send you 6 more books, which you may either purchase at the discount price or return to us and cancel your subscription.

*Terms and prices subject to change without notice. Sales tax applicable in N.Y. Canadian residents will be charged applicable provincial taxes and GST.

If offer card is missing write to: Silhouette Reader Service, 3010 Walden Ave., P.O. Box 1867, Buffalo, NY 14240-1867

BUSINESS REPLY MAIL

FIRST-CLASS MAIL   PERMIT NO. 717   BUFFALO, NY

POSTAGE WILL BE PAID BY ADDRESSEE

SILHOUETTE READER SERVICE
3010 WALDEN AVE
PO BOX 1867
BUFFALO NY 14240-9952

NO POSTAGE
NECESSARY
IF MAILED
IN THE
UNITED STATES

Her hand tightened on the receiver. "Trevor, wait!"

"I'm here."

"How do I do that? Check his heart and respirations, I mean."

She had developed a certain knack for working with horses, but when it came to injury or illness she'd never been called on to do much more than treat skin sores or massage strained muscles. She'd never been around an animal in real trouble before.

She didn't know if Trevor sensed her anxiety or not. In that same impersonally professional tone, he simply told her where to locate the horse's facial artery and to watch its rib cage to count breaths.

"And keep offering him water," he reminded her, much as she suspected he would have anyone else. "Once he starts cooling down, he may start drinking and we can get the 'lytes into him that way."

Trevor made it to the ranch in twenty-seven minutes. His shirt was sticking to his back as he grabbed his brown leather case and two bags of IV solution from a thermal pack in the back of his Bronco. The heat was wearing on him as much as it was everyone else, he supposed. But, normally, a little heat wouldn't have him agitated simply because people expected him to be in three places at once, or because the air-conditioning in his car had gone out two days ago and he hadn't had time to get it fixed. He wouldn't care that he hadn't had a chance to talk to his uncle Cal about building him a place of his own, or that he hadn't had a chance to ride through the hills, or that the days were about six hours too short. But Erin was wearing on him, too, and that was making him testy.

It was bad enough that thoughts of her invaded his waking hours. At night, when there was no work to distract him, the restlessness was so much worse.

That was no one's fault but his own.

If he hadn't kissed her. If he hadn't allowed himself to know how she tasted, how she felt against him, he wouldn't feel like a panther pacing a cage. The troublesome part wasn't just the physical craving churning him up inside. It was finally acknowledging that he'd really hurt her—and that she wasn't going to let him get close enough to do it again.

Deliberately pulling his thoughts to more immediate concerns, he strode past a couple of barn cats lazing in the shade of the garage and headed through the compound.

This morning the Farleys had lost the old cow that had birthed the calf he'd just treated for dehydration. Yesterday, he'd had to put down a mare that had stroked from the heat. Hoping he wasn't about to revisit that scenario with one of his dad's animals, he entered the wide breezeway of the old stable.

The horses that were usually there were all outside, seeking shade and what there was of a breeze beneath the sprawling live oaks in the pastures. The only movement inside the building was the rusted blades of the old overhead fans stirring the stifling air. A huge puddle of water leaked toward the drain on the cement floor and a pair of cross ties hung limply from the metal rings anchored into the wall. But there was no sign of a sick horse. Or of Erin.

Thinking he'd misunderstood and that she was in the new stable, he'd just started out when he heard the soothing, worried tones of her voice and the faint splash of water. Following the sounds, he found her and his patient on the back side of the building. She'd obviously found it more efficient to douse the horse where they normally washed down the animals rather than to drag a hose inside.

This late in the afternoon, only one end of the building cast shade. That was where she had the horse, careful to keep it out of the sun. The big animal's sides were moving like bellows, its massive muscles rippling as it shook. Erin continued to soothe. She stood on a stool beside his left shoulder, holding the trickling hose over its head to let the cool water flow behind his ears and down its massive neck, then stepped down to run a dripping, yellow sponge over its chest.

It looked as if she'd taken the hose to herself, too. As Trevor moved closer, he could see water glistening on the back of her neck, and running in rivulets to the scooped neckline of a sleeveless shirt sporting a logo of a baby whale and its mom. Tendrils of hair that had escaped her topknot stuck damply to her shoulders.

"How's he doing?"

She glanced up, her motions stalling before she looked away. "He's still not drinking."

An old wooden bench sat next to a spray of morning glory growing over a section of the stable's peeling white wall. The regular supply of water from the hoses allowed it to thrive and the trailing plant had overtaken all but the section of bench where Trevor set his veterinary case.

"What's his heart rate?"

"Nearly ninety. I checked a couple of minutes ago."

With a glance toward the wet knees of her jeans, he stopped next to where she crouched on a big, black rubber mat and checked the animal's eyes, its gums, its flared nostrils.

"I wrote down what you asked," she said, inching sideways when his leg brushed her shoulder. "His respirations have slowed a little, but not much."

Ducking under the horse's neck, she moved to the side and pushed back the hair sticking to her cheek. A bead of moisture trailed from beneath the brim of Trevor's hat near his temple, and a wedge of perspiration stained the back of his shirt. But it was his profile that had her attention. His intense expression made his features look chiseled from stone, and the way his jaw tightened as he examined the animal did nothing to alleviate her concern. She'd never worked with this particular horse before. It was part of a work string that was kept on the range with the men, and she didn't even know its name. She just called him ''Big Guy'' and they'd done some serious bonding in the past half hour. She couldn't bear the thought of anything happening to him.

''We need a portable fan. See if there's one in the supply room.''

''Anything else?''

He glanced up at the long wooden pole that held the hose and shower attachment she'd been using. ''Not unless you can arrange for a nice stiff breeze,'' he muttered, and turned back to the horse.

She was back in less than two minutes. In another minute she had the fan plugged into an extension cord and, keeping it well back from the water, turned it on the horse. The entire time she worked, Trevor was moving between the animal and his case.

''His temperature's a hundred and four. Could be worse, but not much. Here. Hold these.''

He handed her a plastic IV bag filled with yellow liquid and a roll of tape, then ripped open a packet of clear tubing with his teeth. After dropping a paper packet into his shirt pocket, he took back the bag, attached the tubing and handed the bag back to her again.

''You're going to have to hold this for me,'' he told her, clearly expecting her to follow him when he moved since he had the other end of the tube. Snagging the stool she'd used earlier with the toe of his boot, he pulled it closer to the horse and slipped around to the other side. "Keep it above his head."

It didn't occur to Erin to balk at his clipped instructions. He wasn't asking anything she wouldn't do willingly, anyway, and it was infinitely easier focusing on what had to be done than on the edgy way he glanced at her. She hadn't seen him since the night he'd proven just how susceptible to him she was, and she was feeling a little edgy, too.

Stepping onto the stool, she held the bag above the horse's ears. From her vantage point, she couldn't see much more than Trevor's broad shoulders and the deep dent in the top of his gray hat as he found the neck vein he wanted and deftly inserted the needle.

"Can you hand me the tape?"

She held out the roll he'd given her. With one hand holding the needle in place, he used the other to rip adhesive.

"Is he going to be all right?"

"I don't know yet. He's young. So that's in his favor. We'll just have to see how he does in the next few minutes."

The fan had to be helping. The breeze felt like heaven to her as it evaporated the moisture on her shirt. The horse had to be feeling some relief. "Hank might be bringing back another one in the same condition."

Trevor's glance met hers, got as far as a whale's tail on her shirt then slid away.

"They had a problem with some cattle," she explained, and related to him what she'd heard Carter tell Hank.

"Then we're going to need more electrolytes. Will you be okay while I get them and a hammer?"

The hand holding the tape moved protectively to the horse's head. "What do you want a hammer for?"

Had Trevor not been so preoccupied, he would have smiled at the alarm in her eyes. Between concern for the animals and trying not to think about what had happened the last time he and Erin had been together, the expression never formed. "I'm going to put a nail in that pole so you don't have to hold that thing."

"Oh." Her hand relaxed. "Trevor?" she called, wondering at the tension in his strides as he moved away. "Would you hurry? I need to make a phone call. I have an interview in San Antonio at three o'clock. I'll never be able to make it."

Trevor automatically glanced at his watch, then back to the woman poised like the *Statue of Liberty* atop the stool. He wasn't sure why, but as he told her he'd be right back and headed for the workshop, he had the feeling she hadn't even mentioned the interview to Hank when he'd commandeered her to help with the horse. She'd simply set her own plans aside to do what needed to be done.

A minute later, watching Hank pull into the compound in a cloud of dust before jumping out to lower the gate of the horse trailer, his only thought was that he was glad she'd stayed.

Chapter Seven

"You're going to have to make that phone call in a hurry." Trevor brought the hammer down on a tenpenny nail, sinking it halfway into the upright four-by-four. Lifting the IV bag from Erin's hand, he turned and suspended it from the makeshift stand. "The other horse is in trouble, too."

Erin stepped from the stool, rubbing her shoulder as Trevor sank another nail halfway into the opposite side of the post. "How's Tom?"

"I don't know. He was sitting in the Jeep, but I didn't really see him. I just told Hank I'd be back to help him with the horse and headed here."

Trevor had jogged to the workshop and back in record time. As quickly as he'd made the two-block trip, she doubted he'd even broken stride when he'd passed Hank and the horse trailer.

"I'll check on him." She backed away, her thoughts

moving in three directions at once. "Annie's down at the bunkhouse with Carter. If Tom needs help, I'll get her."

Trevor didn't ask why Annie was there. Seconds after checking the bay to see if he was responding to the cooling fan and the fluids, guardedly optimistic to find the animal's breathing less labored, he followed Erin around the corner of the building. She was already at the Jeep, talking first to Hank, who was trying to back the horse out of the trailer, then to the young cowhand in the passenger seat. After handing him the towel he'd seen her wet at the faucet, she pointed toward the bunkhouse as if to tell him to go rest, then took off like a shot for the barn.

The sun streamed down like a brilliant white laser, leeching color from the sky and causing waves of heat to shimmer from the dirt and gravel covering the ground. It was too blasted hot for her to be running, Trevor thought.

Overlooking the fact that he hadn't exactly been moving at a Sunday stroll himself, he shouldered a trickle of sweat from his cheek and reached for the flank of the sleek cinnamon-colored cutting horse unsteadily backing down the ramp. The new arrival's chestnut coat and white mane were muddied and dank. Glassy-eyed, she barely responded to the prods and gentle coaxing of the ranch foreman.

"Let's get her out of the sun."

"What do you think I'm trying to do?" Hank muttered, pulling his hat off to wipe away the salty moisture running in his eyes.

Trevor's glance sharpened on the older man's face. The acerbic tone was par for Hank even without stress and heat. What had Trevor scowling was the flush under the man's weathered skin.

"You'd better get out of the sun yourself for a while. Take a break. I've got the horse."

"I'll take a break after the work's done. I've got a mechanic out in section three waiting on gaskets. The pump in the lower well-house quit." He jammed his hat back on. "If the wind'd just come up like it's supposed to and turn the windmills, we wouldn't be having half the problems we're having now. Damn motors keep overheating."

If the wind came up, it would just dry everything out that much faster. The land was turning to tinder as it was.

Trevor would have pointed that out, just for the sake of argument, since he was feeling a little contentious himself. But the horse needed water. She needed to be cooled down, too. Now.

The horse didn't even care that a total stranger was trying to lead her. She didn't shy or snuffle as even the best-trained animal might do when first approached by someone it didn't know. She gave no indication at all that she cared what happened to her. That was not a good sign. Lacking the energy to hold her ground, she simply set one hoof in front of the other, following Trevor blindly to the side of the stable while sweat gleamed on her coppery coat and she shook as if she were freezing.

In less than a minute, he had the mare tethered to the post and a bucket of water under her nose. Shocky as she looked, her nose twitched at the scent of the saving liquid. For a moment Trev thought she might drink. But the Fates were in a perverse mood today. As if the contents of the bucket had suddenly turned to sand, she lifted her big head and stood staring into space.

He'd looked over to make sure the bay wasn't doing anything weird, and was thinking that he could sure use a little help, when Erin came up behind him.

"I'll do that," she said, and shoved a cold can of cola at him.

He'd barely said, "Thanks," and was downing the

blessedly cold contents of the can when she took the hose from him and turned to the horses. She had a knack for taking care of people without making it look as if that was what she was doing. He wondered if she even knew how instinctive her actions were when he saw her glance automatically to their first patient on her way to help the second. Her motions briskly efficient, she started sponging down the mare, talking to her, soothing her, much as she had the horse behind her. He was right there, too, checking the animal's vital signs to see just how bad she was.

They worked together quietly, almost easily, he supposed. When he approached with another bag of solution and packet of tubing, she handed him the tape he'd given her earlier and hung the bag before he could even ask for her assistance. When he took over sponging down the mare, she went back to sponging down the bay gelding. He tried to overlook the smooth shift of the slender muscles in her arms, and the way her scent, warmed by her body, knotted tension low in his gut. He tried not to think about the heat.

Some things simply wouldn't be ignored. He was counting respirations on the bay when he saw Erin take a handful of water from the bucket and splash it on her flushed face. It ran down her neck, sluicing over her chest as she moved to pick up the hose.

Thinking he could use cooling down himself, he stopped her at the horse's side.

"Can I have that for a minute?"

"This?" she asked, lifting the hose.

"Yeah."

She handed it to him, water splashing over their feet and soaking the cuffs of their jeans. Bending from the waist, he held the stream over the back of his neck, letting the tepid water soak into his hair, run over his cheeks and soak the shoulders of his shirt when he straightened. When he handed the hose back to her, she shrugged and did the same thing, not seeming to care a whit that her T-shirt now clung to her like a second skin.

Or maybe, he thought, she just didn't notice. Her movements were artless, her preoccupation with her task complete as she swiped her bangs back with her forearm. He didn't have to wonder if she was wearing a bra. He could clearly see the outline of scalloped lace. But it was the shape of her, the firm fullness that strained against the filmy undergarment and the thin cotton shirt, that kept him from looking away when he knew that was exactly what he should do.

It was then that she saw him watching her—and noticed what he would have had to be dead to ignore.

Erin's glance shot down, her hand automatically bunching the fabric between her breasts to pull it out. When she looked back up, Trevor was already turning away.

"What's with the whales?"

The tightness of his jaw made the question terse.

"What do you mean?"

"The shirts you wear. They've all got a cause on them."

Wolf preservation. Save the rain forests. Today it was whales. His eyes narrowed as another facet of her emerged. "Are you an environmentalist or something?"

"I don't believe in labels. I just think we need to take care of what we have."

He appreciated the philosophy. He would just have appreciated it a lot more if she wasn't wearing it on her chest.

"See if you can get him to drink."

Giving him a look that was part puzzlement, but mostly caution, she reached for the bucket. In the same soft tones she'd used before, she encouraged the animal to take the water. She cajoled. She begged. The bay still wouldn't drink.

"Give him some time," Trevor murmured, seeing worry shadow her face again. "It might take a while." Picking up a sponge, he squatted by the mare's back legs. Five seconds of silence was all it took for him to start thinking about the way the whale's tail curved over her breast. "Where was your interview?"

With his back to her, she couldn't tell if he was truly interested, or if he was just making conversation. It didn't matter. She was grateful for anything that would take her mind off the look she'd seen in his eyes moments ago. "At the Hotel del Rio. They're looking for a new director of public relations."

"Were you able to reschedule?"

"There wasn't time. I just told the woman at the employment agency that we had an emergency and that I'd call her later."

The splash of water underscored the clatter of the bucket handle when she set it down.

"Do you miss anything about it? Los Angeles, I mean."

Definitely just conversation. "A few things. The ocean. Some of my friends." She picked up the hose, letting water trickle into her hand, and held it under the horse's black muzzle. "But not enough to ever want to go back." The horse ignored the water, so she wet his cheek with it instead. "The fantasy wasn't there."

"The fantasy?"

She shrugged. "I'd had this fantasy of what my life would be like when I went back...of how perfect everything would be. All through college, I kept telling myself to be patient. That once I had a job, I'd be happy. Then I graduated and landed the job, and I kept telling myself to be patient, that things would be better when I didn't feel like such a greenhorn.'' A rueful smile formed at the thought. Even her analogies had tried to lead her back to Texas. She'd just been too busy insisting she knew what she was doing to pay attention.

"What happened once you had some experience under your belt?''

"I told myself to be patient,'' she said, diligently concentrating on her task, "that things would be better when I got a promotion.''

"Then the promotion came,'' he coaxed.

Her voice dropped. "I told myself to be patient.''

"Maybe you want something that doesn't exist.''

He hadn't looked up from what he was doing, hadn't hesitated. He'd just dismissed what she sought as something that couldn't be found.

"No, Trevor,'' she quietly countered, needing badly to believe she wouldn't always live with the unsettled feeling that had plagued her for years. "It's out there. I just need to find it. I was just looking in the wrong place.'' The horse sidestepped. She steadied it. "You told me I wouldn't find it there, anyway.''

His glance cut toward her, his brow furrowing as if he couldn't remember having said such a thing.

"I think what you said was that there was no way things could be the way they were,'' she reminded him, "but that I wouldn't be happy until I'd proved it to myself. I was looking for the security I'd lost when Dad died,'' she said quietly, time having mellowed the awful ache of that loss. "It took me a while to figure that out. But I know now that I need to make my own security.

"I know I need a job in a smaller agency, too,'' she added, since she'd been doing a lot of thinking about how to find what eluded her. "Someplace less cutthroat. Or maybe something in a private company's PR department.''

She had a knack for selling ideas, products, other people. She just hadn't figured out where to best sell herself. "Unlike yours, my path doesn't seem all that clear." Her voice dropped another notch. "Maybe that's why the job search is taking so long."

"Maybe something will come of this interview."

His tone was encouraging and, she thought, hopeful. "I hope so," she replied, though she didn't sound particularly convinced.

"You know, Erin," he said, his voice lacking the edge that had crept into it a few minutes ago, "the only reason my path was clear is because what I want isn't all that complicated. I never had the setbacks you did, and I never had big dreams. All I've ever wanted is to work with the land and the animals on it.

"That's still all I want," he told her, his purpose as certain as it had been years ago. "I'll build my own place here and maybe take over Doc Henderson's practice someday. I'd need to bring in another vet if I did that, so I could keep up my end on the ranch, but it could be done."

"What you want is to work yourself into the ground," she murmured.

With his hand on the mare's flank, he rose to check the IV. "This is a great life. I'm doing what I want to do and I'm happy doing it. What else is there?"

The delicate wing of her eyebrow arched, her glance following his movements. Despite the strain that ebbed and flowed between them, she'd found far more about him that was admirable than was not. When he committed to something, his sense of loyalty was unshakable. His affection for animals was as real as his respect for the land, and for his father. He was, she supposed, what the men in this part of the country called a man's man. The kind who knew what it was to love a horse, but not a woman. The kind who relied on himself, and not much of anybody else.

She needed the kind of man who wasn't afraid to share.

"What else?" she repeated quietly. "Most people want a relationship. A family. Don't you want a wife some-day?" she asked, wishing she didn't need to understand him. "Children?"

A few weeks ago, Trevor would have answered that question without a second's hesitation. He'd given as much thought to having a wife and kids as he had to tattoo-ing *Mom* on his biceps and riding off on a Harley. The fact that he hesitated now caught him completely off guard.

"I've never thought about a family." Not until he'd been surrounded by it, anyway. "And we were talking about you," he reminded her, his discomfort with the sub-ject resurrecting the edge in his voice. "Not me."

She ducked her head, her voice dropping as if she'd just been chastised. "I thought we were just talking."

It wasn't until he turned toward her that he caught the agitation in her movements. Her horse had stopped shaking and his eyes had lost their glaze. Erin didn't seem to no-tice. She just continued wetting the sponge and running it down the big bay's neck, using the motions as an excuse to avoid looking at him.

With a quick glance at the mare, who was doing better herself, Trevor walked over to Erin and took the sponge from her hand.

Her glance immediately flew to his. Suddenly seeming as nervous around him as a filly with a stallion, to find him so close, she backed up. "Why did you do that?"

"Because he doesn't need it anymore."

The unease between them could shift from barely per-ceptible to taunting in the space of a heartbeat. Moments ago, it had been veiled. Now, that veil was slipping again, revealing the tension that shimmered between them like heat waves off a tin shed.

It had been a week since he'd touched her. But the feel of her remained fresh in his mind, taunting him as surely as if she'd just stepped from his arms. He'd seen her light on every night when he'd finally finished his chores, and every night he'd forced his feet to carry him to his place instead of climbing the stairs to hers.

Wanting her, restless with the feeling, he skimmed a glance over her mouth, the faint pink sunburn on her shoulders, the gray fabric that had nearly, mercifully, dried out.

He could feel her caution, could appreciate it, too, he supposed. But all he could think about was that she'd wanted that kiss as badly as he had.

She anchored her hand over her opposite shoulder in a less-than-subtle attempt to block his view. "Maybe he'll drink now."

He didn't know why the breathy quality of her voice pleased him. Maybe it was because it betrayed the awareness she wanted to deny. Maybe it was because he hoped she was as frustrated as he was. She'd said she didn't want to get involved with him again. But that wasn't what he saw in her eyes.

"Maybe," he muttered. "Why don't you see?"

The bay drank. Finally. And despite the guardedness she felt, Erin couldn't help but smile as the long pink tongue gingerly touched the water, then began drawing fluid in earnest. Delighted, enormously relieved, she turned that smile to Trevor—and felt her heart stop.

His pewter gray eyes held hers, something in their darkened depths telling her he'd just hit his limit. She couldn't begin to define what had pushed him over, but the thought had no sooner registered than his hand snaked out and hooked the back of her neck.

"Nice job," he drawled, and bent his head to capture her mouth.

The kiss was full, warm and deliberate, a quick and deadly assault that scrambled her senses, melted her bones and left her blinking owlishly at him when he lifted his head and set her back.

"I'd hire you on as my assistant," he told her, liking the way her breathing had altered, "but you're far too distracting."

He let his hand fall, purposely turning his attention back to his patients. She could hear him talking to her, telling her he was going to leave her something to mix in the horse's water after he disconnected the IVs, but it took her a few seconds to grasp what he was saying. It took her a few seconds longer to grasp what he'd done.

It felt as if he'd just staked a claim.

Telling herself she'd been in the heat too long, she forced herself to concentrate on what he was saying—and breathed a sigh of relief when, seconds later, Carter and Tom came wandering around the corner to see how their horses were doing. Both men looked far better than they had when she'd first seen them, and both stayed until Trevor headed for his vehicle to finish making his calls.

Neither of those men seemed to notice the steady glance Trevor gave her after he'd told them all he'd see them later. What that look made clear was that the next time he saw her, he'd make sure they were alone.

Her sense of self-preservation demanded that she beat him to the punch.

The wind Hank had whined about missing came up late that afternoon. Hot, dry and gusty, it blew in the thunderclouds that had hugged the horizon. But the constant flashes and rumbles produced nothing but light and noise. By the time Trevor returned at nine o'clock that night and went into the stable to check his patients, the air was as muggy and miserable as a swamp in August. Not a drop of rain had fallen from the lead black sky.

Weather was still the main topic of conversation everywhere he went. And since it felt as if he'd been just about everywhere within a hundred-mile radius of Leesburg, he figured there wasn't an opinion or complaint he hadn't heard. Now, hot, tired and hungry, he wanted nothing more than to put food in his stomach, stand under a cool shower, then lie naked under the air conditioner in his bedroom. The thought that he'd like Erin there naked with him was dashed away as soon as it formed. He felt frustrated enough without having to admit that he'd let her get to him that afternoon. The thought that he wanted her to feel the same way he did was what had caused him to reach for her in the first place.

"Trevor?"

He'd just walked out the breezeway of the new stable. At the sound of his name, he glanced up and saw Erin on the apartment landing above the old building on the other side of the corral. Standing in the pool of golden light from next to the door, she snagged back her hair to keep the wind from grabbing it and moved to the waist-high railing next to the long flight of wooden stairs.

"Would you mind coming up for a minute? I can fix you something to eat if you haven't had supper yet."

It was the wrong appetite she proposed to satisfy. And he hadn't planned to see her tonight, not with him needing a shower so badly. But since food was on his mind, and his prospects were limited to leftovers in the cookhouse and whatever didn't look like a lab experiment in his re-frigerator, he had no intention of turning down her offer.

"I just checked the horses," he called, figuring that had to be why she wanted to talk to him. "They look good."

"I thought they did, too." She watched him come up the stairs, stepping inside when he reached the small plat-form. "I just checked them a while ago."

She'd already turned to the tiny kitchenette, leaving him to close out the wind and the heat. Cool air enveloped him like an embrace, drawing a sigh that dropped his shoulders and would have had him closing his eyes in pure pleasure had curiosity not been gnawing at his mind.

"Why are you offering to feed me?"

Beneath the short pink shirt she wore, this one lacking any cause at all, her shoulder lifted in a shrug. "Because I figured you'd be hungry…and I want to talk to you."

"Fair trade. As long as it's not about the weather."

A clear vase of hardy wild roses in a deep shade of mauve sat on the old Formica-and-chrome dining table. Picking it up, she set it next to a sewing basket on the coffee table. "I promise I won't even mention it."

"Mind if I wash up first?"

"Go ahead."

He knew where the bathroom was. He'd been in this spare little apartment plenty of times when various trainers had occupied it over the years. He'd stayed in it himself the last few times he'd come home to visit. So he headed through her bedroom, pulling off his hat on the way and tossing it onto the foot of the bed. At the door of the tiny bathroom, he turned around, a frown slashing his brow.

The room itself was painfully neat. Nothing was out of place. The same blue flower print bedspread that had cov-ered the bed the last time he'd slept in it was pulled taut enough to pass military inspection. He'd thought he might find frills and feminine clutter. Except for a couple of magazines and a mystery novel on the nightstand, there wasn't anything in the room that hadn't always been there.

The clutter was in the bathroom. A wicker basket of colorful hair clips, brushes and a curling iron shared space on the back of the toilet with nail polish in shades of pale peach and ripe berry. The small counter beside the sink was lined with lotions, sunscreen, creams and powders. The edge of the tub held shampoos and soaps. From the curtain rod above it dangled a scrap of white satin that could have been a slip or a nightgown and a lacy bra in the pale blue of arctic ice.

The room smelled of her, the combination of light, clean scents creating something that managed to sing along his nerves even though she was nowhere in sight. He understood about pheromones. They'd hooked him when he'd walked past her seconds ago. The scent of a mare could have a stallion knocking down walls to get to her. A wolf could scent his mate for a mile. There was no denying that Erin's scent aroused him. But as he tore his glance from the lace and met his reflection in the medicine cabinet mirror to wash his face, he couldn't begin to imagine why she had a piece of straw taped to the glass.

"Do you want milk, or iced tea?"

"Tea."

Erin glanced cautiously toward Trevor as she reached for the jar of sun tea she'd brewed on her little porch that afternoon. He'd combed his hair, but the hat dent remained. She shouldn't have found that so appealing, but she did—and that was the very sort of reaction she didn't trust.

It was also one more reason that what she needed to do was so very necessary.

"I hope sandwiches are all right," she told him over the clink of ice cubes dropping into a glass. "I didn't think you'd want anything hot."

"Whatever you've got is fine."

She knew he was watching her. She could feel his eyes on her back while she poured tea, ice cracking, and set the glass on the table. That unnerving sensation remained as she returned to the counter to stack lettuce and tomato atop slices of cold chicken. As long as she had something to occupy her hands, she'd be fine. That way, he wouldn't know she was nervous. Self-assurance was critical in any negotiating session—even if it had to be faked.

"Here you go." Setting the plate on the table, she glimpsed at the strong line of his jaw. She could understand her physical attraction to him. It was the emotional one that worried her. She didn't want to be touched by his efforts with the children. She didn't want to be impressed by his professionalism, his decisiveness, his skill. His strength. But if she had to be drawn by any of that, she needed to change the direction of her thinking. And his.

"Get started on this while I make you another one. Will two be enough, or do you want three?"

Trevor's eyes narrowed on Erin as she moved back to the counter. Her manner was briskly efficient, her tone as pleasant as he imagined it would be with a total stranger. She seemed remarkably at ease to him—except for the way she avoided his eyes. That alone told him just how unsettled she was.

"Trev? How many?"

He opted for three, and downed them with the sweet tea and a handful of Oreos she pulled from the back of a cabinet. The way the package had been stashed, he might almost have thought she'd been hiding them from herself, but he was too curious about the little domestic routine she was engaged in to do much more than marvel at her lack of logic.

As if he ended every evening at her table, she asked how his day had gone. Then she busied herself putting away the sandwich makings and wiping down the scarred beige counter while he told her he'd had worse, but that he was glad it was over. With a soft smile, she told him she imagined he was, then mentioned that she'd heard from Hank that the men had moved the last of the herds into the sections with the most trees.

It was quiet, almost companionable conversation, and since he felt quite comfortable where he was, he saw no need to rush her. She'd said she wanted to talk, but he was dead certain it wasn't cattle on her mind. He was just getting curious about how long it would take for her to stop fussing and get to it when she reached to refill his glass.

He caught her wrist, intending only to keep her from pouring more tea into the tumbler. But the instant his fingers closed around the fragile bones, her entire body went still.

"I don't want any more. Thanks."

"Oh," she whispered, swallowing hard. "Then I'll just take your glass."

He didn't let go. He simply waited while her glance skittered away and she gave a faint tug.

Any intention he had of letting her call the shots vanished. He could feel the fine tremor in her hand. Beneath his fingers, her pulse raced.

"Do you want to tell me what's going on?"

"Will you let go of me?"

He took a little longer than she thought necessary to consider the request before his hand slipped away. But even as he settled back, she had the distinct feeling that she'd just lost a slice of the home court advantage. Determined to retrieve it, she picked up his glass and carried it to the sink.

"I called the employment agency back," she said, beginning her little speech just as she'd planned. "After I talked to the counselor about rescheduling, she mentioned that the position won't even be open for another month. Even if something does come of it, that means I'll be stuck here for at least that long."

The possibility of her being around for another four weeks should have had Trevor groaning. The sooner she left, the sooner he could stop spending his nights wrestling the sheets. But the argument failed to appease him. If anything, the thought of her not being there didn't hold nearly the appeal it once had.

His brow furrowed at that little realization. But it was the fact that she was so agitated that bothered him even more.

"Are you going to keep looking in the meantime?" he asked mildly.

"Of course. But that's not what we need to talk about. What happened the other night…and this afternoon," she prefaced, hoping to dilute the significance of having dissolved in his arms by stating her piece over the sound of running water, "shouldn't have happened. Since I'm still going to be here for a while, that means we'll keep running into each other and I don't want to complicate our situation any more than it already is." A truce was one thing. Sleeping with the enemy, so to speak, was something else entirely. "I don't think you do, either."

The blinds on the window over the sink were closed, so she couldn't check the reflection to see how he reacted to her conclusions. When all she could hear behind her was dead silence after she turned off the water, she could only assume he was still listening.

"Since we don't want to complicate it," she continued, "maybe we should try thinking of each other as brother and sister. After all, in a way, that's what we are. Sort of."

For a moment the only sounds to be heard were the wind whistling past the window, the long, low rumble of thunder and the squeak of towel against glass as she nearly dried the wildflower pattern off the tumbler. She needed to believe that she'd learned from her mistakes, and if she just hadn't fallen in love with him so long ago, there never would have been a problem. She knew now to avoid that particular pothole. And because the way she'd felt about him in the past was getting all tangled up with how she was feeling about him now, the only sensible thing to do was straighten everything out before the situation got more knotted up.

The silence behind her was practically screaming when she opened the cupboard to put the glass away. It was then that she heard the abrupt scrape of chair legs on the floor.

A heartbeat later Trevor turned her around.

"Erin," he began in the flat, deliberate tone one might use with the slow-witted. "Let's get one thing straight right now." His hands flattened on either side of her, trapping her between his big body and the hard edge of the counter. He leaned toward her, his face inches from hers and his features drawn tight with patience. "You are not my sister. I have never thought of you as one, and I can't see that I ever will. Your mother happens to be married to my father. I had nothing to do with that particular circumstance, so as far as I'm concerned, their relationship is their business and my relationships are mine. If you need to play mind games with yourself because of what's going on between us, then you go right ahead. I'm going to find some other way to deal with it."

She swallowed. Hard. "I just thought it might be easier."

His eyes narrowed on hers, searching. "Can you honestly think of me as a brother?"

Her lashes swept down as she ducked her head.

He tipped her chin right back up. "I didn't think so." Considering the subject closed, he brought her lips to his.

Erin's breath caught. The only places he touched were her face, when he slipped his callused hand to her cheek to angle her head, and her mouth, which he proceeded to alternately plunder and caress. With nothing more than those two points of contact, he made her breasts ache and her womb feel empty. Yet, when her knees started to go and she reached for him, he captured her hand in his and raised his head.

His eyes glittered like polished pewter. "If you don't want that to happen again," he said, his breathing a tad ragged, "all you have to do is look me in the eye and tell me. You do that," he whispered, meaning every word, "and I promise, I won't touch you again."

She opened her mouth, but her glance faltered even before the words stuck in her throat.

"You don't play fair," she finally whispered.

"And you should never play poker. At least, not with me."

Hunger gnawed inside him, but he ruthlessly banked it and let her go. He didn't trust the need he felt to kiss her again, and he no longer trusted himself to stop with a few kisses if he were to pull her into his arms. She was no longer the headstrong, emotional girl he'd once known. She'd grown into an intriguing, complicated, passionate woman who had him wound up in knots, and he honestly wasn't sure if her presence in his life was a blessing or a curse. She had his well-ordered life as unsettled as hers.

Thunder rumbled again, the lights flickering as Erin watched Trevor move away. The heavens were taunting the earth as surely as he was taunting her, but her only thoughts were how separate he regarded himself from the family, and that he'd completely dismissed everything she'd said.

She scarcely had a chance to wonder why he'd done that when he walked out of her bedroom with the hat he'd left there and opened the door. A blast of warm wind swirled inside as he looked back to where she stood stiffly by the counter.

"Thanks for dinner."

At a loss, all she could say was, "You're welcome."

Holding the brim of his hat to keep the wind from snatching it, Trevor ducked out the door and pulled it shut behind him. He bounced down the steps and was halfway across the compound, frustration fueling his stride, when he felt the hair on his arms prickle and the scent of ozone burned his nostrils. In the same instant, a bolt of lightning streaked across the sky above the trees. A deafening crash shuddered the windows in the barn and the buildings around him. Blinding white light turned night into day.

The horrific shriek of horses curdled his blood as he spun around in the gravel and blowing dust. The electrical lines that ran to the stables were sparking like fireworks on the Fourth of July as they whipped and arced near the hay bales stacked at the entrance. The security lights that had been glowing only a moment ago had already shorted out.

The sound of wood splintering joined an ominous crackle. But it was the acrid smell of smoke the wind whipped past him that shot pure fear through his veins.

One of the stables had been hit. Trevor just couldn't tell which one as he bolted through the darkness at a dead run.

Chapter Eight

Erin could rarely be still when she was agitated. If she could pace, she would. If she could clean something, scrub, rearrange, so much the better. For as long as she could remember, the only time her surroundings were totally free of her usual, haphazard clutter was when she was upset.

For the past month, the only thing that had been out of place was her.

Because she'd needed to move when Trevor had walked out, she'd picked up the vase of wild roses to return them to the table. They were now on the floor. Somewhere. The timber-rattling boom of thunder had startled her so badly that she'd dropped them.

She hadn't even heard the vase shatter, but she knew it had because glass crunched under her feet when her hand fell from the base of her throat and she reached toward the counter. The flash of light had been so brilliant that the plunge into darkness left her momentarily blinded. But even as her eyes adjusted, she could hear the high-pitched whinnies of the horses.

She wasn't sure where the lightning had hit. She just knew that it had, and that it had been far too close.

Later she would deal with the need to distance herself from Trevor. Now her only thought as she groped for the door was to call him back to help her check the animals.

The door opened with a burst of wind. Ducking her head against the sting of swirling dust, her hammering heart nearly stopped.

Smoke.

"Trevor!"

When Trevor rounded the corner of the old stable, he could see an eerie orange glow outlining the jagged teeth of broken glass in the new stable's windows. He didn't question the relief that swept through him when he saw Erin's shadowy form racing down the stairs. His only thought was to keep her from running into the stables herself. Flames were already licking around the end of the newer building, lapping greedily at the wood-shingled roof.

"The horses!" she cried, heading right where he knew she would go. "We've got to get them out!"

He caught up with her twenty feet from the burning stable, grabbing her by the arm to whip her around. Beyond them, wooden walls shuddered under the assault of horse hooves seeking to batter them down. "I'll get the horses." He'd already let her go and was backing toward the open breezeway. "You get Hank and the men."

"There isn't time!"

"Damn it, Erin."

He swore because he knew she was right. He swore because he knew he couldn't stop her. He swore because the smoke was getting thicker by the second, and there was no way he could unlatch all the stalls himself before the flames began tearing along the ceiling and igniting all the hay on the floor.

The fire extinguisher inside the door would be useless.

"You take the right side." The fire seemed to be spreading slower there. "Keep your head low and stay close to the walls."

There were twenty stalls. Ten on each side. He didn't know how many of them were occupied, but the cacophony of shrieking whinnies and battering hooves was horrendous. Nothing frightened a horse like fire. And a panicked horse wanted only to flee. Anything in its path would literally be trod into the dust.

The only light came from the flames. Dark smoke billowed, sucked along the breezeway by the wind. Though the worst of it roiled along the ceiling, it stung his eyes, blurring his vision as he neared the end stall. The entire back doorway was already engulfed, blocking escape from that direction. Heat searing his side, he slid back the latch and swung open the gate.

He didn't even try to control the horse. The little chestnut was out like a bullet, instinct throwing her headlong into a gallop as she shot down the breezeway and into the night.

Glancing behind him, he slipped the second latch, sending a pinto free, and saw Erin crouched in front of the stall she'd just opened. The big sorrel inside was on its back legs, its front hooves clawing the air and its eyes wild as the fire bubbled the paint on the walls.

Trevor had her by the shoulders and pressed against a post six feet away even as the great beast's legs smashed through the front grill of the stall, making matchsticks of the front panel. He didn't know if he'd shoved her head to his shoulder or if she'd turned it there herself, but the horse had no sooner bolted past them, the ground shuddering beneath its hooves, than the roar of the fire consuming fresh fuel snapped her head back up.

Fear, stark and unashamed, marked her fragile features. The encroaching flames were dancing along the ropes and leather lead lines on a burning post ten feet away.

"You okay?"

Gamely, she nodded. "You?"

"Go."

Erin was out of his arms before she could think to question their verbal shorthand. Thinking didn't seem like a good idea, anyway. She'd never been brave. Strong-willed and stubborn. Impulsive and reckless. But never brave. If she thought too much, she didn't doubt for an instant that fear would send her bolting, too.

The two horses that had been closest to the fire were out of danger, but it would only take minutes for those hungry flames to reach the rest. Already the wall that had been bubbling was covered with a shimmering wash of yellow and orange. The horses couldn't avoid the smoke by moving lower. Their heads were barely below the thickening cloud, and every one that reared up to lash at the walls would get a lungful of that tainted air.

The next two horses collided in their dash from their stalls, their massive bodies connecting in a sickening thud. Clearly panicked, they managed to keep their legs under them and vaulted past their pacing stable mates, their necks stretched like contenders at Pimlico.

They'd turned out two more and she'd shooed out a barn cat when she heard Trevor start to cough. Hurry, she silently begged him. Or maybe she spoke the plea aloud. She wasn't sure of much of anything as she crawled along the cement floor, mindless of the dirt she ground into her pants and her palms, trying not to breathe.

Lightning flashed. Over the snap and crackle of flames, thunder boomed, rattling the few windows that hadn't already blown out. She thought she heard shouting off in the distance, male voices raised over the crackle and roar. She could feel the heat, searing waves of it fanned by the wind. Smoke shifted, blinding her as she groped for the next latch. Coughing, eyes tearing, she raised her arm to cover her face and kept going.

"Erin?"

"I'm okay."

"Don't breathe it."

Don't think. Don't breathe.

Another horse had thundered past when she felt a hand on her arm. Strong and gnarled, that hand pulled her far enough back to get her out of the wave of smoke and shoved a wet handkerchief toward her.

Blinking rapidly, she coughed into the filtering cloth Hank had given her and saw him motion one of his men toward Trevor.

"You two the only ones in here?"

She nodded, coughed again and fumbled open the latch. She didn't have to open the gate. The sorrel mare she and Trevor had treated just that afternoon butted it open herself, leaving Erin and Hank to flatten themselves against the outside of the stall to avoid getting trampled.

The man who'd come in with Hank was now helping Trevor. She couldn't tell who he was. She could only see shapes on the other side. Odd, wavering shapes that looked like black-and-orange silhouettes through a haze of gray. The shapes were clipping leads to a horse too terrified to recognize the route of escape.

"You don't need to be in here breathing this smoke," Trevor yelled at Hank, who was coughing already. "We need to clear the other stable in case this spreads. Erin, go with him.''

Hank was already backing up, his arm covering most of his face. "How many more are in here?"

"One on this side." Trevor hauled on the line, the strain in his muscles evident in his voice as he pulled the yearling into the breezeway. "How many over there, Erin?"

"Two."

"We've got 'em," he called back, his voice clipped.

She had Hank by the arm. Towing him out with her, she hurriedly told him she'd get the horses if he'd get more help. She hadn't even thought about the old stable until Trevor mentioned it, but it wouldn't take much more than a spark on its tinder-dry roof and it would be in flames, too.

The wind still whipped the dust around, and her eyes stung from smoke, but she could hear help coming. Hank shouted for hoses to be brought up from the barn. Someone else yelled that he'd get shovels. She heard Hank holler for Carter to help her clear the old stable.

Within minutes she and the veteran cowhand had led most of the dozen horses from the older building to the cattle pens behind the breeding barn. She took the last four herself, leaving Carter free to help fight the fire, and was on her way back when she caught sight of her mother standing well back from the chaos. Samantha held the flashlight that had lit her path from the house. Her other hand covered her mouth. Michael, in jeans and no shirt, ran in front of her with a grim-faced Logan, each carrying an end of the long extension ladder from the workshop.

In the glow of leaping flames, Erin watched her mother's gaze follow her husband and son. Anxiety, sympathy and concern etched deeply in her features. When she noticed Erin walking toward her, only the sympathy vanished.

"Erin!" Her glance darted over her daughter's soot-streaked face and shirt. "*You* were in there? Hank said you were in the *old* stable taking the horses out."

"I was. But we had to get them out of the new one first."

"Are you all right?"

"I'm fine. Honest," she repeated, because her mother's expression hadn't changed.

"Are the horses okay?"

"Yeah," Amy echoed. "Are they okay?"

Both Erin and her mom turned to see the bobbing beam of a flashlight moving toward them. Behind the beam was Amy, her hair wrapped in a towel and wearing a bathrobe. She held Mandy's right hand. From the little girl's other hand dangled a doll dressed in a nightgown that matched her own. Zach was two steps behind them, his untied shoelaces peeking from the bottoms of his pajamas.

"I told you to stay up at the house with the children," she said to Amy, catching Zach by the shoulder to keep him with her.

"We couldn't stay up there," the teenager explained, looking as if she couldn't understand how her mother could expect such a thing. "Are the horses okay?" she repeated.

"And the cats?" Mandy asked, her little voice sounding very small.

"As far as I know, they're all fine." Erin offered the assurance to both sisters and automatically reached to soothe Mandy's troubled little brow. Seeing the shadow of dirt on her hands from crawling along the stable floor, she settled for a smile. "They were scared, but they're all safe now."

"Really?"

"Really."

Her glance cut anxiously toward the inferno. The entire structure was now involved, the breezeway engulfed in a molten mass of swirling flame. It was burning hot and fast, and putting it out was impossible. The only thing the men could do was soak down the roof of the old stable and hope the wind didn't shift. Two men were on the roof now, wetting it down with hoses. Everyone else was beating out the little fires that had started in the dry grass beyond the burning building with wet blankets.

Erin's focus wasn't on the fire, morbidly fascinating as it was. She was looking for the man she was determined not to care about, even though she was presently worried sick about him. He'd been concerned about her breathing smoke. And he'd sent Hank out within seconds of the older man entering the burning building. But he'd been in the worst of it himself, and for far longer than she had.

Wiping her gritty eyes with the back of her hand, she tried to spot his big, broad-shouldered frame among the half dozen men ahead of them. A couple wore only jeans and boots; the rest had loose shirttails. Every one of them, though, had tied his handkerchief over his nose and mouth, making the lot look like a bunch of bandits that had been pulled from their card game or bunk or wherever it was they'd been when the lightning hit.

"Have you seen Trevor?" she asked when she couldn't spot him.

"I'm right here."

He came up behind her, his glance sliding to her mother before he surreptitiously scanned Erin's soot-streaked face.

He coughed into his fist, then used the ragged, wet towel he'd retrieved from the old stable's storage room to wipe at his eyes. "I see they're all out."

He was referring to the horses. Thinking he must have gone to the old stable to see if she'd needed help, she gave him a nod, her own glance shifting over his face when he wiped the back of his neck. He'd lost his hat somewhere, and his dark hair was stuck to the perspiration glittered on his brow. Soot darkened his face and tears from the irritation of smoke and dust had left their tracks in the gray film on his cheeks. As astute as he was, he must have caught the concern she tried to mask.

With four pairs of eyes trained on them, all she could see in his expression was caution.

"We've got some spooked horses running around here somewhere," she said to him.

"We'll find them tomorrow."

"Do you think they're okay?"

It was really him she wanted to ask about. He sounded all right, though. His deep voice betrayed none of the rasp she might have expected, considering the smoke he'd inhaled, and he wasn't gasping for air or coughing that much. Even streaked with soot, he was as commanding and controlled as always.

She thought it monumentally unfair that he should be so together when, inside, she was shaking like the proverbial leaf.

"Won't know for sure until we find them. I'm betting they're all right, though. They weren't in there that long."

Trevor dragged the wet towel off his neck, aware of Samantha's glance bouncing between him and her daughter. If the woman hadn't been there, he would have reached over and wiped the smears of soot off Erin's cheeks himself. He would have asked, too, if she was all right. The way her arms were coiled around her waist, he wouldn't be surprised if she was trembling.

Torn between a sense of possession he didn't understand

and the need for distance, which he understood perfectly, all he did was hand her the towel so she could wipe the smears herself.

"I'd better go help the men," he said, holding her glance as she took the worn piece of terry cloth. "If you have anything in the apartment you don't want to lose, now's the time to get it."

His last words were all but lost in a thunderous crash as the back of the burning structure collapsed. A flume of flame and sparks shot into the air, drawing gasps from Samantha and Amy and a wide-eyed "Wow" from Zach. Mandy screamed.

"Amy, take the children back to the house," Sam ordered, swatting at the air as ash rained down on their heads. "I'll be there in a while."

"But, Mom—"

"Don't argue with me. Just do it. And you be careful, Trevor."

He hadn't heard her.

Blinking from the smoke, Erin watched Trevor jog away to grab a shovel. Within seconds, he was beside his dad, throwing dirt on an arc of burning grass. She knew if it spread in the direction it was headed, it could destroy thousands of acres of dry sagebrush, mesquite and cedars before it burned itself out.

Her mom touched her arm. "I'll help you get your clothes out," she said. "We'll wet down your towels out here for the men. They're going to need cold drinks, too, so we'll take whatever you have and get more from the house."

By two o'clock in the morning, despite Hank's constant muttering about the need for a deluge, the clouds that had generated the damage had departed without sparing a single drop of rain, and the new stable was a pile of glowing embers. When Erin made her third trip back from the house, the men were reducing those embers to sodden ash and steam with the hoses.

The various little grass fires had been extinguished and, by some miracle, the old stable had been spared. The stars were out, the air balmy, though the smell of burned wood and wet ash hung heavily over the relatively quiet compound.

Her mom had wanted her to spend the night at the house, but Erin couldn't sleep until she'd taken care of the horses. In their haste to get them somewhere safe, they'd simply released them into the long, narrow pens. They hadn't even unclipped the leads, which meant several of the horses that had been trained to ground tie, were standing pretty much where they'd been left.

The lightning had only taken out the power to the two stables and the security lights on the south end of the compound. In the pale yellow light that hung under the eaves at the back of the massive barn, she wedged open the section of wood railing she and Carter had used as a makeshift gate. The lines of chutes stretched on for acres, looking like some sort of macabre maze that disappeared into the darkness surrounding her. Except for Logan's prize bulls snorting in their private enclosures somewhere on the opposite side of the building, there was nothing else on that side of the compound except wide-open, and very black, space.

Adrenaline had been pumping when she'd been there a few hours ago. And, most of the time, Carter had been with her.

Trying not to think of how creepy it was with nothing but the glow of a measly little sixty-watt bulb between her and total darkness, she gathered the leads of the two nearest horses. The night had been traumatic enough for them without the animals picking up fear from her. They were uneasy and skittish being in the unfamiliar place, as it was. So she promised them that everything would be fine once they were back in their cozy stalls, though it was actually herself she was reassuring. It wasn't unheard of for a wolf or coyote to come snooping around, and there was still as much city as country flowing in her veins. She liked her canines domesticated.

"What are you doing down here?"

Erin spun around, her hand flattening at the base of her throat.

"Trevor." She said his name half in relief, half as epithet. "You scared the hell out of me."

He could see that. He could also see that, like him, she'd found time in the past couple of hours to clean the soot from her face. She hadn't changed her clothes, but she had pulled her hair into a slightly listing ponytail. Cartoon-character princesses danced around the scrunched up fabric that held it in place.

It occurred to him, vaguely, that she must have borrowed the hair thing from Mandy. On a more immediate level, all he cared about was that she was the last person he wanted to deal with right now. "I thought you were spending the night up at the house."

"I came down to take care of the horses."

"What are you planning on doing with them?"

"I thought I'd take them back to the stable if it was safe," she explained, matching his scowl. "Or take off their leads and bring them water if it wasn't. Since the fire's almost out, I'm taking them to the stable."

"Nothing goes back in there tonight."

"Fine." She wouldn't ask him why. He looked as irritable as he sounded, which meant the more they spoke the greater the chance for an argument. Considering the late hour, the stress everyone had been under and how tired he had to be, at least one of them needed to exercise a little prudence. "Then I'll bring them water."

"They'll be better off in the upper corral." It was a sign of his fatigue that he used the makeshift gate rather than simply jumping the fence. "These rails are too low and too close for horses. One of them gets antsy and tries to jump out, it'll wind up breaking its neck."

"The corral it is." With deliberate patience, she clipped the lead back into place. There was a water trough in the corral so she wouldn't have to haul buckets, a task that hadn't appealed to her, anyway.

"Easy, sweetie," she soothed when the jittery animal backed up, bumping into one of the low rails. "I'll have you out of here in just a minute."

"No, you won't," Trevor muttered. "I'll do it. You don't need to be down here this time of night."

"What I don't need," she informed him, prudence strained as she reached for the lead of the horse behind the yearling, "is you telling me what to do."

"Somebody needs to."

"Excuse me?"

"You're down here in the dark with a dozen agitated horses and no one else around. You could get hurt and nobody'd even know." He shook his head, wonder joining the lines of fatigue etched in his face. "Do you ever stop to think about what you're doing?"

It suddenly occurred to her that he must have seen her heading for the barn and dropped whatever he'd been doing to see that she stayed out of trouble. He'd had that same protective response when he'd sent her to the less-dangerous side of the burning stable and when he'd insisted that she get out the instant other help arrived. But he'd been just as insistent with Hank, so she wouldn't allow herself to believe his protective instincts toward her were particularly significant. That was just the sort of man he was. The fact that he found her lacking common sense effectively overshadowed her kinder thoughts about his actions, anyway.

"Only when it comes to you," she muttered and snagged one more lead before heading for the gate.

That was not the response Trevor expected. But when it came to Erin, he never quite knew what to expect from her anymore. Half the time he had the feeling she didn't know what to expect herself.

One thing was for certain, though. The woman was as stubborn as sin and just as hard to resist.

"Would you get the gate for me, please?"

"Damn it, Erin."

"Is that a yes or a no?"

It was a yes. He told her so with the exasperated glare he shot at her just before he gathered a few horses himself. He'd intended to have one of the men help him take care of them in a while, anyway, so he led three horses through the gate while she held it for him. Then, with the leads of two of the animals in his fist, he swung up on the back of a snuffling roan while she closed the gate. She couldn't mount without a saddle horn to grab on to. Holding two leads in her hand, she used the side rail of the chute to give herself a boost and mounted a chestnut.

They made another trip that same way, each riding one and leading two others. They said little, working together in the moonlight as if they'd done it all their lives. They didn't even speak each time they reached the corral and he lifted her from her mount.

Twice he reached up and caught her by the waist. And twice she hesitated before curving her hands over his wide shoulders. Since the horses were large, his assistance made it far easier for her to dismount, and refusing his help would have been foolish. Accepting his help seemed foolish, too, considering what he'd done the last time he'd been that close. But he made no attempt to do anything other than help her down.

Still, each time his fingers spanned her waist, she felt the bridled tension in his big body flowing into hers. And each time, she was aware of how tightly he held himself when their bodies brushed on her way to the ground. Yet he let her go the moment she had her feet under her and immediately turned away to tend their charges.

She'd thought the less they said to each other, the better. No words. No arguments. Yet, as the silence stretched into their last trip back into the compound, she began to think arguing preferable to the distance he'd managed to put between them. That distance wasn't physical. He was only four feet away. Yet, he'd isolated himself as surely as if it had been four hundred miles.

The smoldering ruin had been abandoned, now that it had been reduced to charred log and ash. The only sounds to mar the quiet as they passed it were the chirp of crickets and the clink of metal clips on the leads dangling over their shoulders. Trevor walked with his eyes straight ahead, his stride steady.

Walking two paces back from him in the dark, her eyes fixed on his broad back, she found herself wondering if he'd ever felt the need to lean on anyone. If he'd ever felt the need for a pair of arms, the way she so often did. It was hard to imagine him ever needing comfort, ever allowing anyone to take care of him. In many ways, he was almost like the island no man was supposed to be. Even surrounded by people tonight, working with the men, he had somehow been separate.

As they reached the pitch-black breezeway of the old stable, she couldn't help thinking that he was keeping himself separate now.

I'll find some other way to handle it.

Was he going to push her away again? Was that what he had decided to do?

The thought made her chest burn. He shouldn't be able to do this to her. "I'll put the leads away," she said, wanting to pretend the burning wasn't there.

The moonlight carved his face in planes of shadow. "I've got 'em."

"It's okay. I'm going into the supply room, anyway."

"What for?"

"I want a flashlight," she explained, deliberately overlooking the tightness in his voice. "I'm going to stay here in case any of the other horses come back tonight. Someone will need to put them in the corral."

"I know what they'll need," he assured, completely disregarding her plans. "I told Dad I'd stay down here in case the fire flared up again. I can't see that it will, but you never know."

Instead of giving her his leads as she'd requested, he slipped his hand under the leather straps hanging over her shoulder and lifted them away. Before she could do much more than open her mouth in protest, he was striding into the yawning black hole of the stable's doorway, calling back, "You don't need to stay."

She watched him disappear, blinking in disbelief at his abrupt dismissal. As quiet as it was outside, she heard him bump a wall and swear. A few moments later she saw a light go on. The dim glow had to be from the heavy-duty flashlight she'd intended to get herself.

She was inside the breezeway before she could even

acknowledge that her quota of patience for the night was shot.

He'd left the flashlight on the shelf above the feed bins. The pale glow cast a wedge of yellow light over the concrete floor and illuminated part of the open stall across the breezeway. Catching Trevor's arm as he turned to hang the leads on the tack wall, she lifted the leather straps out of his hand the same way he'd taken them from her.

"I told you I'd take care of this. It makes no sense for you to be up all night when you have to work tomorrow."

His eyebrows slammed together at what she'd done. "Tomorrow's shot, anyway." The edge in his voice was sharp as a blade. His expression was no softer. "I told you, I'm staying. There's no need for both of us to be down here."

She couldn't have agreed more. "Accidents happen when people are tired," she countered, trying to sound reasonable, certain she didn't. The man could take care of everyone but himself. "You were the one who just accused me of not considering how dangerous working around animals can be. You might think you're invincible, but I doubt even you can exercise perfect judgment without sleep. If you're tired tomorrow, you could do something stupid and wind up with a broken neck yourself."

She jerked a lead over a peg, jamming down the anxiety she felt as an image of him hurt and bleeding flashed in her mind. A picture of him illuminated by flames had already burned itself into her brain.

Think of him as the devil, she told herself.

"You need rest anyway," she insisted, her chest tight at the thought of what could have happened to him. "I don't know how much smoke you breathed in tonight, but you need to take care of yourself. Go to bed and get some sleep. I'll watch the barbecue pit."

"I'm not leaving you out here alone."

The lead fell off. Swiping it up, she slapped it back over the hook and added two more.

"I sleep alone thirty feet from here every night."

"That's different."

"The horses are my responsibility while I'm staying here," she snapped. Metal clattered as every lead she'd hung fell from the overloaded peg and she whirled back to face him. "Just because I can't seem to handle much else about my life, doesn't mean I can't take care of this."

She bent to pick up the leads, the lines of leather coiled like snakes at her feet. The way she felt at the moment, no self-respecting snake would dare strike at her. She snatched up the nearest one, which happened to be draped over Trevor's boot.

Stress. That was all it was. And fatigue. Emotions had run a little high in the dash to get the fire out before it destroyed anything else, and she was sure the edginess she felt now had as much to do with residual fear as with the frustration she felt with her life. Most especially, the frustration she felt with Trevor. She didn't want to care about him. She didn't want him to make her chest burn, or her heart ache, or her body go weak with need.

The least he could do was move.

The thought had no sooner occurred to her than she felt his hands close around her upper arms.

"Leave them."

"No."

"Leave them," he repeated, hauling her upright. "And look at me. I didn't mean to imply that you couldn't handle this. I just don't think being together right now is a good idea."

"Damn it, Trevor." She jerked her arm back. Glaring

up at him, she swung at his biceps. "You could have been hurt in there."

She slugged him. Not hard enough to hurt. Granite didn't have feelings.

"Hey," he growled, grabbing her fist.

"Let go."

He seemed to consider it. For about two seconds. Then he caught the suspicious brightness in her eyes. With a gentle twist of his wrist, he slipped her arm around her back and drew her to him. "Hey," he repeated, murmuring the word this time.

Hating that the burning in her chest had somehow wound up behind her eyelids, she brought her hand to his shirt and blinked hard. Definitely tired, she told herself, trying to ignore the brush of his thigh, the heat of his arm seeping into her shoulder. She needed to push him away. She needed him to hold her. Torn, she bunched his shirt in her fist.

She shouldn't have slugged him.

The thought barely registered when his free hand closed over hers and he loosened her fingers. As he did, he slowly drew her other hand from behind her back. But when she stiffened to pull away, he just held both of her hands in his until she raised her glance as far as his chin.

"I'm not going to hit you again," she said, thinking he was probably weighing that possibility.

"I'm not worried," he told her, and lifted her hands to his shoulders.

Her heart knocked against her breastbone as his fingers trailed back down the length of her arms. Shaping her ribs, he bent slightly to settle his hands around her waist. The old familiarity of what he'd done had her glance jerking to his. The moment she looked up, he slowly drew her against him.

The heat of his body seared her from her breasts to her knees. But it was the look in his eyes that tore the breath from her lungs. She'd been afraid for him, and something about that knowledge exposed the hunger banked and glittering in those dark depths.

"This is why I wanted you to leave," he said in quiet warning, and closed his mouth over hers.

The last time he'd kissed her, she'd felt as if she'd been branded. Now what she felt was a combination of curbed frustration and an unexpected tenderness that annihilated any defense she might have had. He brushed his lips over hers, coaxing lightly, until her lips parted with a shuddering breath. The contrast of his softly caressing mouth and his hard, male body sapped her strength, along with her will.

Erin rose up, her fingers slipping over his shoulders to clutch the fabric at the back of his neck. He tasted faintly of smoke and mints, and the part of her that needed him to be all right overrode the part that ached at the thought of him pushing her away. He wasn't distancing himself at all. He was getting as close as he could.

The hunger he'd kept in check moments ago broke free as she clung to him. With a groan his tongue swept hers, his mouth seeking, devouring. One hand slipped low on her hip, pulling her against the bulge straining his zipper. The other slid to her back, drawing her up. That one small movement hitched his breath, and he eased her back down, curving his hand on her ribs.

Her own breath caught an instant later. With his fingers splayed at her side, his thumb slowly swept the undercurve of her breast, grazing the edge of her nipple. He did it again, coaxing the bud tighter, and drank in her soft whimper.

"I remember the first time I touched you." His words

were dark and rough against her ear. "Do you remember, Erin?"

Trembling, she gave a little nod, his breath heating her temple when he touched his lips there.

"Do you remember where we were?" His fingers snaked into her hair. The scrunchee holding it loosely on her head landed by his boot, silken tendrils tumbling over his hand. "We were right here." He tipped her head back, drawing a line of kisses along the side of her throat. "But we're going to be in that stall behind us in about thirty seconds unless you back away right now."

He was the one with the iron control. He was the one who could hold his passions so ruthlessly in check. She would have reminded him of that. But all she could think about at the moment was that he had been the man who'd awakened her sensuality. And he was the only man who had ever filled her with the raw need consuming her now. What she felt, she felt only with him. Only for him. She didn't know how it had happened, how he'd managed to breach every defense she possessed, but she'd fallen in love with him all over again.

"There's fresh straw in there."

She felt his body go still.

"I need a shower," he murmured against her collarbone.

Soot streaked his shirt—hers now, too—where he'd rubbed against her. She could smell smoke in his hair, his clothes, though the night air had diminished its scent. Mostly she was aware of the soap he'd washed up with, and the primitive essence of warm, musky male. "I don't care."

"Erin."

Her name was a warning. The last one she was likely to get.

She slipped her hand down his side. "Trevor," she whispered back.

He raised his head, something feral sweeping his expression. But there were no more warnings. He'd told her before that he could fight himself. That he could fight her. But he couldn't fight them together. With his eyes locked on hers, he slipped one arm behind her knees, braced the other at her back and scooped her into his arms. A moment later he swung her around so she could grab the flashlight off the shelf, and he pulled a saddle blanket off the stack on a sawhorse.

The flashlight landed in a corner of the confining little stall, half-buried in the straw. The blanket landed next to it when he lowered her to the ground.

Breathing in the scent of animals and sweet hay, she saw Trevor's large shadow move on the wall as he reached for her. Framing her face with his hands, he lowered his mouth to hers.

Moments ago, she'd thought of his indomitable control. That was what he seemed to exercise as he slowly, systematically sensitized her nerves, tightening her in some places, softening her in others. She'd thought, too, about how he'd seemed to stake some sort of claim earlier that night in her apartment. As his mouth continued to work over hers and his fingers unhurriedly released the buttons on her shirt and the front clasp of her bra, she couldn't help thinking that was exactly what he was doing now.

"Look at me, Erin."

He'd opened her blouse and eased back the lace to bare her gently rounded breasts. Though her body was in shadow, self-consciousness struck as she lifted her head. Only then, when her eyes were on his, did he touch her. When he did, any thought that he might find her less than he remembered ceased to exist. The sensation of his hand cupping her, his thumb pebbling her nipple while his eyes turned dark on hers, nearly buckled her legs.

She didn't know what he saw in her face, but the look in his bordered on pain in the moments before he claimed her mouth again. He edged her back, dragging her to her knees, and flipped open the blanket with one hand. Impatient for the feel of him, she slipped her hand from his neck to pull his shirt from his pants and work open the buttons.

The moment the buttons were free, he yanked the soot-streaked chambray off himself, biceps flexing, and flung it aside. His body was ridged with hard muscle, his shoulders broad, his chest thick. She reached out, running her hands over him, tasting the salt on his skin, almost afraid to believe she could actually touch him this way. But when she reached for his buckle, he caught her hand, his control looking precarious as he nudged her back on the blanket and fumbled for the flashlight.

"Nobody's coming in here," he said, his voice a low rasp. "But just in case…"

Trevor let the thought trail off as he thumbed the switch. The light went out, enveloping them in darkness, in each other. Each time he'd had his hands on her in the corral, he'd forced himself to let go, when what he'd really wanted to do was pull her into his arms. Now that was exactly where she was and restraint was the last thing on his mind. There was nothing but the need burning in his blood, a need that had been there far too long.

He lay half over her while his hand swept her body, slipping away denims, shoes and a filmy scrap of satin. Straw rustled over the sounds of their breathing, the clink of his belt buckle, the rasp of his zipper.

She tried to reach for him, slipping her hand down his belly, but he trapped her hand by her head and told her that touching him now would be a mistake. She could have her turn later.

She said that wasn't fair.

He told her that was too bad and nuzzled aside her blouse to kiss his way up to her mouth. Because the blanket was wool and would scratch her sunburned skin, he'd left her shirt on her. It wasn't in the way, anyhow. Nothing was. Stretched out beside her, drinking in the taste of her, he stroked her bare stomach, her hip, the shape of her leg. Every breath he drew brought her scent, driving him a little crazier, making the need that much greater.

He groaned her name.

She whispered his back.

He nuzzled her breasts, drawing deeply, making her moan.

She threaded her fingers through his hair, holding him closer, feeling his hunger.

The need to slake that hunger finally had him groping in the dark for his jeans. He pulled out his wallet and the foil packet inside, not at all sure why he hesitated before he opened it. He always used protection. Always. Yet something fundamental in him now begrudged the need to use it with her. He didn't question what that something was, nor did he indulge it. He just ripped the packet open with his teeth, unrolled the condom over himself and pulled her back to him.

He wished he could have left the light on. He wanted to see her eyes when he entered her. He wanted his name on her lips, his imprint in her mind. He wanted her to know she was his. He should have been her first. Her only. There was a catch in such thinking, but with her small, soft hands roaming his back and the uninhibited way she tangled her tongue with his, he could think of little beyond the need to possess.

He moved over her, pushing his hand under her hip to nestle himself between her legs, entering her slowly when what he wanted to do was bury himself in one strong stroke. He didn't want to hurt her, small as she was. He wanted to take his time. But Erin had other ideas. She arched up, taking him in with a quiet breath, her fingers biting into his hard buttocks, urging him closer. He moved inside her, sheathed in her heat, his heart thundering, control shot.

His only thought before his brain shut down and sensation took over was that once would never be enough.

Chapter Nine

Erin hadn't realized she'd fallen asleep until voices woke her. Deep, male voices that grew steadily closer and forced consciousness to return with a jolt.

In the space of a heartbeat she became aware of the itch of straw that had worked between her shirt and her back, the heat of Trevor's breath against her ear when he swore softly and lifted himself on his elbow, and the feel of his calloused hand brushing her tender breast when he pulled her shirt around her.

Sliding his arm from beneath her head, he rolled away and snatched up his jeans. ''Hank's coming.''

Sunlight poured through the high, narrow window above them. Weather grime filtered the light considerably, but Erin could easily see the taut muscles of Trevor's beautifully sculpted back bunch and shift as he pulled on his jeans and snatched up his shirt. His bare shoulders and chest looked a mile wide when he turned and cocked his head toward the stall door. "Dad's with him," he muttered, slapping his shirt against his thigh.

Already upright herself, she'd fastened the catch on her bra and was working on her blouse buttons when Trevor held out a filmy scrap of white satin he'd removed from her a few short hours ago.

In his big hand, her underpants looked impossibly dainty. Taking them, she glanced up at the hard angles of his face, and his eyes locked on hers. It was impossible to tell what he was thinking at that moment. She wasn't sure what she was thinking herself.

"Dad will be looking for me." His voice carried nothing but warning as he skimmed his hands along her shoulders, brushing away straw. His touch was quick, designed only to rid her of evidence. Or so it seemed as he turned away and swiped up the torn foil packet. "Get yourself together while I head him off."

The consequences of what had happened between them seemed to loom larger by the second to Erin. There was just no time to consider them. Or to indulge the anxiety waiting to be acknowledged. Within seconds, he pulled on his boots, tucked, zipped and was striding out of the stall, leaving her to scramble into the white denims that would soon become cutoffs because the knees were shot from crawling around in the fire, and to shove her underwear into her pocket before someone stumbled in on her.

"Hey, Hank. There he is," she heard Logan say, his voice sounding as near as the main doorway. "Mornin', Trev." The greeting met with a chuckle, the pleasant sound melding with the chirp of birds perched under the eaves and the rustle of straw as she searched for her left shoe. "What did you do? Sleep in there last night?"

"Yeah," Trevor muttered. "Matter of fact, I did."

"What time did you finally turn in?"

"I don't know. Three. Four. Somewhere around there."

"Had to be closer to four," Hank pronounced. "You and Erin were still moving horses when I turned in at three. Speaking of which, have you seen her this morning? She's usually with the stock by now."

Erin's heart nearly stopped when she heard the thud of booted feet on cement. It sounded as if someone, presumably Hank, had started inside.

"I'm sure she's around here somewhere," she heard Trevor reply. "Listen, I need coffee. Let's get some while you tell me what you want me to do to help with that mess. We have horses to round up, too."

It was Logan who responded. Since Erin had both hands in her hair shaking out the straw, she couldn't make out what he said. But moments later Hank drawled that he could use another cup of joe himself, and the clump of boots disappeared.

Holding her breath, she dared a peek around the edge of the door frame to see the three men walking away. Two, big and broad-shouldered. The other, bow-legged and grousing about something as he poked the air with his unlit cigar. A quick glance in the other direction revealed nothing but empty paddock and open stall doors.

Air leaked from her lungs. Trevor had taken over, taking command in a way that seemed second nature to him, and averted what would have been a decidedly awkward situation. Since avoiding awkward situations was her only goal at the moment, she focused on getting around the back of the building and up the stairs to her apartment. But she'd been inside less than a minute when she realized that avoiding one might not be entirely possible.

She could shower because she had a towel—the one she'd forgotten on the towel rack when she'd grabbed the sets from the closet for the men to use. But the clothes she and her mom had hastily packed last night were in suitcases outside the door of the barn. Even the T-shirts she'd finished for Lindsey were there. She hadn't wanted to drag everything up to the house, so she'd just stowed them out of the way.

She didn't know how that little detail managed to eke through the dismay blooming in her chest, but it did. It registered as she started to strip for a shower—which was about the time the anxiety hit.

She was in love with him. Again.

Still.

She'd very probably never stopped loving him. Somewhere in the back of her mind he had always been the standard by which she'd measured every other man—and every other man had fallen hopelessly short. That had to be why she'd never had a serious relationship until she'd met Scott. And *that* had to be why she'd ultimately been willing to settle for the pleasant illusion she'd allowed Scott to lure her into. Yet, even with the illusion, she'd never felt the sense of rightness, and of passion, she had with Trevor.

She'd thought the lack was in her. But Trevor had shown her there was no lack. With him, she'd felt the rightness, the passion and, incredibly, a sense of the security she craved. In his arms, she'd felt grounded and safe, and those were things she hadn't felt in a very long time. Not since he'd held her when she'd been sixteen.

With a defeated little moan, she leaned her head against the wall. She had a gift, it seemed, for needing the unattainable. Even if he weren't practically allergic to the concept of family, even if he hadn't admitted to having no idea what love was, the last time she told him she loved him, he'd stopped speaking to her.

The thought of banging her head against the tiles occurred just as she heard a thump from somewhere outside. The sound was followed by a quick, heavy knock on the door.

Pulling her shirt back on, she hurried past the broken glass on her kitchen floor and edged back the filmy curtain on the door window. Trevor had already reached the bottom of the stairs. He didn't look back. He didn't slow his stride. He did nothing but disappear around the end of the building.

When she opened the door, she found her soft-sided blue bags on her porch.

What he had done was undeniably thoughtful. Yet the fact that he hadn't stayed to say anything to her put a knot the size of a prizefighter's fist in her stomach. She knew that when they'd wakened, he'd been intent on sparing them an embarrassing encounter. They hadn't had a second to spare. Now his dad and Hank were undoubtedly waiting for him. But he could have said something, even if it was just that he'd see her later. Or, she thought, growing uneasier by the moment, that he wouldn't.

Turning inside with the bags, she closed the door with her shoulder. Knowing him as she did, she wouldn't tease herself with the thought that what had happened meant anything significant to him. But as she carried her clothes into the bedroom and finally stepped into the shower, she also tried very hard not to think about what he'd said to her the night of her mom's and Logan's party—that he'd once wished he'd slept with her years ago, just so he wouldn't have to keep wondering what it would be like.

The shower helped. So did activity. Within half an hour, she'd braided her hair, donned clean jeans and her green rain forest T-shirt, put her minimal wardrobe away and was on the floor in the kitchen cleaning up wilted flowers and glass shards. She had the radio on, more to distract her from her thoughts than because she was interested in the weatherman's prediction of another miserably muggy day or the latest country-western hits. Because she had the volume up—way up—she didn't hear the heavy stomp of boots on the stairs, which was why the sharp knock on the door sent her heart to her throat.

Through the filmy curtain on the door's window, she caught the familiar shape of a tall, broad-shouldered male.

The knock came again, louder, more insistent.

Just don't let him know he's got you by the heart, she coached herself, modifying one of her mentor's mottoes as she disposed of the damp paper towel she'd used to pick up the last splinters and slapped at the Off button on her portable radio. She'd play it close to the chest, or the vest or whatever that expression was.

You should never play poker. At least, not with me.

Ignoring the warning he'd given her, she opened the door—and looked up at her stepdad.

Logan had never come to the apartment before. At least, he'd never come to it while she'd been there.

"I'm glad you're up," he said, tipping back the brim of his dusty beige hat. "Until I heard the music, I thought you might be sleeping in," he added, looking a little weary himself. "Your mom needs you up at the house."

Faced with Logan rather than his son, anxiety plummeted, giving way to a smile that still managed to feel awfully strained.

"No problem. I'll go up as soon as I feed the horses," she told him, since she'd been less than a minute away from doing just that. "I'm on my way to the corral now."

"I've got your chores covered this morning. Archie's already taken feed up to the corral, and he'll turn the horses into the pasture."

"What about the ones that bolted?"

"Most of 'em came back on their own," he said as she stepped out and closed the door.

"Are they all right?"

"Trev's checking them now. If the other three aren't back soon, we'll go look for 'em. Horses know their way home. If they're not back, that means they're hurt." He motioned her toward the stairs, absently gripping the smooth wood railing and wiggling it as if to make sure it was still secure. "Don't you worry about anything down here."

She wasn't going to argue with Logan. After all, the horses belonged to him and if he chose to give her duties to someone else that morning, the prerogative was certainly his. Still, she couldn't deny the twinge of insecurity she felt at having her job—temporary as it was—usurped. It was all she had right now.

"I can see what Mom wants, then come back and take care of them," she offered. The unpleasant odor of charred wood drifted by as the breeze shifted. Wrinkling her nose as she reached the ground, she glanced up at the man behind her. "I want to help, Logan."

Weathered lines fanned from the corners of his silver-blue eyes. They deepened when his brow pinched. "You already have," he told her, sounding as if he couldn't believe she didn't know that. "That's the reason I came myself instead of sending one of the kids to get you. Samantha told me you were in the fire last night. And a while ago Trev said you headed straight for the stable as soon as you realized it had been hit.

"I've got to admit," he continued, shaking his head, "there have certainly been times over the years when I thought you had more guts than good sense. And this is probably one of them. But I appreciate what you did, Erin.

You and Trev saved me some good stock.'' He reached out a callused hand and pulled her to him. ''I'm just really grateful that neither of you got hurt.''

She could see that gratitude in his hard, handsome features, could feel it in the big bear hug he wrapped her in a moment later.

It wasn't often that Logan displayed affection with her. Just as her mom had never tried to mother Trevor, Logan had never tried to be her dad. He was different with Michael and Amy, as much a father to them as he was his blood children, but with Erin, he'd been more of a quietly commanding presence who'd somehow understood her struggles without ever saying a word about them.

She hugged him back. ''I'm really sorry about your stable, Logan.''

''Me, too. Cal put a lot of hard work into it. But it can be rebuilt.'' Giving her a quick squeeze, he let her go, then stood pondering the wreckage. ''Like I said, the important thing is that nobody got hurt and we didn't lose an animal.''

In the bright morning sunlight, they stood side by side, arms crossed, surveying the pile of blackened debris on the far side of the training corral. A trail of gray smoke, or maybe it was steam, threaded upward like a wide, undulating snake at one end. Near the middle stood a single post, charred and scored like blackened alligator hide. Incredibly, tack still hung from a hook, as scorched as everything else but easily identifiable.

She looked back to the man who'd taken on her family. ''You think I've got guts?''

He slanted her a look. ''That's not quite the way I said it, but yeah. In a lot of ways, I think you do. So does my son.''

At the mention of Trevor, she felt herself hesitate. "He does?"

"He thinks you're stubborn, too."

For some reason, that didn't sound quite so flattering. "That sounds more like Mom."

"True. She says you got that gene from your dad. It's not one of the ones she wanted him to pass on."

His mouth quirked in a smile. Considering that he had to feel awful about his stable, she liked that she'd been able to make him do that.

"I think my dad would have liked you, Logan."

The smile settled deeper. "I think I'd have liked him, too." He gave the end of her braid a gentle yank. "You'd better get going. Sam has a meeting and needs you to watch the kids while she runs into town. You don't have to be anywhere else this morning, do you?"

"No, I don't. But where're Amy and Michael? Can't one of them watch them?"

"They're going in with her. Michael's working for Cal this week and Amy has a dental appointment.

"Oh, and Erin," he said, turning back just as he turned away. He hesitated, suddenly looking uneasy, which didn't look like him at all. "I really appreciate that you and Trevor got past your differences. I know it's been a long time coming." He gave her a nod, his jaw tightening much the way his son's did when there was something on his mind that he wasn't entirely comfortable talking about. "That means a lot to me."

Erin's smile felt decidedly forced, but Logan didn't seem to notice as he headed toward Jett's truck, which was pulling up by the workshop. From the way he'd acted toward her, she didn't think he suspected anything of what had happened between her and his son. He was just grateful that she and Trevor were finally speaking.

Knowing how very much that meant to him was one of the little complications she'd been trying to drown out with the radio when he'd come knocking on her door.

By eleven o'clock that morning, Erin had seen Trevor twice. Both times at a distance. Once on her way up to the house, where he'd been talking with Carter and Archie by the barn. And ten minutes ago, on the way into the compound with the kids. Then he'd been with Hank by the equipment shed.

Now she could see him slipping into the training corral with his dad to check another of the horses that had wandered back. He'd found his hat somewhere and, like his dad, he had it pulled low, though heavy clouds obscured the sun. The two men were talking as they moved around the frisky little mare, but even if Erin hadn't been thirty feet away, she wouldn't have been able to hear a word they said.

The ranch owned a John Deere loader that was used to move everything from hay bales to cow carcasses. At the moment, Jett was using it to hoist large scoops of wet, charred wood onto the metal floor of an old flatbed truck. Between the roar of the loader's diesel engine and the awful grinding of the truck's gears as it backed up for another load of burned stable, she could barely hear Zach and Mandy's chatter, and they were only two feet from her elbow.

Zach had heard the loader from the house when it had started up a while ago and immediately started begging to come down to watch. Mandy had joined him seconds later, adding a plaintive, "Pleeeeze, Erin?" Seeing the excitement in their eyes, she hadn't the heart to refuse. That was why they were now propped on hay bales watching the machine belch puffs of black smoke, while she watched the man who'd barely glanced at her and had yet to say a word.

The cacophony decreased considerably after the truck had backed into place.

"I think I recognize that look."

Between the noise and her preoccupation, Erin hadn't noticed Annie approach. Pulling her attention from Trevor, she met the quizzical expression playing over her aunt's pixieish features, then jerked her glance to the dark-haired little boy tugging on the hem of his mom's khaki shorts.

Pleased to see them both, preferring to ignore the observation, she bent down and gave Ricky a raspberry kiss—his favorite—on the side of his neck. He'd tucked his head to his shoulder and was giggling for her to do it again when she straightened to talk to his mom.

"What are you doing here?" she asked Annie.

"I brought Ricky over to watch his dad on the tractor."

"That's what Zach and Mandy are doing. As far as they're concerned, it's better than a video."

"I noticed you weren't watching," Annie casually observed, plopping her son on a hay bale beside his cousins.

"Ranch equipment has never been my thing."

"Just ranchers who happen to be vets?"

Caught snagging back the hair the stiff breeze blew across her face, Erin's smile faltered.

"I was afraid of that," Annie said with a sigh.

"I didn't say anything!"

"Do you think you need to? It's written all over your face."

"We're not supposed to write on ourselves, Erin," Mandy piped in, her tone admonishing. "Mommy said."

"It's just an expression, sweetie," Annie explained. "Erin didn't really write on herself.

"Anyway," she continued, lowering her voice to avoid

further comments from little people with big ears, "a woman doesn't stand around chewing her lower lip while she's watching a guy unless she's worried about something."

"I'm not worried."

Annie considered her, then looked up to catch Trevor glancing away from them. "Maybe not," she conceded, not sounding at all convinced. "But after what your mom said when she called this morning, I think *she* is."

Her mother? Erin thought, caution creeping through her. "What did she say?"

"Mostly she talked about the fire and how relieved she and Logan were that all that was lost was a building. But she did mention that you and Trev seemed rather concerned about each other."

"We were," she admitted, seeing nothing extraordinary about that. They'd been concerned about Hank, too. And the horses. "It was scary in there."

"She also said she didn't know how it was that you two happened to be there at the same time."

Erin hesitated. Trevor had been nearby because he'd just left her apartment. And he'd just left her apartment because she'd invited him up so she could tell him they couldn't get any more involved with each other than they were. Or had been. For all the good it had done.

"I don't think I need to explain that."

"Of course you don't. You're a grown woman. And frankly," she added, sensitive to both her sister and her niece, "there are some things a mother truly doesn't want to know. But I know she's concerned about you getting involved with him again. Seeing you now, so am I." The breeze picked up, feathering her short hair, making her look more like an imp than a woman pushing forty. "A couple of weeks ago, you were at least trying to put up a fight.''

The knot of anxiety in Erin's stomach was big enough without having to contend with her family. Not that she begrudged her aunt's interest. She just didn't want to say anything to betray how hard she'd fallen, or how much she was wishing last night had never happened.

"I'm not admitting anything, Annie."

Her aunt nodded, sympathy softening her smile. "I'm not asking you to. I really didn't come out here to give you the third degree. Honest. And don't be upset with your mom. She's just thinking about what he did to you the last time and how it affected the whole family. She has to. It's her job.

"As for me," she added, giving her arm a pat, "I just don't want you to get hurt again. I know what it's like to want a man who doesn't know how badly he needs you."

Even if Annie hadn't turned to keep Ricky from climbing higher on the stacked bales so he could play airplane, Erin would have let the matter go. She knew her aunt meant well. Annie probably even thought she understood the chaos she was feeling. But Annie now had her man. And as for Trevor, Erin knew he didn't need her. He had his life all mapped out and she, and the family she wanted someday, weren't part of his plans.

The reminder of how he'd hurt her before hadn't been necessary, either.

Having returned her son's interest to the noisy green machine, Annie turned back to say something else. The kids' squeals of delight over the boom of another load landing on the truck bed kept her silent, though, and in that moment her thoughts seemed to shift.

"Buck up, kiddo," she warned. "He's headed your way."

The feeling that slithered through Erin at Annie's announcement felt distinctly like panic. Trevor and his dad were walking toward the old stable, which would take them right past the little hay-bale bleachers the children were perched on.

"I should take the kids up to the house," Erin said, feeling a sudden need to be occupied. "It's getting awfully windy out here. It's almost time for lunch, anyway."

Zach didn't care for her conclusions at all. "We want to watch the tractor!"

"Yeah, Erin," Mandy whined. "You said we could stay."

"Stay! Stay!" Ricky chanted, though he wasn't going anywhere, anyway.

"What have we got here?" Logan's deep voice carried toward them on the breeze, drawing the kids' attention and effectively thwarting escape. "Is this the peanut gallery?"

Erin made herself smile as the men drew closer. Afraid she'd find Trevor looking anywhere but at her, she let her glance get as far as the sweat-ringed collar of his pale blue shirt before turning that smile on Logan. She halfway expected Trevor to hang back. Or to keep going to take care of whatever task they'd been on their way to tend. But he kept coming, walking right up and stopping with his dad three feet in front of her and Annie and the kids.

Speculation lurked in Annie's eyes as she offered him a reasonably friendly hello, then glanced back up at his father. "Jett's got an audience."

"I see that." Sleeving sweat from his brow, Logan reached out and ruffled his youngest son's hair. "I can't believe they've stayed still this long. Is there glue under there?" he asked, drawing laughter from his little girl when he picked up Mandy and set her back down.

Ricky, who'd taken off one shoe, scrambled to his feet

to assure his uncle there was no glue under him, either. In his haste, he knocked the shoe to the ground.

Annie didn't seem to notice. Her attention was on Logan and the children while he teased with the kids, and while she told him she was sorry about his stable. What they were saying barely registered to Erin, though. Aware of Trevor watching her, more aware of the uneasy sensation in her chest, she turned to get the shoe herself. As she did, she felt the brush of his hand on her shoulder.

"I'll get it." His hand immediately fell, but instead of going around her, he stepped between her and her aunt. "Are you all right?" he whispered, his warm breath brushing her ear before he bent to retrieve the miniature sneaker.

With his back to the others as he straightened, his eyes met hers. He seemed to know he only had a couple of seconds before the others would notice them, but those seconds were long enough for her to see the concern she'd heard in his question.

She'd primed herself for everything but that. She hadn't expected him to consider that she'd be shaken by what had happened. Nor had she anticipated the hunger tightening his expression when his glance dropped to her mouth.

A strange form of relief swept through her as she took the shoe he held out. She wasn't all right at all, but she felt herself give him a little nod as his hand curved under hers. His thumb moved across her wrist, the motion deliberate, possessive, if that were possible. It was almost as if he wanted her to know he had a right to touch her.

At the betraying leap of her pulse, a muscle in his jaw bunched. But an instant later he'd stepped back, looking up to see the truck rumble by.

The roar of the tractor died.

"You about ready for lunch, Trev?" she heard Logan ask in the startling silence.

"Sure." Pushing his hands into his pockets, he spared his dad an easy glance. "Whenever you are," he said, and turned with him and Annie to watch Jett walk toward the little gathering.

He'd no sooner turned than Mandy was scrambling to stand up on her hay bale to get his attention.

"You know what Jasmine did, Trevor?"

"What?" he returned, jerking a hand from his pocket to steady her.

"She piddled on the floor."

A smile tugged at his mouth, relieving some of the tension that had settled in his big frame. "Puppies will do that. Are you letting her outside when you're supposed to?"

"Most of the time. And you know what else?" she demanded. "I'm teaching her to sit up. 'Cept she keeps rolling over."

Erin watched his smile deepen, struck by the ease of his conversation with the little chatterbox. He wasn't anywhere near as reluctant with Mandy as he'd once been. With any of the children, for that matter. When Jett reached the group and swung his son onto his hip, Trevor's glance followed the sturdy little boy.

Or maybe, she thought, aware of a subtle shift in his expression, what had his attention was the brief exchange between husband and wife when Jett, holding their son between them, leaned down to kiss Annie.

"How's it going over there?" asked Logan when his brother looked up.

The contented pleasure in Jett's lean features faded to mild annoyance. "It's bad enough that it feels like a sauna out here, but this wind is blowing ash all over the place. I'm going to wait until it dies down some." He glanced at his watch, then back at his brother. "I'm getting hungry, anyway. Seems like a good time for a break."

That was what Logan and Trevor had thought. Logan told him that, too, frowning himself as the warm wind suddenly billowed dust and bits of leaf around them. The clouds had built up today as they had for weeks, making the hot air humid and toying with the prospect of rain. But the clouds had cried wolf too often for anyone to pay them any attention now. The wind was new, though. It had only started getting in on the act yesterday.

"I'd better get the kids inside," Erin said. "This is getting nasty."

She'd just reached for Mandy when she saw Logan glance at his arm. Dark spots were forming on the sleeve of his shirt.

"I don't believe it," he muttered, taking Zach by the shoulder to hand him over to her. He tipped his head back. "Look."

Big fat drops of water were falling from the leaden sky. The ground was so dry that every drop that hit dirt raised a little puff of dust, beading on the surface for an instant before sinking into the earth. The drops that landed on the roof of the metal shed by the barn nearly sounded like hail. But mutterings of disbelief and comments about how it was about time it rained quickly changed to hurried goodbyes before Erin shooed Zach and Mandy toward the house and Annie and Jett, with Ricky on his shoulders, headed for their respective vehicles.

Erin had heard Logan tell Jett to go, that he'd bring the loader in, and Trevor had headed to the barn for tarps to cover the hay. But she and the kids hadn't even made it to the road leading past the house when the rain turned to a downpour.

They were just passing the workshop when Mandy

stopped dead, wanting to be carried. Zach had pulled his shirt over his head, and his bare back was getting wet. Rather than letting the children get soaked, she grabbed their hands and hauled them inside. She'd lived in Texas long enough to be familiar with its summer "monsoons." There were times when the sky could open up, and the rattle of thunder and lightning would make a person think it was the end of the world. Minutes later the sun would be out, making a rainbow, covering the land with a blanket of steam and everyone would be wondering what all the fuss had been about.

This particular storm cell, however, didn't peter out that way. Instead of letting up after a couple of minutes, the rain came down heavier, harder, arrowing at a sharp right-hand angle and dropping the temperature a full ten degrees in half as many minutes.

The workshop was no place for children. Power tools were bolted to metal stands that occupied various places on the cement floors. Above two long workbenches hung an array of hand saws, axes, chisels and hammers. Spools of barbed wire were stacked along the back wall. But Erin wasn't worried about the children getting hurt. Afraid of the thunder booming in the distance, fearing lightning was going to start another fire, they were glued to her sides like splints.

She was wondering how long they'd be stuck there when she saw Trevor and his dad jog past. As if he sensed her, Trevor's head turned toward the open double doors where she and the kids were standing. Grabbing his dad's arm, he jerked his head in their direction.

Water poured off the brims of their hats as they hit the doorway, and their shirts stuck to their shoulders and chests as if they'd been blasted with a firehose.

"Doesn't look like this is going to pass," Trevor said,

as if he'd known she'd thought to wait it out. "There's not a break in the sky anywhere."

Eyeing his shirt, trying not to think about the hard muscles it molded, she ran her hand protectively over Mandy's head. "The kids are going to get soaked if they go out there."

With his dad at his elbow, Trev's incisive glance fell to the children clinging to her legs. "Hang on a second."

She didn't know where he thought they would go, or what he was doing as he rummaged through a metal storage cabinet. But when he came back moments later, he was cutting slits in the sealed ends of green trash bags with his pocket knife.

"Good idea," Logan muttered, swiping water from his face as he reached for one and slipped Zach into the makeshift raincoat. "We'll help Erin get the kids up to the house and get something to eat." He glanced back at the little waterfalls pouring off the roof. "Then I'd better check the weather report."

Trevor was first to reach the back door of the house. The screen slammed behind him, but he left the inner door open to set Mandy down on the mudroom floor and catch the puppy that slid in to greet them. With the wriggling animal in one hand to keep it from darting into the deluge, he turned Mandy around and pulled off the green plastic that had covered everything but her face. Water droplets flew everywhere.

"That was fun," she said, her pink cheeks dimpling as she smiled and took the dog he handed her.

Holding open the screen, Trevor watched Erin and his dad, carrying Zach, hustle for the house. "You think so, huh?"

"Yep. 'Cept for the thunder."

"Thunder can't hurt you," he replied, as Erin slipped past him and lowered the wet plastic from her head. "By the time you hear it, the part you need to worry about is over."

Twisting her head to avoid the dog's tongue, Mandy's brow furrowed. "What part?"

"The lightning." Plastic rustled as Erin stuffed her makeshift raincoat into the utility sink. Picking up the one he'd pulled off Mandy, he handed it over so she could stuff that one in the sink, too. "It's already hit by the time you get to the part that scares you."

Erin knew Trevor wasn't talking to her. His back was even to her as she turned from the sink and pushed back the wisps of hair that had loosened from her braid. But she couldn't help thinking how facing what she felt for him was a little like that lightning bolt.

Logan and Zach blew in with the wind.

The little room was far too small for so many people. Bodies bumped as Erin unbagged her little brother and the men toed off their muddy boots.

"Mandy. Zach. Out," Logan ordered, since the kids were clean and dry. Boots off, he hung his wet hat on its customary peg. "I'll get you a dry shirt," he told Trevor and headed off to get the same for himself.

"I'm hungry," Zach announced from near the kitchen table.

"Me, too," Mandy echoed.

"In a minute," Trevor told them and pulled the door closed.

Erin was in front of the washer, preparing to take off her own boots, when she glanced up. But she'd no sooner realized that they were alone than Trevor's hands were skimming her shoulders, slipping up to cup her face.

He looked like a man doing battle with himself in the

scattered seconds before he caved in and closed his mouth over hers.

The taste of him filled her. The feel of him drugged her. In the space of seconds, whatever rational thoughts lurked in her mind were vaporized, and her body responded by flowing toward his.

With a lone moan he dropped his hand down to catch her hip. Aligning her to him, he pressed against her. The wet denim covering his heavy thighs soaked into her jeans; the wet shirt covering his hard chest dampened the fabric covering her breasts. He was making her remember how she'd responded to him, eliciting those same responses now. But even as the heat raced through her, he eased back, reluctantly pulling his body from hers until only his lips touched her mouth and his hands held her face.

"Erin. We're hun-gry," Mandy whined, punctuating each syllable with a bump against the door.

"I've thought about that all day," he murmured, one hand on her neck, the other closing over the knob to keep his insistent little sibling from opening the door. "I can't believe how many people there are around here." He brushed her lower lip with his thumb. "If Dad and Hank hadn't been standing there waiting for me this morning…"

He let the thought go, but the look in his eyes before he dropped another kiss to her mouth told her exactly why he'd taken off the way he had when he'd brought her bags. She hadn't realized he had an audience. "Help me with the horses later?"

"Er-rin."

She didn't know what he wanted help with. But she nodded as he opened the door and caught Mandy, who'd been about to bump against it again.

"You can have your sister now," he told the little girl,

and gave the puppy squirming in her arms an absent pat on his way through the kitchen.

Erin leaned against the doorjamb, vaguely aware that Mandy was telling her she wanted tuna and Zach wanted peanut butter and jelly. She felt as if she'd just been sucked up the funnel of a tornado and dumped, like Dorothy, in Oz. The man walking away from her had just scrambled her senses, turned her knees to wax, then calmly walked off to change his shirt.

"I'd appreciate a sandwich, too," she heard Logan say when he appeared in the doorway on the far side of the room. "Whatever you're fixing for the kids is fine for me and Trev."

Feeling a little numb, she pushed herself away from the door and headed for the fridge. Her biggest fear had been that Trevor would pull back from her. But pulling back wasn't what he seemed to have in mind at all. That was all she cared about at the moment. She would deal with the rest of it—the consequences with the family, the consequences with her heart—when she didn't have four hungry people to feed.

Chapter Ten

"If you and the kids can't leave in the next few minutes, go stay at Cal and Lindsey's. I just talked to Bill Farley. He said the wash out by his place is already running."

Trevor stood with his back to the wall in his dad's office. Their empty plates sat on the corner of the desk among the production reports, accounting ledgers and weight charts that always covered it. His dad had called the weather service, then Trevor had called Verna to see if everything was still under control at the clinic. While he'd been on the phone, his dad had used the ranch's short-wave radio to contact the camps to make sure there were no problems at any of them. Now he was talking to Samantha.

It seemed that his dad always had his wife in the back of his mind. He'd had that same impression of Jett from time to time, too: that Annie was somehow never far from his thoughts.

"I promise I'll be careful, but I can't ask the men to do something I won't do myself. You know that." His dad paused. Then whatever Sam said made him smile. "I love you, too, babe. *You* be careful."

He broke the connection with a sigh that puffed his cheeks and rose, seat springs squeaking, from the worn red leather chair he insisted was too comfortable to replace.

"I need to run supplies out to the camp in section three," he said, his back to the topographical map of the ranch that took up nearly an entire wall. "I'd planned to have Archie run them out this morning, but he was working with Jett cleaning up the fire and I forgot all about 'em. They're already low out there. If it starts flooding and they get cut off, they'll be down to nothing."

"I'll do it."

"You sure?"

"Doc has everything covered. When he heard about the fire this morning, he said he didn't expect me to be available today, anyway."

"That'd be great. If you'll take care of the supplies, I'll have a couple of the guys bring that bunch of calves we were working yesterday into the barn and we'll finish them in there." The calves were late drops that had to be ear tagged, dehorned and vaccinated. There weren't many, but the job needed to be finished. Rain didn't stop chores. It just added to them. "What about the two horses that got hurt last night?"

In the panic, one horse had run into something rough and peeled the hide open on his shoulder. Twenty stitches, a walloping dose of antibiotic and a bandage had taken care of that. Another had pulled a muscle in her right fore-leg.

"The palomino will need a dry bandage. I'll stable him

and change it before I go. The other needs hot and cold packs. I'll talk to Erin about them both.''

''You'd better tell Hank what to do for them. I need Erin here. Sam may stay in town tonight, and I have to be able to leave if something comes up.''

Trev hesitated. He actually trusted Erin more with the horses than he did Hank. Considering that the old cowhand had decades more experience, he knew that wouldn't make much sense to his dad. He wasn't sure it even made sense to himself. Or maybe it wasn't so much that he trusted her more, but simply that he knew the job of tending the animals was important to her.

Not questioning why that mattered to him, he picked up the plates, since he was going to the kitchen, anyway, and headed past the grandfather clock ticking quietly in the hall.

Turning into the kitchen a moment later, he saw Erin, her back to him, at the long white counter by the sink. Rain beat against the window in front of her, running in rivulets down the glass. The gloomy daylight turned the outdoors gray, but this room was bathed in brightness. The overhead lights glinted off the streaks of gold in her intricate braid, reminding him of how soft her hair had felt in his hands when he'd buried them in it.

He banked the thought, his glance sliding across the long breakfast bar that cut the room in half. Zach and Mandy sat at the old pine table unscrewing sandwich cookies and dipping them in their milk.

Plates clattered over their childish chatter as he came up behind Erin and set them in the sink. ''Thanks for lunch.''

She'd obviously been preoccupied. Startled, she whirled around, nearly dropping the cantaloupe half she'd just wrapped in cellophane.

''Easy,'' he coaxed, taking it from her before it wound

up on the floor, anyway. He set it on the counter, backing up a step. He wouldn't touch her. Not with the kids fifteen feet away.

She seemed to sense that. But, just for good measure, she picked up the melon and headed for the refrigerator. "What's the word on the weather?"

"No letup before morning. Washes are already flooding."

"I guess that means I'll be staying here for a while. Mom might get stuck in town."

"It's a possibility," he confirmed, wondering at her easy acceptance. On a ranch the hands had to be adaptable, to pitch in where necessary. He'd never considered that it worked that way in families, too. "Dad just talked to her. I guess that means you'll sleep here."

And that means I won't get you alone tonight.

He knew she caught his implication the moment he saw her glance dart to his. Standing with one hand on the open refrigerator door, she gave the door a nudge to swing it closed, then turned to lean against it. From the way she met his eyes, he could practically read her uncertainty about what was happening between them.

As far as Trevor was concerned, what had happened last night had been inevitable. It had been coming for years. He just hadn't expected the possessiveness that had surfaced with the intimacy they'd shared. Or the reluctance he felt to back away, when he knew that was exactly what he should do. Erin wasn't someone he could walk away from without repercussions. But now that he knew how she responded to him, he wanted her with a fierceness that would have stunned him had he allowed himself to consider it.

All he considered was Erin's caution. He couldn't blame her for being wary of him. But he didn't want her uneasy with him. He didn't want to hurt her, either. That was why, as difficult as it would be, he would let her call the shots. He wouldn't push. Not hard, anyway.

"We need to talk."

"I think that would be a good idea."

Their eyes held. In the distance, thunder rolled across the plains.

"We'd better get going," his dad said, passing between them on his way through the kitchen. "I'll help you load up one of the Jeeps. You okay with staying here for me, Erin?"

She glanced away, unnerved to find her hand trembling when she reached to put the cookies away. "Fine."

"Good. I'll call up if I leave the compound. Otherwise, that's where I'll be."

The caution Erin felt changed quality as Trevor moved down the counter. If his dad was going to help him load a Jeep, that meant he was going out on the range, not to work for the clinic.

"And you?" she asked, thinking of the times she'd seen her mom's concern when Logan had gone out in weather like this. She'd always thought it had something to do with the way her dad had left for work one day and never come home. That still probably had something to do with her mother's fears. But now Erin understood part of that concern was simply because she loved him.

"I'm just delivering supplies to section three."

"How far away is that?"

She knew the road and the horse trail to the homestead where Annie and Jett lived and the route to the shaded rise above the river where she liked to watch the sun set, but she really knew little about the ranch beyond the stables. Her world, like her mother's, had never included the rough, rugged cattle land that had always been the men's domain.

"Ten miles. Give or take."

If he was taking a Jeep, then he wasn't going to one of the remote camps accessible only by horse. Still, ten miles was a long way over dirt roads in this weather.

"Listen," he continued, suddenly remembering, "I didn't get the files on the calls I made yesterday back to the office. If Doc gets a call on one of them, he'll need—"

"Drop them off here and I'll read your notes to him over the phone."

"Thanks. And if he does call, tell him I told Arlie Fullbright we're going to have to do surgery on that heifer's eye before it gets infected. Arlie's thinking about it, and he'll get back to us. I can do it tomorrow morning unless Verna's got another procedure scheduled."

"Anything else?"

"Can't think of anything…unless you should happen to get down to the stables later," he amended, obligations easing the faint strain threading between them. "I'll tell Hank what to do for the two injured horses. One has stitches in his shoulder that need to be kept dry. The other has a pulled muscle," he added, because he hadn't had a chance to tell her about them yet. "Hank won't have time to work the muscle, but I'll leave hot and cold packs down there in case you have time later."

"If I can get down there, I will."

He was sure she would.

"Be careful?"

He couldn't imagine why she thought he wouldn't be. Then he noticed the concern in her eyes and even with his thoughts so occupied, he felt something indefinable shift inside him. It was the same sensation he'd felt in the early hours of the morning when he realized she'd been worried about him in the fire.

"Sure," he murmured, and looked up to see his dad quietly watching them both.

Without a word, Logan tossed him an olive-colored slicker, then cast a speculative glance toward Erin.

Catching the thin garment, Trevor headed for the door, fighting the urge to look back.

Samantha didn't get stuck in town. When she and Amy arrived an hour after the men departed, she told Erin there had only been a couple inches of water on the pavement when she'd come through the section of road five miles out of Leesburg that always flooded when it stormed. But after her mom called Logan down at the barn to let him know she was home, she called Lindsey to let her know she'd made it home safely and learned that the road situation had already changed.

Lindsey had heard from a waitress who'd been listening to the police scanner at the café that the wash Samantha had come through a half an hour ago was getting higher and swifter by the minute. It had already claimed one vehicle. A little sedan had tried to cross it and was now stuck in the middle with water covering its floorboards. The sheriff and one of his deputies were down there getting the driver out.

"That means all the washes are running in the lowlands," Erin heard her mom say as she hung up the phone a few moments later. "I hope Logan doesn't have to go out there."

Erin stood in the doorway of the mudroom, Michael's slicker in one hand and eyeing Amy's boots. With her mom back, she could see to the animals Trevor had told her about. "Is that where section three is?"

"What?"

"Section three," she repeated, not wanting to worry. "Is it in the lowlands?"

Leaning against the counter by the phone, Samantha distractedly ran her fingers through her hair. She'd had an umbrella in her car, so she hadn't gotten as wet as she could have in her mad dash into the house. But the shoes she'd left by the back door had wet grass stuck to them, and her stockings were splattered with rain. "I think so. I know there are washes there. They feed into Tumbleweed Creek in that section. Why?"

"How did you know that?" She'd heard that there were hundreds of little creeks and streambeds out there. "What creek they feed into, I mean?"

The silver necklace her mom wore over her coral shift shimmered as she shrugged. "I've spent a lot of time looking at that map in Logan's office. He tells me where he's moving cattle and what's going on with the land, just like I tell him what's going on in town." Her head tipped, curiosity entering her warm brown eyes. "Why the interest in section three?"

"Just wondered." Plastic rustled as she checked the slicker for anything gross. Michael was into bugs. Hard telling what was in his pockets.

"Is Trevor out there?" her mom quietly asked.

She apparently didn't need to say a word for conclusions to be drawn when she glanced up. But at least she wasn't subjected to a tsking "Oh, Erin," the way she once would have been when she'd done something that exasperated her mother. Her mom didn't even tell her to remember what happened the last time she'd gotten involved with him. Or warn her of how the fallout from another disastrous end to the relationship would, in some way, affect them all.

"He knows the land," she said, the assurance in her

voice that of a woman who understood another's worry. "He cut his teeth on it."

Clutching the turquoise stone at the end of the necklace, she leaned against the breakfast bar that cut the room in half. Behind her, polished oak cabinets and copper pots gleamed. Near her elbow, three ceramic ducks marched toward the stick-figure drawing Amy had handed her before she'd raced off to battle her brother for the remote control. "Are you still looking for a job in Austin?"

The question was nowhere near as off-the-wall as it sounded. It was also as transparent as glass.

"Or San Antonio," Erin replied. She wasn't naive. Not anymore. She wouldn't weave dreams around him; wouldn't let herself imagine anything beyond what had already happened. She'd come here with a purpose, and her goals, ambiguous as they sometimes felt, hadn't changed. "I have no reason to alter my plans."

She'd thought she would see relief in her mother's expression. Surprisingly, there was none.

"Has he ever realized how much he means to you?"

The directness of the question caught Erin as off guard as its scope. For a moment she just stood in the mudroom doorway, her eyes on the face that was so familiar she rarely noticed how much it betrayed. A lifetime of hurts, worries and concerns were revealed in the faint lines etching her mom's delicate brow. A wealth of pleasures were visible in the tiny creases near her peach-tinted lips, formed there over the years by thousands of smiles. It was the face of a woman who'd been there—a woman who understood.

In the face of that understanding, denying that she cared about Trevor seemed pointless. She just didn't have to admit how much.

"What do you mean?" she asked, not quite certain what her mom was after.

"You've always cared about him," she said simply. "I just hope he respects that." She fingered the stone. "I keep reminding myself that circumstances are different now. That you're both adults and that he's changed. Changing, anyway," she amended, looking somewhat ambivalent about the admission. "He's made an effort to be less distant with us, and Zach and Mandy adore him. But some feelings die hard."

Erin draped the slicker over the utility sink, her brow furrowing as she watched her mom across fifteen feet of shining hardwood floor. "Whose feelings?"

"Mine."

"About Trevor?"

Her mom considered her for a moment, her hesitation speaking more of how to phrase what she wanted to say, rather than reluctance to say it.

"Remember when you first knew him?" Dropping the stone, she crossed her arms. "That was such an awful time for all of us," she reflected, shaking her head as if to dispel the memory. "We were all trying to cope with losing Jim," she said, speaking of Erin's father, "and I was trying to start our lives over and do a job that certain people...like Logan," she muttered, "didn't want done.

"I think it was worse for you, though. You were angry with me for moving you here and you had no friends and you were rebelling at...everything," she concluded because there was no point dragging up what had been resolved years ago. "But Trevor was like an anchor for you. I was so afraid of what was happening between you two. You were so young and he was so...mature," she decided, for lack of a better way to describe the boy who'd been a man even then. "Yet in a way I was grateful to him for being there for you, because you needed to be able to open up to someone. But just when you started acting more like yourself with the rest of us, he stopped talking to you.

"I was so upset with him for doing that to you," she admitted over the steady beat of rain on the windows. "But I was relieved, too, because I think you'd have run off with him in a minute if he'd asked. Logan kept assuring me that wouldn't happen. 'I know my son,' he'd say. But I knew how crazy you were about him, and women don't tend to be anywhere near as practical as he says men are.

"Anyway," she said, her sigh saying she knew those concerns no longer applied, "I hope he's not encouraging you unless he's serious. As much as he meant to you before, I don't think it would take much for you to fall for him all over again. Just be careful, will you, honey?"

She offered the request with a little smile, tipping her head as if to seek her daughter's agreement. She wasn't interfering. She wasn't warning. Not exactly. She was just asking that Erin protect her heart.

It was already too late for that. It had been too late the minute he'd returned. "Don't worry about this, Mom," Erin said quietly, wanting to relieve all the concerns her mom was forcing herself not to mention. "I'm not going to let what happened the last time happen again." What Trevor didn't know couldn't hurt her. Or something like that. "I'll be moving soon, anyway."

Her rationale seemed more evasion than an explanation, but the reminder that she'd be leaving soon finally brought a hint of relief to her mother's eyes. Releasing a deep breath, Samantha pushed herself from the counter and, focusing on her next task, slipped off her necklace to change clothes.

"If you haven't found a job by end of next week," she said, the long chain dangling from her hand as she worked open the zipper at her nape. "I could use some help with the brochures for the Winterfest. Your eye is better than mine for that sort of thing."

Her "eye" was what she got paid for. "I'll help even if I've got a job," she told her, picking up the raincoat again and pulling it on. "I like doing layouts. Oh, do me a favor, would you?" she asked, her sleep-deprived brain suddenly remembering Trevor's requests as she stuffed her stockinged feet into the bright pink rubber boots. "I called Verna and gave her a message Trevor needed passed on, but Doc Henderson might need information from one of the files he worked yesterday. If Doc calls, the files are in Logan's office and yesterday's notes are on top. Okay?"

Catching the opened zipper between her shoulder blades, her mom replied with a quiet, "No problem." But Erin thought the faint little lines in her mom's forehead looked a tad pronounced before she left the room.

There really was no need for her to worry, Erin told herself. She truly had no intention of letting history repeat itself. She just needed a little time to figure out what she was going to do when she saw him again. Since he assumed she was spending the night up at the house, she figured she had at least until the morning to work on it. At the moment she hadn't a clue.

She was just as clueless the next morning. But the rain granted her a reprieve.

The sky was still lead gray and leaking like crazy when Logan told her that Trevor hadn't come back last night— that he'd stayed out on the range to help move cattle to higher ground and that he'd asked if she would call Verna for him so they could reschedule whatever surgery it was they'd talked about. He told her, too, that he needed every man he had out on the range so she was on her own with the horses, then asked if she'd mind helping her mom put together a couple dozen sandwiches for the men because he'd sent Leon, the compound cook, to the north range to help with a problem out there. Twenty hours of steady rain had turned the land to mud, and he needed every hand to dam swollen streams to protect the camps in the valleys and pull cows out of muck.

Erin knew it was dirty, dangerous and demanding work. She'd been there before when such storms had hit. That had been a long time ago, though, and years in the city had made her forget how intimately man sometimes battled nature when he worked so closely with it. In a city of concrete, storm drains and skyscrapers, such a tempest could snarl traffic, cause accidents and make people late for appointments. In the country, it could wash away precious topsoil, ruin crops and cause an animal to break his neck, or a man to risk his trying to save it.

She'd never considered the matter before, but it seemed to her now that life became more immediate when a person looked out an open stable door at a rain-lashed tree bending with the wind, than when she looked through rain-splattered glass at the little vignettes in the windows of the office building towering across the street. She had a greater sense of appreciation for things she once took for granted, such as the sun when it came out just before it set that evening to turn raindrops to glittering jewels on the trees, and the sounds of the birds when they grew raucous with the passing of the storm. And oddly, when she climbed the stairs above the stable that night after dropping off casseroles for the men's supper and finishing her chores, she found the thought of moving into an apartment building, no matter how cute, or cozy or trendy, enormously depressing.

Trevor had once said he'd never wanted anything but to

come back to the ranch, to work with the land, with the animals. She was beginning to understand why. But thinking of Trevor brought the unsettled feeling she'd tried all day to ignore, so she turned on the radio and headed for the shower, hoping to drown the concern nagging at her. Last she'd heard, Trevor was still out on the range. Even if he came in tonight, as late as it was and as tired as he'd be, stopping to let her know he was all right would be the last thing on his mind.

Or so she was thinking when she turned off the hair dryer twenty minutes later and, over the bluesy melody on the radio, she heard a faint, tapping sound.

At first she thought it was the wind starting up again. But when she lowered the volume on the radio and heard it again, there was no mistaking its insistence.

Snagging her freshly dried hair back from her face, she left the radio on low and padded barefoot through her bedroom. Seconds later, edging aside the curtain on the door's window, her heart bumped her ribs even as the breath she'd held leaked out.

Trevor stood on the other side of the door, his head lowered and his hand clasped over the back of his neck. His hand fell when she turned on the overhead light and his head came up when she opened the door with a faint groan of old hinges. But when he saw her standing there in her nightgown with her hair tumbling around her scrubbed face, he said nothing. For a moment he just stood there, filling the door frame with his wide shoulders, a black Stetson pulled low and lines of fatigue etched into the carved angles of his face. He looked haggard and weary and, seeing the caution in her concern, not entirely sure of his welcome.

"I know it's late," he finally said, his eyes steady on

hers. "But I need you to do something for me. I'd do it myself, but I can't."

His voice was gravelly with exhaustion. His shoulders were slumped with it. Stepping back to let him in, she watched him duck to avoid hitting the top of the door frame. He didn't take his hat off as he usually did when he entered a house. He simply walked in, floorboards squeaking beneath his weight, and stopped by the little kitchen table.

His glance drifted over the modest, white-eyelet-trimmed sleep shirt that bared her arms and skimmed her knees. "Were you in bed?"

"I was just getting ready." She closed the door with a quiet click, breathing the clean scent of soap and fresh air that lingered where he'd passed. His shirt and jeans were clean, and the hair at his nape looked damp. "When did you get back?"

"About twenty minutes ago."

"You look exhausted."

"I guess I prefer a bed to a bedroll these days. I've slept on the ground two nights in a row and barely managed six hours between them."

One of those nights, he'd managed less than two. Thinking it best to overlook the reason for that at the moment, she watched him knead the knotted muscle in his shoulder. "What is it you need for me to do?"

He glanced toward the basket of laces and thread she'd returned to the coffee table.

"You sew, right?"

One eyebrow arched. The man was practically dead on his feet and he wanted her to sew something? "What did you tear?"

"I didn't tear anything." He pulled out the nearest chair,

scraping its legs over scarred linoleum. "I ran into something."

He dropped into the seat, finally taking off his hat and setting it next to a vase of bright baby sunflowers. His dark hair was damp, a deep glistening sable that smelled of his shampoo. But it was the handkerchief his hat had covered that had her attention. More specifically what was bleeding under it.

"What did you run into?" she asked, stepping between his legs to get a closer look.

"A horse's hoof. I tried to sew it up myself..."

"Of course you did."

"...but when I winced I couldn't see."

"How bad is this?" she asked, gingerly lifting the square of blue fabric.

"Not as bad as it looks. Head wounds can bleed like crazy. One of the guys at the camp put a butterfly on it, and the bleeding had pretty much stopped. It started up when I showered and washed my hair."

"Why did you do that?"

"Because I smelled like the horse I'd been riding," he muttered, digging in his front shirt pocket. "Here. Use this stuff."

The flow of blood had pretty much been stanched again. She could easily see a slightly curved, inch-long gash near the crown of his head. Someone had used a razor to shave away a little hair on either side, presumably so the butterfly would have some skin to stick to.

She glanced at the paper packets he'd dropped on the table, listening to the tear of paper as he ripped one open. When he laid it back on the table, she could see it held a threaded suture. Apparently he'd raided his veterinary supplies.

"Can't I just put another butterfly on it?"

"It won't hold. Just stick a couple of stitches in it."

"Trevor, I can't—"

"Two stitches. Three max. The curved needle makes it easy."

"It'll hurt."

"Having that horse rear over me when I was pulling on that steer hurt. Damn hooves are sharp. I lost a good hat, too. My other one's trampled into eight inches of mud."

"Do you do this a lot?"

"All the time. Just go in near the lip on one side, come out the other and make a double knot."

She glanced at his scarred knuckles. Below the rolled-up sleeves of his shirt, the deep bramble scratch he'd inflicted on his forearm a couple of weeks ago had faded to pale pink. A few more scratches had been added in the past thirty-six hours. Bright red ones that indicated another bout with something with stickers. "I mean batter yourself."

She couldn't see his face. But she saw his broad shoulders rise with a deeply drawn breath. "Use this first," he muttered, ignoring her comment to rip open a packet containing an alcohol pad.

She didn't want to do this. The very idea of sticking a needle into someone's flesh was enough to raise goose bumps on hers.

Pretend it's a Thanksgiving turkey, she told herself.

Air hissed between his teeth when she touched the pad to the slightly gaping wound.

"Sorry," she murmured, hating that she'd hurt him.

"Don't worry about it. Just talk to me."

"I can't. I need to concentrate. You talk to me. Tell me what it was like out there."

"It was a mess. At one point, we had two hundred head stuck in a ravine, and they were up to their knees in water and mud.'' Braced against the sting, he wearily grumbled, ''This is all Hank's fault.''

''It is?''

''Sure. Three days ago he was praying for a breeze, and we got a windstorm that brought lightning and set the stable on fire. Two days ago, he was praying for rain to put out the fire, and we get this. If you hear him praying for snow, gag him.''

It sounded to Trevor as if there was a smile in her voice when she assured him she would. But he couldn't see her face. All he could see were the folds of white fabric covering her stomach and skimming down to her knees. There were tiny pink rosebuds embroidered along the edge of the lace around her hem, and the fabric was so delicate it was almost virginal. But when he glanced down at her bare feet, he saw that her toenails were painted a sophisticated dark burgundy.

The woman was a walking contrast, he thought, and fell completely silent.

Conversation wasn't necessary to take his mind off what she was doing. All he had to do was think about her and he'd be distracted enough. She stood between his legs, her fingers in his hair, her scent toying with his mind and having predictable effects on his aching body.

He closed his eyes, digging his fingers into the denim covering his thighs as she apologized again. In the bedroom, the radio was playing, something low and mellow from a deep-throated sax. It wasn't the sort of music he usually listened to, but something about it made him think of a velvet black sky shot with stardust and a soft, gentle breeze.

If he'd had the energy to be surprised at himself, he would have been, mostly because it wasn't like him to think of anything even remotely poetic, if that was what it was. But the music, like the bright flowers he'd noticed on her table, held a quiet appeal that almost seemed... soothing.

He had to be exhausted to be thinking of such things, but he was too tired to care. The irony of the thought nearly escaped him as he tried to concentrate on the feel of her leg brushing his instead of the sting and pull on his scalp. But even as he acknowledged that he probably wasn't thinking too clearly, he let himself absorb the feelings brought by her surroundings, her touch.

She'd been on his mind all day, so the fact that he'd headed straight for her as soon as he'd washed off the trail dirt didn't disturb him at all. There was nothing particularly complicated about his sex drive. He wanted her. Even with his muscles aching, a knot on his head and generally feeling as if he'd been bucked off a bull, he wanted her. What surprised him wasn't that the need was there even as lousy as he felt; what surprised him was that he wanted her because he felt that way.

"I'm almost done," Erin quietly encouraged, conscious of how still he remained. He sat with his head slightly bent, his hands braced on his powerful thighs. What she was doing had to hurt, but he remained stoic—and silent.

She didn't doubt for a moment that he wanted her to hurry and get this over with. Tired as he seemed, he had probably wanted only to crawl from his shower into his bed, which was where he'd be right now if he hadn't re-opened the little injury. He'd come to her tonight only because he couldn't fix it himself, but the fact that he'd sought her help instead of someone else's sparked the hope she'd promised herself she wouldn't feel.

Reaching past him, she set aside the tube of ointment she'd just applied and straightened to cover the wound with a small adhesive square. Reminding herself to remember the dog he'd so easily given away, she smoothed his thick hair over the bandage, covering it with the shining, still-damp strands.

"There," she said, moved by his appearance on her doorstep despite herself. "All finished."

She thought he'd look up. Or maybe touch his fingers to the bandage. What he did was lift his hands and settle them on the outsides of her thighs.

She'd been ready to move away, to let him go. It was what she thought he would want. Certainly it was what she should do. Instead, he held her rooted between his spread legs while his hands slid to her hips, bunching her gown with them as he tugged her forward. Without looking up, without a word, he slipped his arms around her hips, pulling her close and rested his forehead between her breasts.

His broad shoulders rose with a deeply inhaled breath. When he released it, his whole body seemed to relax.

He'd come to her to take care of him, to comfort him. He hadn't said the words. She doubted he could. But as she hesitantly touched the top of his head, almost afraid to believe what he was letting her see, she knew that was what he had done.

Her fingers sifted through his hair, cautiously cradling his head. She never could imagine him needing anyone, much less caving in to the feeling. But there was something terribly vulnerable about the way he held her, something that spoke of lowered defenses and weariness that went soul deep. It spoke of need. And the thought that he needed her, even if it was only for that moment, totally destroyed the defenses she knew she should be raising.

It also worried the daylights out of her.

"Trevor?" Her voice was hushed, and heavy with concern. "Are you all right?"

He didn't move. He just let her hold him to her, much as a mother might a tired child. But he allowed himself the respite for only a few moments before he drew another breath and leaned back enough to let his hands rest on her hips again.

"Yeah," he agreed, his hands flexing lightly against her. "It's been a long day."

"How bad does your head hurt?"

"Not that bad."

"Maybe you should have a doc—"

"This happened hours ago. I'm fine."

He was not. "You need sleep."

She brushed back the hair from his forehead, thinking he would agree when he tipped back his head to look up at her. But he said nothing. His gray eyes intent on hers, he just watched her while her hand fell away and the heat of his palms burned through the thin fabric of her gown.

His thumbs flexed against her hip bones, his glance moving to the gentle swells of her breasts, unrestrained under the soft cotton. Her body stirred beneath that knowing visual caress, heat pooling low when his fingers flexed against her flesh.

"Probably," he finally said, rubbing the fabric against her skin. "But what I want is you." He drew her closer. "Do you want me, Erin?"

"Trevor—"

"That's not an answer," he said, leaning forward to nudge the fabric covering her breast with his mouth. The motion was gentle, almost needy. "Yes or no."

It wasn't a question of want. It was a question of self-preservation.

"Yes or no," he repeated, nuzzling the bud hardening at his touch.

"Are those my only choices?"

"Yes."

Heat shot through her as his hand rubbed over her stomach. Moments later, echoing his response, she felt his breath shudder out, its warmth heating her skin before he drew back far enough to see her face.

He pushed the gown up slowly, shaping her with his hands as the hem moved past her hips, her waist, revealing white satin and lace. He pushed it higher, coaxing her arms up, revealing the soft swells of her breasts to him, and pulled it over her head. But he didn't touch her the way she thought he would. He just looked at her with hunger stark in his eyes and brushed her cheek with the back of his knuckles.

The touch was incredibly, impossibly tender. That same tenderness was in his kiss when he caught her mouth as he rose over her, and in the way he held her in his arms in the long moments before he guided her to her bed.

There was none of the frenzied heat that had caught them before. In its place was gentle exploration as clothing was cast aside and their bodies sought each other like old lovers. That gentleness created its own heat, an exquisitely slow burn that was somehow more shattering than mindless passion and ultimately left Trevor feeling more reluctant than he ever had to leave a woman's bed.

But tired as he was, and as difficult as it was to leave that quiet, comfortable place beside her, he dragged himself away and left her sleeping.

Chapter Eleven

The dull roar of the old John Deere loader encroached on the early-evening silence as Erin drove past the mile of white pasture fence lining the road from the old highway into the RW. The interview she'd had to reschedule had been at four o'clock that afternoon. It was now well after eight.

She crested the hill above the compound, listening to the chug and snort of the diesel engine grow louder as she took the curve past the house. With another hour of daylight left, it wasn't unusual that the men would still be working. They invariably went back to tend chores after supper, especially in the summer. Logan was anxious to start rebuilding the stable, and nothing else could be done until everything was cleared.

She should be anxious to start rebuilding, too, she told herself. And she now had the perfect opportunity to move on with her life. She just couldn't feel the excitement she should have. What she felt instead was something close to the awful anxiety she'd experienced when her family had first left California. And that made no sense at all. No one was uprooting her. She wasn't losing anything she actually had.

The job was hers if she wanted it. The interview had gone so well that it had spilled over into dinner. She could start next week. The PR director of the exclusive three-hotel chain wanted her to start as soon as possible so Erin could be up to speed when the current assistant left.

Erin knew she should be thrilled. The position entailed advertising and promotion for the chain and, as small as the operation was, she'd be involved in every aspect of it. The company's offices were in the chain's flagship hotel on San Antonio's famed River Walk. There were charming apartments and condos nearby. The lovely little city itself was only an hour and a half from the ranch, a quick jaunt by Texas standards, so family would be near. It was everything she should have wanted.

But it wasn't.

Blowing a long, low breath, she angled toward the garage. She'd told herself before that she wouldn't toy with impossible dreams, and she had no intention of doing it now. Despite Trevor's need for her last night, he'd been careful not to say anything to indicate what she might mean to him, or what he wanted from her other than physical comfort. He was a wonderful lover, giving, caring. But she wanted—needed—far more than that. She wanted his heart. And she was desperately afraid that what she needed, Trevor would never be able to give.

His black Bronco was in the long, open garage. Pulling in between it and an old truck with the bottom half of a bow-legged cowboy sticking out from under the front end, she gathered her purse and jacket, concern battling self-protection. She was relieved to see that he was home because she wanted to know how he was feeling. But another part of her remembered the hollow sensation she'd experienced when she'd wakened to find him gone. She knew why he hadn't stayed. There would be talk if someone noticed him coming from her apartment at dawn, and he didn't want anyone to know they were involved, either. Even if he'd done it solely to protect her, she couldn't live that way.

"Hey, Erin…er, ma'am," Archie amended, seeing high heels and stockinged legs emerge from her car rather than the expected jeans and boots.

"Hey, Archie," she replied, smiling at the wiry red hair his hat usually hid.

The thought that she was going to miss that shy, sunburned face hit just as he ducked back under. Telling herself not to dwell on such things now, that it was too soon to start missing anything, she headed for her apartment to change clothes.

From the hill above the compound, she'd seen the blackened spot in the landscape where the stable had been. Approaching the area now, she could see a trio of plaid-shirt-and-denim-clad males leaning against the corral fence watching the loader scrape away the last of the burned debris. Trevor was elbow-to-elbow with Hank and his dad, one booted foot resting on the lower rail and his forearms propped on the upper one.

It was Hank who noticed her coming. Lifting the brim of his battered hat, he nodded at her, which caused the two men with him to check out who he was looking at.

Logan smiled when he saw her.

Trevor dropped his foot from the rail and slowly straightened.

In the space of seconds, he'd taken in the smooth twist

of her hair and the gold glinting from her ears, the smart cream-colored sheath, the matching jacket draped over her arm and the camel pumps that made her legs look a mile long.

"She cleans up real nice," Hank muttered around his cigar.

"She looks like her mother," Logan drawled, appreciation in his voice.

Trevor said nothing. Memories of last night crowded his head, luring, warning. Feeling like a steer caught between leaping a canyon for water or dying of thirst, he just watched Erin glance toward the stairs leading to her apartment as she approached them, her slight hesitation making him think she debated whether she should just wave or come over.

Seeing that the other men expected her to be sociable, she moved toward them, her easy smile greeting them all.

"You look like the men I saw a while ago in San Antonio," she said to no one in particular. "There was a backhoe digging a hole across from the lot I was parked in and ten guys in business suits were standing around supervising. What is it with boys and machinery, anyway?"

"Same thing as women and dress shops, I expect," Logan replied, tipping back his hat. "Different things appeal. How'd your interview go?"

"Good. Thanks."

Trevor saw her glance slide toward him. She seemed careful not to study him too closely as her guarded hazel eyes swept his face, then followed the scratches on his neck beneath his pale blue collar. The long bramble marks were still as angry looking as they'd been last night, but he couldn't tell if she was remembering how she'd kissed them or if the caution in her eyes was because she thought they might still hurt.

Quite deliberately she lifted her glance to his hat. "How's your head?"

"Better," he admitted, conscious of the way her hands were clasped in front of her. They were nearly hidden by the jacket draped over her arm, but he glimpsed her thumb working over her knuckles. Considering how composed she looked otherwise, the motion was decidedly agitated. "Doc noticed it at the clinic this morning and said you did a good job. Thanks," he added, because he hadn't said it last night.

"Still say there was no reason for you to go bothering Erin with that last night," Hank muttered, his words muffled as he rubbed his mustache. "Would'a' made more sense for me to do it. My trailer's right next to yours."

Trevor glanced blandly at the grumbling old coot. "Her needlework's neater than yours."

"She's got a better disposition, too," said Logan, popping the dense old guy in the arm before turning back to the show.

The noise of the loader muffled whatever Hank mumbled at his boss's good-natured jibe, but he propped his elbows back up on the fence, returning his attention to the discussion they'd been having about building the stable out of brick this time.

Trevor remained where he was, six feet away, his hands on his hips and his eyes shifting from her to the men beside him and back again. Eight hours of solid sleep had done a remarkable job of clearing his mind, and what he'd realized when he awakened was that he was getting in over his head.

He'd never felt anything like the unquestioned need that had driven him to her last night, and that lack of control threatened him. No one had ever affected him like that before. That was why he thought he'd step back for a couple of days, keep his hands to himself, if for no other reason than to prove that he could.

But something wasn't right with Erin, and he wanted to know what it was. He didn't need to touch her to talk. He just needed to get her away from his dad and Hank.

"I'm going to check that palomino's shoulder," he said to them, speaking of the horse that had torn its hide, "then I'm heading in. I'll see you tomorrow."

He caught Erin's eye, wondering if she'd take the hint and come with him.

Her hands tightened, but she managed an easy smile. "I'm on my way, too. As soon as I change, I'll see if Archie needs help with the feed."

"He just finished," Hank informed her, watching the big shovel raise a puff of black-and-gray ash. "Didn't know how late you'd be, so me and Archie took care of the horses. No need for you to bother with anything in there tonight."

She thought she saw Logan's glance narrow at his foreman as she offered her thanks, but he could just as easily have been frowning at the big old barn cat screeching at an even bigger tabby over by the hay shed.

"Tell Mom I'll talk to her in the morning, will you, Logan?"

Still pondering the construction of his new stable, he assured her that he would. As he did, Hank raised his hand without looking back to acknowledge their departure. But she saw Logan look back a moment later, his glance moving between her and the mountain of muscle in denim that had fallen into step beside her.

Trevor's hands were in his pockets, his normally long

stride checked to keep pace with a woman in heels and a narrow skirt.

In the long evening shadows, she saw his glance skim her face, lingering on her mouth long enough to harden his jaw before he turned his focus to the bits of hay the breeze blew in front of them.

"Did you mean what you said to Dad, that your interview went well?"

"Yes, it did," she quietly replied, not looking forward at all to talking to him about her decision.

"Then why do I have the feeling it didn't?"

The warm breeze loosened a few strands of hair near her temple. She tucked them back, seeming to stall as she drew a deep breath.

Fighting the urge to tip her chin toward him when she remained silent, Trevor nudged her with a quiet, "Erin?"

"Really," she quickly insisted, forcing a smile toward his chin. "It went great. They offered me the job."

That confused him. Not that they wanted her. He didn't doubt for a moment that she was very good at what she did. Her lack of enthusiasm just wasn't the reaction he would have expected. Her smile didn't fool him a bit.

"It must not be what you're looking for, then."

"Actually," she said, ambivalence clawing at her. "It has a lot going for it."

"Then what's the problem?"

"I never said there was a problem."

The considering look he gave her took in the calm denial in her expression, the slight challenge in the tilt of her chin and the stranglehold she had on her jacket. When his eyes reached hers, their droll glint told her she'd have to do better than that.

"Do you want to tell me about it?"

"Not really."

"Do you want me to badger it out of you?"

He was making what she needed to do even harder, she thought. At that moment, he sounded very much like the old friend he'd once been—the friend who'd listened, who'd helped her sort through alternatives. But she really had no alternatives, and she'd lost that friend once. She was desperate not to do it again.

He cast a glance at his watch, then looked toward the horizon. The sun was obscured by the usual string of heavy clouds, but it wouldn't be long before the gathering dusk turned to darkness. "I'll be up in about an hour."

Knowing she had to talk to him sooner or later, Erin had told Trevor that an hour would be fine and headed upstairs to change her clothes and pace a rut in the linoleum while she repeatedly told herself that taking the job was the only thing she could do. Telling him wasn't that big a deal. After all, it wasn't as if he was going to care that much if she left.

That was precisely what she didn't want to face; the very reason she would have put this particular conversation off forever if she possibly could. She didn't want to talk to him about her move because she would then know exactly where she stood with him.

She'd never thought of herself as an ostrich before. Finding the mental image far from flattering, she continued to pace. On her fourth trip through the tiny apartment, she decided that pacing literally wasn't getting her anywhere and that what she needed was something to clean. The problem, however, was that the apartment was spotless. She could go downstairs and polish tack, but she needed better light than she'd have in the stable and she didn't want to drag up bridles, harnesses, polish and saddlesoap, then have to haul it all back down again.

What she didn't mind hauling up was the little pony saddle she'd found buried in the back of the storage room while she'd been cleaning it a couple of weeks ago. But she'd only reached the pool of light on her porch with it when she heard Trevor behind her.

"I won't ask."

"Good," she said, hoisting the little brown saddle higher on her hip.

"Give it here."

He took it in one hand, carrying the fifteen pounds of wood and leather as if it weighed no more than a rope, and reached past her to open her door.

"On second thought, yes, I will," he mumbled, changing his mind as soon as they were inside the cozy little room. He hoisted the miniature object, cinch lines swaying. "What are you going to do with this?"

"I'm going to clean it up so Mandy can use it." Had she not felt so edgy, she might have smiled at his expression. He was accustomed to rugged work saddles. He was frowning at the downsized version as if it had sat out in the rain and shrunk. "She wants to learn to ride."

"Where did it come from?"

"Your dad bought it for Amy years ago." Setting down the spray bottle of leather cleaner she'd also brought, she watched him drape the heavily tooled leather over the back of the nearest kitchen chair, the horn pointing toward the overhead light and little stirrups dangling down the chair back. Stepping back, she asked, "How's the palomino?"

"It looks good," he said, his eyes narrowing on her crossed arms as he leaned back against the counter to mirror her position. "So what's the deal with the job? This is the one for the hotel, right?"

The inevitable was invariably hard to postpone.

Feeling the need for movement, she walked over to the

sink, reaching beneath it for a sponge while she easily confirmed that it was for a hotel, then briefly outlined what the position entailed. There was enough natural enthusiasm in her voice when she spoke about the woman she'd be working under to distract him from the lack of it in her expression. But she had her back to him while she squirted soap on the sponge and went to work on the saddle's skirt, so he couldn't see her face, anyway.

And she couldn't see his.

"You said you wanted to work in a smaller operation than what you were used to," he reminded her, his tone completely unremarkable. "Is this one small enough?"

She told him it was.

"And you like the location?"

Lifting one shoulder in a slight shrug, she went to work on the back of the seat. He wasn't sounding as if he had any problem at all with her moving an hour and a half away. "San Antonio's nice."

"Salary's okay?"

"That," she said with a smile, "could always be better."

She heard him shift, his boots shuffling against the floor. From the corner of her eye, she saw that he'd crossed his feet at the ankles, his posture deceptively casual.

"Why do I get the feeling it's not exactly what you want?"

Because you see too much, she thought, returning her attention to her task. "Because it's not," she allowed, just to get him to back off. "But it's close enough."

"You don't have to settle for close enough. If it's not exactly what you want," he said, sounding utterly reasonable, "don't take it. Something else will come up."

She stared at the lathered sponge for a moment, afraid

to hope, unable to help it. "Like what?" she asked, looking up.

For a moment he said nothing. He just remained with his lean hips against the counter, his big body dwarfing the appliances on either side of him and his expression as unreadable to her as the Dead Sea scrolls.

"Maybe you'll find something in Austin."

The tiny bubble of hope flattened. "No, Trevor," she said quietly, suddenly aware of how careful he was being not to touch her. "I won't find what I'm looking for in Austin. I'm taking this job." She pressed her hand over the nerves knotting in her stomach. "I need to leave here."

Silence suddenly hummed in the quiet little room, growing heavier by the moment as he considered the way she avoided his eyes, the distinct uneasiness of her motions. A couple of months ago, he'd wanted nothing more than for her to disappear. He'd gotten over that. And a while ago when he'd realized she might be leaving, his only thought had been that the distance would be exactly what he needed. She wouldn't be so far away that he couldn't see her once a week or so without a half dozen people watching their every move, but she'd be far enough that she wouldn't be constantly on his mind.

He had a strange feeling, however, that she wasn't thinking along those lines.

"*Need* to leave?" His tone was amazingly mild; the look in his eyes was not. He slowly straightened. "What are you talking about?"

She started to push back her hair, more out of agitation than necessity, then remembered the soap on her hands.

"I'm talking about being sensible...which is something I haven't always been," she admitted, turning on the water at the sink. "And about doing what I can to salvage a relationship that means a great deal to me."

"Whose relationship?" he asked, his voice laced with caution.

Pipes clattered when she twisted the knob to off. "Ours," she said softly, and turned around to get a towel.

Trevor had already pulled the rectangle of bright yellow terry cloth from the refrigerator handle. Holding it out to her, he eyed her evenly. "I'm listening."

His features were a mask, his eyes guarded. He wasn't going to give her a clue as to what he was thinking, but he obviously wanted her to finish whatever it was she had to say.

It would be so much easier if she could just tell him how very much he meant to her. Then he'd understand how hard it was for her to be with him, loving him and constantly having to suppress thoughts of a future. Or maybe, she reminded herself, he wouldn't understand at all.

Whether he would or not really didn't matter. She wouldn't say the words. As she carefully dried her hands, she knew she absolutely would not tell him she loved him and watch that shuttered look fall over his face again. Or have him avoid her when she came home. Or sit as far away from her as he possibly could at a holiday meal.

"I want to protect what we just got back," she said, speaking of the caring that had finally resurfaced. "And I'm afraid that if we get more involved, we're going to ruin everything. It's not as if what's going on affects only us, either." She hurried on, thinking it safer to turn the focus from her heart. "We have family to consider. My mom. Your dad. Your dad," she emphasized, grasping at a reason she knew he would appreciate, "is so happy that we're finally getting along. I couldn't bear to disappoint him if something happened to ruin that."

She twisted the towel, smoothed it out. "It's not as if

we can ever be totally free of each other," she continued, knowing he'd already learned that. "And if you think things were uneasy between us before, you know they're only going to be worse if we let this go any further before something happens to end it. You know it will, too. End, I mean," she added quietly. "You don't want what I want, and I can't be in a relationship like this that has nowhere to go."

She couldn't hang up the towel because he was blocking the fridge. Taking it from her, he looped it through the handle, his hands fisting on the dangling ends. He'd heard every word she'd said. He even agreed with ninety-nine percent of it. But what stung like the venom of a snake bite was his impression that she'd rather take a job she didn't really want than stay there with him.

"So you're running."

She'd been watching his hands. The flatly delivered statement snapped her focus back to the hard angles of his face. "What?"

"You heard me. You're running. It's what you do." She was just doing it a little better this time, he thought. She'd been looking for a job when he arrived, so there wasn't a soul on the place who would think a thing of it when she hightailed it to San Antonio. He alone would know that she was leaving because of him. "Something gets to be more than you can handle, you split."

"Trevor—"

"You did it when you ran to Seattle, remember?" He posed the question in an easy, deliberate tone that totally belied the disquiet filling his chest. "You couldn't go to L.A. because your mom caught you, so you went to your aunt Annie's instead, but it still got you away from Leesburg for a while. Then you ran back from L.A. when things got rough there," he elaborated, not feeling particularly good about the way she blanched. "I'm not saying I blame you. I'm just saying it's what you do."

She did it when she was hurt. He knew that. He would have mentioned it, too, except he knew that, at some level, he was hurting her now.

"I'm not running," she insisted, her bewildered eyes searching his. "I'm trying to cut losses. I don't want to fight with you, Trevor. I don't want us to go back to not talking again. I want us to be friends and stay friends and the only way that's going to happen is if we don't do something like this."

Something like disbelief flickered through his expression. Or maybe it was disgust.

"You told me before that we should think of each other as brother and sister." The tension that had slowly tightened his body slipped into his voice, honing an edge in it. "I told you that wouldn't work. Now you want us to be friends," he muttered, his tone making it clear he didn't think that would work, either. "Why?"

Why? "Because I care about you," she said, thinking that much should be obvious. Or maybe, to him, even that wasn't. "Just because you don't invest your emotions doesn't mean no one else does, Trevor. I don't want to completely lose you again."

She didn't know if it was her admission or the accusation that caused him to go silent. Whichever it was, he pulled a breath that filled his chest, then turned away with the muscle in his jaw working like crazy.

Trevor made it as far as the little saddle over the chair near the door before he glanced to where Erin stood by the sink. She had her arms crossed tightly enough to cut herself in half. "When do you leave?"

"In a few days. They want me to start Monday. I'll stay at the hotel until I find an apartment."

An unfamiliar ache had settled under his breastbone. Not totally sure what he was feeling, but knowing defensiveness was part of it, he jerked open the door. It was a lot easier for a man to admit anger than hurt.

"Let me know if you need help loading your car."

He was out the door in the time it took her to get a breath past the constriction around her heart. Pressing her fingers to her mouth, she watched the curtains until they stopped swaying.

It was no wonder he'd chosen to work with animals, she thought, swallowing hard. He was really lousy relating to people.

"You're going to ruin that shovel, son." The sound of metal hitting rock rang clear in the warm morning air as Trevor's dad approached the fence near the garage. The neat crisscrosses of white pine had broken away from the corner post, which was tipped drunkenly to the right. "What are you doing?"

"Fixing this post. It's listing."

"I can see that," he said, splaying a gloved hand over the top of the post to right it. "Why is it listing?"

"I ran into it."

Logan looked at the black Bronco parked ten feet away. White paint marred the right front fender near the headlamp. "When I asked what you were doing, I meant why are you fixing it? I'll get Archie up here. No need for you to be late for an appointment because of this."

Wiping sweat from his forehead with his sleeve, Trevor shoved the blade back into the ground. In the past two days, he'd had to run an entire set of tests at the clinic twice because he hadn't paid attention the first time, and he'd been late for an appointment because he'd spent the night battling the sheets and overslept. Now, he'd creamed the fence. "I wrecked it. I'll take care of it."

Planting his foot on the heavy metal, he put his considerable weight into his task. If he'd been paying attention, he would have realized he was cutting the corner short. But he'd just noticed Erin across the compound talking to one of the men, and he'd been so busy trying to ignore the hollow feeling in his gut that he hadn't even seen the post he'd driven past a thousand times.

He'd be fine once she was gone. The hard part about letting something go was having it around to remind a person it was leaving.

"This wouldn't have anything to do with Erin leaving, would it?"

The shovel hit rock, shooting pain up his arm.

Trevor swore.

"I thought it might," his dad muttered, stepping aside so Trevor could attack from a different angle. "I've seen the way you watch her and the way she looks at you. Sam and I both suspected there was something going on with you two."

Eyeing his father evenly, he shoveled dirt around the rock that still had his shoulder tingling. "There isn't anymore. She broke it off."

"What did you do?"

"What did I do?" he asked, disgruntled to think his dad would take her side. "What makes you think it was my fault?"

Brawny muscle bunched under beige cotton as his dad shrugged. "Experience. The girl's crazy about you. How do you feel about her?"

Frustrated. Angry. Confused. "I don't know."

"Are you going to miss her?"

"She hasn't gone anywhere yet."

"Are you going to miss her?" he asked again.

"I haven't thought about it."

With a knowing nod, his dad picked up one of the cross-pieces now that the post was back in place and pulled the long slat against it. The post would need to be set with cement later, but the temporary patch job would keep the stock from wandering out of the pasture. But it wasn't what his dad was doing, so much as the familiarity of it that struck Trevor just then. Something about the subject and what they were doing reminded him of another fence they'd patched together years ago, and a similar talk. Only then he'd been the one asking the questions of his dad. About Samantha.

If Trevor remembered correctly, his dad had seemed pretty frustrated himself.

"You know, son," Logan drawled, "I'm not much on advice where women are concerned. But I found that a man's stubbornness can sometimes stand in the way of what he really needs. I'm not pushing anything here. But you and Erin just might have something you aren't going to find anywhere else. You might get a better idea of how you feel about her if you'll consider how it's going to be without her around anymore."

Trevor looked doubtful. "Then what?"

Logan shook his head, slapped his son on the shoulder. "If you find what I think you will, marry her."

One box and one suitcase were already stowed in the trunk of Erin's fiery red Mustang when she approached it with her last bag. She'd said goodbye to her family and the hands and the horses and was reminding herself that she'd be back in a week not a year when she heard Trevor's Bronco coming down the drive.

Her heart promptly slid to her throat, a moan of defeat

right behind it. She hadn't seen him since he'd walked out of the apartment she'd just vacated, and she'd practically said a novena praying he'd be on calls this morning.

The big, black vehicle crested the hill and headed straight for the garage, rumbling by her and pulling into the space next to her car. He hadn't glanced toward her, hadn't given any indication he'd even seen her as he cut the engine and opened his door.

The sound of it closing echoed like a rifle shot, sending the relentlessly cheerful birds scattering from the trees behind the newly repaired fence. In the dappled sunlight, she watched him move toward her, his strides measured and his expression somewhere between guarded and grim.

"Is this all you've got?"

He'd said he would help her load up. The fact that he actually intended to do it caused something painful to squeeze around her already tender heart. She forced a smile, though, absolutely determined to make their parting as pleasant as possible.

"You didn't come all the way back just to say goodbye, did you?"

"No," he said flatly.

He reached past her and took the suitcase from her hand, the clean scents of soap and warm male tugging at a host of unwanted memories. Stepping back, she tried to ignore the heat moving up her arm where his hand had brushed hers, then frowned when he dropped the bag by the tire.

"What are you doing?"

Beneath the shadowing brim of his black hat, his darkly attractive features had grown tense. That was pretty much how the rest of him looked, too, when he clapped his hand over the back of his neck, drew a breath that expanded his chest, then let it slowly leak out.

"You don't need to leave," he finally said. "You don't want to go, so you shouldn't.''

"Trevor, it's very kind of you—"

"I'm not being kind," he countered, looking annoyed with the thought. "I'm being practical. You'd probably do just fine in the city, but you'd do better here. You belong on the ranch as much as I do.''

She thought she knew what he was trying to do, and the thought that he would try to be friends took the edge off the anxiety gnawing inside her. She truly appreciated the concession, but he had entirely missed the point.

"I might want to be here," she began, hating the thought of having to explain her feelings all over again. "But I can't stay. You told me once that you couldn't fight us both. Well, I can't either. If I'm not around that much, things won't have a chance to get more complicated.''

"What if we both stop fighting?"

He posed the question quietly, his eyes steady on hers. A wealth of caution hung in the sudden silence.

Feeling that same caution herself, she watched him step closer, the slow thuds of his black boots sounding vaguely predatory. The shirt covering his broad shoulders was a shade of pale gray that turned his eyes the silver of polished tack. He towered over her, his body blocking the sun, blocking everything but him.

"I'm not sure what you mean," she said, seeming to absorb the fine edge of tension radiating from his big body.

"I mean," he began, touching the tiny gold dolphin dangling from her ear, "that I can see where our situation could get more complicated if we let it go the way it had been." He lifted the little shape with the tip of his finger. "But it doesn't have to be that way.''

He drew his hand from the miniature sea creature, marveling at the sheer variety of what attracted her. She was drawn by wolves and whales and flowers. Music with a twang and music that soothed. He'd seen her currying horses, tending sick ones and looking like a model in a magazine coming home from an interview. She coddled puppies, small children and cranky old men. And she seemed to care about a man who knew he needed her but hadn't known why.

She also seemed enormously wary of that man now. She said nothing, though. She just watched him, looking as if she wasn't about to let herself trust what she was hearing.

"I talked to Dad." He stepped back, not wanting to crowd her, needing a little space himself in case she decided to turn away. "He got me thinking."

The statement was absurdly simple, considering what the result had been. But Trevor knew that the conclusions he'd drawn in the past couple of days would have hit him sooner or later, anyway. He just hoped he wasn't too late with them already.

"Remember how you said you'd missed family while you were gone? And how you were sure I'd missed the ranch?"

Afraid to acknowledge the persistent little bubble of hope that had just reared its shiny little head, Erin gave him a hesitant nod.

"Well, I did miss it. The whole time I was gone, I felt as if part of me just wasn't there." It was a yearning, he supposed. A longing. And that was exactly the way he felt about Erin. But with her, the feelings were so much stronger, so much more vital to his survival. With her, it felt as if the piece that wouldn't be there was his soul.

"And you remember when you asked me if I'd ever thought about having a family of my own? A wife and children?"

Though she gave him another little nod, it seemed as if the rest of her body had gone completely still.

"I think I told you then that I don't know what love is," he said, searching her face. "But if it's feeling like part of me is missing at the thought of you leaving, then I'm in love with you. You got into my blood a long time ago, Erin. And I don't know when you got into my heart, but I expect it was about then, too.

"I know I'm lousy with the words a woman probably needs to hear," he quietly confessed, needing her to know he was doing the best he could. She hadn't moved. To him, it didn't even look as if she was breathing. "But I need you. And I need all the things you made me see around here." He stepped closer, letting himself touch her cheek. "I like the idea of having what Dad and my uncles have. I like the idea of sharing my life with you, and of you sharing yours with me. Getting you pregnant wouldn't exactly be a chore, either," he murmured, drawing his thumb over her mouth. "If you'll be my wife, that is."

Her eyes looked a little shinier than they had a few moments ago, and her breathing seemed a little uneven. He thought she looked a little stunned. Or maybe, he thought grimly, she was upset and trying to think of a polite way to turn him down.

"Say something, will you?"

Erin breathed in, blew out. "Would you do something for me, please?"

He let his hand fall, preparing himself for what he probably deserved.

"Sure."

"Would you put your arms around me?"

She thought she saw relief sweep his face in the moments before his strong arms closed around her. She knew that was what washed through her as her arms went around his neck and he hauled her against his chest. More than anything, what she felt was joy, disbelief and, as his embrace tightened, an incredible sense of coming home.

"I think you said everything just fine," she whispered against his neck. "And, yes, Trevor. I'll be your wife."

He pulled back her head, something primitive flashing in his eyes. But whatever he'd been about to say was lost. That glittering gaze fell to her mouth and he claimed her in a kiss filled with as much promise as passion, as much possession as need.

It was the need that spoke to her heart and filled it near to bursting.

"If I tell you I love you, will you still speak to me?" she asked, long moments later.

Stroking back her hair, his hand stalled at the side of her face. He knew exactly what she was referring to. "Yeah. I'll still speak to you. I might have to tell you I love you, too," he added, dropping another kiss to her mouth, "but we're not going through that again."

"Our parents will be relieved to know that," she told him, and would have smiled had her forehead not just pleated in a thoughtful frown. "You talked to your dad about us?"

"And your mom. That's where I just came from. I missed her here this morning so I went to her office. It seemed kind of strange asking my dad for your hand so I asked her."

The thought of him approaching her mom with such an old-fashioned gesture had her touching her palm to his cheek. What he'd done was terribly sweet, but she was also aware of her mother's ambivalence toward him. "What did she say?"

"That if I don't take good care of you, she'll have my hide." He grinned. "She also said it's about time."

Erin's smile was like the sunshine beaming overhead as she pulled his head toward hers. "I think everyone's going to feel that way."

Epilogue

Erin and Trevor wanted to get married in September, since that was the month they'd met. They also wanted something small and simple, because September was only a month away, and that didn't leave a lot of time for planning.

When they announced their intentions to their parents and their aunts and uncles, everyone thought September was a fine month. Everyone also axed the idea of small and simple. The women in the family did, anyway. The men took their drinks and Trevor into Logan's office and left the women to work on Erin. His departing words to her were that whatever she wanted to do was fine with him.

Erin barely had a chance to accuse him of abandoning her before Lindsey took her by the shoulders and informed her that it required no time at all to put together a wedding. Her own wedding had been concocted in an hour and it had lacked for nothing. She also mentioned that Cal had just finished the restoration of the Leesburg Community Church and that the altar would look lovely banked with flowers.

Annie then reminded Erin that she'd once dreamed of a big wedding, and said she knew that her sister wanted the fairy tale for her daughters.

When Annie looked to Samantha to confirm the claim, Erin's mom headed for the kitchen to get tissues.

That was why, at two minutes to noon on a beautiful fall Saturday, Erin stood in the bride's room of the church in a flowing gown of white satin with a bouquet of white lilies, two bridesmaids, a matron of honor, two flower girls and two hundred fifty-seven friends of the Whitakers seated in the pews.

"You look stunning," her mother said, smiling as she lifted filmy tulle over the braid of pearls anchoring Erin's veil. Trying not to cry and ruin her makeup, she lowered the blusher over her daughter's radiant face. "I hope he knows how lucky he is."

"I know how lucky I am," Erin said, smiling as she squeezed her mom's arm.

Pulling a deep breath, she turned to the door Amy had just opened.

It was time, and she couldn't believe how excited and nervous she was. Those nerves stayed with her as her aunts gathered her train and they all lined up in the vestibule. The knots in her stomach seemed to clone themselves when Ricky and Zach, her tuxedoed ring bearers, and Mandy and Caitlin, adorable in their sapphire blue organdy dresses preceded Lindsey and Annie, her matron of honor, through the tall double doors. And when the organ struck the first chords of the wedding march and she saw the entire congregation stand as she started down the aisle, she really wished she and Trevor had done what they'd talked about last week and eloped.

Then, amazingly, the knots dissolved, and the nerves calmed. Trevor was there, as handsome as she'd ever seen him in a black tuxedo, waiting at the foot of the flower-strewn altar. His uncles stood with him, along with Michael and Gabe, Cal and Lindsey's seven-year-old son. Logan stood tall and proud in the first pew with her mom. But her focus was on the man whose eyes were fixed on her.

She was oblivious to the other people watching her. She wasn't even sure she heard the music as she moved toward him. In Trevor, she had the friend she cherished, the lover her heart craved and the security she had always sought. He was her anchor, the one person in the world who probably knew her better than she knew herself.

"How are you doing?" he whispered when she reached him.

"I'm fine now," she whispered back.

Possession, pride and affection filled Trevor as he searched her eyes. He now knew for certain what love was. It was the thing that opened possibilities, moved a man beyond his own limited vision and made him so much more than he was alone. As he took in the flowers Erin held, the pearls gleaming on her ears, the smile on her lovely mouth, he knew he needed her like he needed the very air he breathed, and he couldn't believe he'd ever considered life without her.

"Me, too," he murmured, and felt his heart swell with the love that had taken root so very long ago as he took the hand of his bride.

* * * * *

Silhouette ® SPECIAL EDITION ®

presents **THE BRIDAL CIRCLE**, a brand-new
miniseries honoring friendship, family and love...

THE BRIDAL
CIRCLE

by
Andrea Edwards

**They dreamed of marrying and leaving their
small town behind—but soon discovered there's
no place like home for true love!**

IF I ONLY HAD A...HUSBAND (May '99)
Penny Donnelly had tried desperately to forget charming
millionaire Brad Corrigan. But her heart had a memory—and a
will—of its own. And Penny's heart was set on Brad becoming
her husband....

SECRET AGENT GROOM (August '99)
When shy-but-sexy Heather Mahoney bumbles onto secret agent
Alex Waterstone's undercover mission, the only way to protect the
innocent beauty is to claim her as his lady love. Will Heather
carry out her own secret agenda and claim Alex as her groom?

PREGNANT & PRACTICALLY MARRIED
(November '99)
Pregnant Karin Spencer had suddenly lost her memory and
gained a pretend fiancé. Though their match was make-believe,
Jed McCarron was her dream man. Could this bronco-bustin'
cowboy give up his rodeo days for family ways?

Available at your favorite retail outlet.

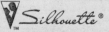

TM *Silhouette* ®

Look us up on-line at: http://www.romance.net   SSETBC

If you enjoyed what you just read,
then we've got an offer you can't resist!

Take 2 bestselling love stories FREE!

Plus get a FREE surprise gift!

Clip this page and mail it to Silhouette Reader Service™

IN U.S.A.	IN CANADA
3010 Walden Ave.	P.O. Box 609
P.O. Box 1867	Fort Erie, Ontario
Buffalo, N.Y. 14240-1867	L2A 5X3

YES! Please send me 2 free Silhouette Special Edition® novels and my free surprise gift. Then send me 6 brand-new novels every month, which I will receive months before they're available in stores. In the U.S.A., bill me at the bargain price of $3.57 plus 25¢ delivery per book and applicable sales tax, if any*. In Canada, bill me at the bargain price of $3.96 plus 25¢ delivery per book and applicable taxes**. That's the complete price and a savings of over 10% off the cover prices—what a great deal! I understand that accepting the 2 free books and gift places me under no obligation ever to buy any books. I can always return a shipment and cancel at any time. Even if I never buy another book from Silhouette, the 2 free books and gift are mine to keep forever. So why not take us up on our invitation. You'll be glad you did!

235 SEN CNFD
335 SEN CNFE

Name	(PLEASE PRINT)	
Address	Apt.#	
City	State/Prov.	Zip/Postal Code

* Terms and prices subject to change without notice. Sales tax applicable in N.Y.
** Canadian residents will be charged applicable provincial taxes and GST.
   All orders subject to approval. Offer limited to one per household.
® are registered trademarks of Harlequin Enterprises Limited.

SPED99   ©1998 Harlequin Enterprises Limited

And Baby Makes Three

FIRST TRIMESTER

by

SHERRYL WOODS

Three ornery Adams men are about to be roped
into fatherhood...and they don't suspect a thing!

And Baby Makes Three

APRIL 1999
The phenomenal series
from Sherryl Woods has readers
clamoring for more! And in this special collection,
we discover the stories that started it all....

Luke, Jordan and Cody are tough ranchers set in
their bachelor ways until three beautiful women
beguile them into forsaking their single lives for
instant families. Will each be a match made in
heaven...or the delivery room?

Available at your favorite retail outlet.

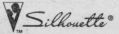

Look us up on-line at: http://www.romance.net   PSBR499

Coming soon from

Silhouette® SPECIAL EDITION®

A captivating new miniseries duet from bestselling author
Susan Mallery

BRIDES OF BRADLEY HOUSE: If the family legend comes true, two close-knit sisters will dream of the men they are destined to marry when they don an heirloom nightgown on their twenty-fifth birthday. But before those wedding bells chime, Chloe and Cassie must discover the meaning of everlasting love!

DREAM BRIDE (#1231, March 1999)
The sophisticated skeptic: *That Special Woman!*
Chloe didn't believe in fairy tales until a ruggedly handsome stranger swept her off her feet....

DREAM GROOM (#1244, May 1999)
The hopeless romantic: Innocent Cassie yearned to discover true passion in the arms of her reserved, devastatingly gorgeous boss....

You won't want to miss the unforgettable Bradley sisters—and the irresistible men they vow to have and to hold...forever!

Available at your favorite retail outlet.

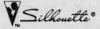

Look us up on-line at: http://www.romance.net   SSEBOBH

Silhouette ROMANCE™

In March,
award-winning,
bestselling author
Diana Palmer joins
Silhouette Romance in
celebrating the one year
anniversary of its
successful promotion:

VIRGIN BRIDES

*Celebrate the joys of
first love with unforgettable
stories by our most beloved authors....*

March 1999:
CALLAGHAN'S BRIDE
Diana Palmer

Callaghan Hart exasperated temporary ranch cook
Tess Brady by refusing to admit that the attraction they
shared was more than just passion. Could Tess make
Callaghan see she was his truelove bride before her time
on the Hart ranch ran out?

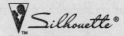

Silhouette®

Available at your favorite retail outlet.

Look us up on-line at: http://www.romance.net   SRVB99

SILHOUETTE® **Desire®** is celebrating the 10th Anniversary of **MAN OF THE MONTH**

For ten years Silhouette Desire has been giving readers the ultimate in sexy, irresistible heroes.

M of the MAN Month

So come celebrate with your absolute favorite authors!

JANUARY 1999
BELOVED by Diana Palmer—
SD #1189 Long, Tall Texans

FEBRUARY 1999
A KNIGHT IN RUSTY ARMOR
by Dixie Browning—
SD #1195 The Lawless Heirs

MARCH 1999
THE BEST HUSBAND IN TEXAS
by Lass Small—
SD #1201

APRIL 1999
BLAYLOCK'S BRIDE by Cait London—
SD #1207 The Blaylocks

MAY 1999
LOVE ME TRUE by Ann Major—
SD #1213

Available at your favorite retail outlet, only from

Silhouette®

Look us up on-line at: http://www.romance.net   SDMOM10

Coming in May 1999

BABY *Fever*

by
New York Times Bestselling Author

KASEY MICHAELS

When three sisters hear their biological
clocks ticking, they know it's
time for action.

But who will they get to father their babies?

Find out how the road to motherhood
leads to love in this brand-new collection.

Available at your favorite retail outlet.

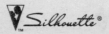

Silhouette®

Look us up on-line at: http://www.romance.net   PSBF